'Haunting, lively, tactile. *Austerlitz* possesses a harrowing emotional power ... a powerful and resonant work of historical imagination'
*The New York Times*

'Extraordinarily atmospheric. This novel is about many things: the resistance we put up to memory and the compulsion to remember, the need to know oneself and the fear of self-knowing. With this superb book Sebald has confirmed his reputation as a major novelist'
*Sunday Telegraph*

## ABOUT THE AUTHOR AND TRANSLATOR

W. G. Sebald was born in Wertach im Allgäu, Germany, in 1944. He studied German language and literature in Freiburg, Switzerland and Manchester. In 1966 he took up a position as an assistant lecturer at the University of Manchester, and settled permanently in England in 1970. He was Professor of European Literature at the University of East Anglia until his death in December 2001. He is the author of *On the Natural History of Destruction*, the long prose poem *After Nature* and three works of fiction in addition to *Austerlitz*: *The Rings of Saturn*; *Vertigo*; and *The Emigrants*, which won a series of major awards, including the Berlin Literature Prize, the Heinrich Böll Prize, the Heinrich Heine Prize and the Joseph Breitbach Prize. His selected poems, *Across the Land and the Water*, are also published in Penguin.

Anthea Bell was born in Suffolk and educated at Somerville College, Oxford. She has worked as a translator for many years, primarily from German and French. Her past translations include works of non-fiction, literary and popular fiction; books for young people; and classic German works by the Brothers Grimm, Christian Morgenstern, E.T.A. Hoffmann, Freud, Kafka and Stefan Zweig. She has served three terms on the committee of the Translators' Association of the UK, and has received a number of translation prizes and awards. In 2010 she was awarded an OBE for services to literature and literary translation.

# Austerlitz

## W.G. SEBALD

*Translated from the German by Anthea Bell*

With an introduction by James Wood

PENGUIN BOOKS

PENGUIN BOOKS

Published by the Penguin Group
Penguin Books Ltd, 80 Strand, London WC2R 0RL, England
Penguin Group (USA) Inc., 375 Hudson Street, New York, New York 10014, USA
Penguin Group (Canada), 90 Eglinton Avenue East, Suite 700, Toronto, Ontario,
Canada M4P 2Y3
(a division of Pearson Penguin Canada Inc.)
Penguin Ireland, 25 St Stephen's Green, Dublin 2, Ireland (a division of Penguin Books Ltd)
Penguin Group (Australia), 250 Camberwell Road, Camberwell, Victoria 3124, Australia
(a division of Pearson Australia Group Pty Ltd)
Penguin Books India Pvt Ltd, 11 Community Centre, Panchsheel Park,
New Delhi – 110 017, India
Penguin Group (NZ), 67 Apollo Drive, Rosedale, Auckland 0632, New Zealand
(a division of Pearson New Zealand Ltd)
Penguin Books (South Africa) (Pty) Ltd, 24 Sturdee Avenue, Rosebank,
Johannesburg 2196, South Africa

Penguin Books Ltd, Registered Offices: 80 Strand, London WC2R 0RL, England

www.penguin.com

First published in German by Carl Hanser Verlag 2001
First published in Great Britain by Hamish Hamilton 2001
Published in Penguin Books 2002
Reissued with a new introduction in this edition 2011

003

Copyright © W. G. Sebald, 2001
Translation copyright © Anthea Bell, 2001
Introduction copyright © James Wood, 2011
All rights reserved

The moral right of the authors and of the translator has been asserted

The photograph at the bottom of p.3 appears courtesy of the Wittgenstein Archive, Cambridge

Set in Monotype Perpetua
Typeset by Palimpsest Book Production Limited, Falkirk, Stirlingshire
Printed in Great Britain by Clays Ltd, St Ives plc

ISBN: 978–0–241–95180–4

www.greenpenguin.co.uk

MIX
Paper from
responsible sources
FSC
www.fsc.org    FSC™ C018179

Penguin Books is committed to a sustainable
future for our business, our readers and our planet.
This book is made from Forest Stewardship
Council™ certified paper.

ALWAYS LEARNING                    PEARSON

In the summer of 1967, a man — who remains unnamed but who resembles the author W. G. Sebald — is visiting Belgium. At the Centraal Station in Antwerp, he sees a fellow traveller, with fair, curiously wavy hair, who is wearing heavy walking boots, workman's trousers made of blue calico, and a well-made but antiquated jacket. He is intently studying the room and taking notes. This is Jacques Austerlitz. The two men fall into conversation, have dinner at the station restaurant, and continue to talk into the night. Austerlitz is a voluble scholar — he explains, to the book's narrator, about the slightly grotesque display of colonial confidence represented by Antwerp's Centraal Station, and talks generally about the history of fortification. It is often our mightiest projects, he suggests, that most obviously betray the degree of our insecurity.

Austerlitz and the Sebald-like narrator meet again — a few months later, in Brussels; then, later still, on the promenade at Zeebrugge. It emerges that Jacques Austerlitz is a lecturer at an institute of art history in London, and that his scholarship is unconventional. He is obsessed with monumental public buildings, such as law courts and prisons, railway stations and lunatic asylums, and his investigations have swollen beyond any reasonable *raison d'être*, 'proliferating in his hands into endless preliminary sketches for a study, based entirely on his own views, of the family likeness between all these buildings'. For a while, the narrator visits Austerlitz regularly in London, but they fall out of touch until 1996, when he happens to meet Austerlitz again, this time at Liverpool Street station. Austerlitz explains that only recently has he learned the story of his life, and he needs the kind of listener that the narrator had been in Belgium, nearly thirty years before.

And so Austerlitz begins the story that will gradually occupy the rest of the book: how he was brought up in a small town in Wales, with foster parents; how he discovered, as a teenager, that his true name was not Dafydd Elias but Jacques Austerlitz; how he went to Oxford, and then into academic life. Though clearly a refugee, for many years

Austerlitz was unable to discover the precise nature and contour of his exile until experiencing a visionary moment, in the late 1980s, in the Ladies' Waiting-Room of Liverpool Street station. Standing transfixed for perhaps hours, in a room hitherto unknown to him (and about to be demolished, to enable an expansion of the Victorian station), he feels as if the space contains 'all the hours of my past life, all the suppressed and extinguished fears and wishes I had ever entertained'. He suddenly sees, in his mind's eye, his foster parents, and also 'the boy they had come to meet', and he realizes that he must have arrived at this station a half-century ago.

It is not until the spring of 1993, and having suffered a nervous breakdown in the meantime, that Austerlitz has another visionary experience, this time in a Bloomsbury bookshop. The bookseller is listening to the radio, which features two women discussing the summer of 1939, when, as children, they had come on the ferry *Prague* to England, as part of the Kindertransport: 'only then did I know beyond any doubt that these fragments of memory were part of my own life as well', Austerlitz tells the narrator. The mere mention of the name

'Prague' impels Austerlitz to the Czech capital, where he eventually discovers his old nanny, Věra Ryšanová, and uncovers the stories of his parents' abbreviated lives. His father, Maximilian Aychenwald, escaped the Nazis in Prague, by leaving for Paris; but, we learn at the end of the book, he was eventually captured and interned in late 1942, in the French camp of Gurs, in the foothills of the Pyrenees. His mother, Agáta Austerlitz, stayed on in Prague, insouciantly confident of her prospects, but was rounded up and sent to the Terezín ghetto in December 1942 (better known by its German name of Theresienstadt). Of the final destination of Maximilian and Agáta, we are not told, but can easily infer the worst: Věra tells us only that Agáta was 'sent east' from Terezín, in September 1944.

This short recital, poignant though its content is, represents a kind of vandalism to Sebald's beautiful novel, and I offer it only in the spirit of orientation. It leaves out, most importantly, all the ways in which Sebald contrives *not* to offer an ordinary, straightforward recital. For what is so delicate is how Sebald makes Austerlitz's story a broken, recessed enigma, whose meaning the reader must impossibly rescue. Though Austerlitz, and hence the reader too, is involved in a journey of detection, the book really represents the deliberate frustration of detection, the perpetuation of an enigma. By the end of Sebald's novel, we certainly know a great deal about Jacques Austerlitz – about the tragic turns of his life, his family background, about his obsessions and anxieties and breakdowns – but it can't be said that we really know him. A life has been filled in for us, but not a self. He remains as unknowable at the end as he was at the beginning, and indeed seems to quit the book as randomly and as unexpectedly as he entered it.

Sebald deliberately layers and recesses his narrative, so that Austerlitz is difficult to get close to. He tells his story to the narrator, who then tells his story to us, thus producing the book's distinctive repetitive tagging, a kind of parody of the source-attribution we encounter in a newspaper: almost every page has a 'said Austerlitz' on it, and sometimes the layers of narration are thicker still, as in the following phrase, which reports a story of Maximilian's, via Věra Ryšanová via Austerlitz, and collapses the three names: 'From time to time, so Věra recollected, said Austerlitz, Maximilian would tell the tale of how once, after a trade-union meeting in Treplitz in the early summer of 1933 . . .' Sebald borrowed this habit of repetitive attribution from the Austrian writer Thomas Bernhard, who also influenced Sebald's diction of extremism. Almost every sentence in this book is a cunning combination of the quiet and the loud: 'As usual when I go down to London on my own,' the narrator tells us in a fairly typical passage, 'a kind of dull despair stirred within me in that December morning.' Or, for instance, when Austerlitz describes how moths die, he says that they will stay where they are, clinging to a wall, never moving 'until the last breath is out of their bodies, and indeed they will remain in the place where they came to grief even after death'. In Thomas Bernhard's work, extremity of expression is indistinguishable from the Austrian author's comic, ranting rage, and his tendency to circle obsessively around madness and suicide. Sebald takes some of Bernhard's wildness, and estranges it — first, by muffling it in an exquisitely courteous syntax: 'Had I realized at the time that for Austerlitz certain moments had no beginning or end, while on the other hand his whole life had sometimes seemed to him a blank point without duration, I would probably have waited more patiently.' Second, Sebald makes his diction mysterious by a process of deliberate antiquarianism. Notice the slightly quaint, Romantic sound of those phrases about the moths: 'until the last breath is out of their bodies . . . the place where they came to grief . . .'

In all his fiction, Sebald works this archaic strain (sometimes reminiscent of the nineteenth-century Austrian writer Adalbert Stifter) into a new, strange and seemingly impossible composite: a kind of mildly agitated, pensive contemporary Gothic. His characters and narrators are forever finding themselves, like travellers of old, in gloomy, inimical places (East London, Norfolk) where 'not a living soul stirred'. Wherever they go, they are accompanied by apprehensions of uneasiness, dread and menace. In *Austerlitz*, this uneasiness amounts to a Gothicism of the past; the text is constantly in communion with the ghosts of the dead. At Liverpool Street station, Jacques Austerlitz feels dread at the thought that the station is built on the foundations of Bedlam, the famous insane asylum: 'I felt at this time,' he tells the narrator, 'as if the dead were returning from their exile and filling the twilight around me with their strangely slow but incessant to-ing and fro-ing.' In Wales, the young Jacques had occasionally felt the presence of the dead, and Evan the cobbler had told the boy of those dead who had been 'struck down by fate untimely, who knew they had been cheated of what was due to them and tried to return to life'. These ghostly returnees, Evan said, could be seen in the street: 'At first glance they seemed to be normal people, but when you looked more closely their faces would blur or flicker slightly at the edges.' In the curiously empty village of Terezín, not far from Prague, Austerlitz seems to see the old Jewish ghetto, as if the dead were still alive, 'crammed into those buildings and basements and attics, as if they were incessantly going up and down the stairs, looking out of the windows, moving in vast number through the streets and alleys, and even, a silent assembly, filling the entire space occupied by the air, hatched with grey as it was by the fine rain.'

This is both a dream of survival and a dread of it, a haunting. To bring back the dead, those 'struck down by fate untimely' — Jacques's parents, say, or the imprisoned victims of Theresienstadt — would be a miraculous resurrection, a reversal of history; yet, since this is impossible, the dead can 'return' only as mute witnesses, judging us for our failure to save them. Those resurrected dead at Terezín, standing in 'silent assembly', sound very much like a large court, standing in judgment against us. Perhaps, then, the guilt of survival arises not just from the solitude of success (the 'success' of having been lucky, of having outlived the Nazis), or the irrational horror that one's survival involved someone else's death (an irrationality that Primo Levi explores in his work). There is also guilt at the idea that the dead are at our mercy, that we can choose to remember or forget them. This is finely caught by Theodor Adorno, in an essay on Mahler, written in 1936: 'So the memory is the only help that is left to them [the dead]. They pass away into it, and if every deceased person is like someone who was murdered by the living, so he is also like someone whose life they must save, without knowing whether the effort will survive.'*

Saving the dead – that is the paradoxically impossible project of *Austerlitz*, and it is both Jacques Austerlitz's quest, and W. G. Sebald's too.

* 'Marginalia on Mahler', in Theodor W. Adorno, *Essays on Music*, ed. Richard Leppert (Berkeley: University of California Press, 2002).

This book is like the antiques shop seen by Jacques in Terezín; it is full of old things, many of them reproduced in the photographs in the text: buildings, an old rucksack, books and paper records, a desk, a staircase, a messy office, a porcelain statue, gravestones, the roots of trees, a stamp, the drawing of a fortification. The photographs of these old things are themselves old things – the kind of shabby, discarded picture-postcards you might find at a weekend market, and which Sebald greatly enjoyed collecting. If the photograph is itself an old, dead thing, then what of the people caught – frozen – by the photograph? (Flickering slightly at the edges, as Evan the cobbler describes the dead.) Aren't they also old, dead things? That is why Sebald forces together animate and inanimate objects in his books, and it is why the inanimate objects greatly overwhelm the animate ones in *Austerlitz*. Amidst the photographs of buildings and gravestones, it is a shock to come upon a photograph of Wittgenstein's eyes, or a photograph of the rugby team at Jacques's school. The human seems to have been reified – turned into a thing – by time, and Sebald knowingly reserves an entire page for his shocking photograph of the skulls in mud (supposedly, skeletons found near Broad Street station in 1984, during excavations). Towards becoming these old things, these old head-stones in mud, we are all travelling. (In the North of England, a cemetery used to be called a 'bone-yard', the phrase somehow conveying the sense of our bones as mere lumber or junk.)

Yet some are travelling faster than others, and with more doomed inevitability, and there is surely a distinction between, on the one hand, the photograph of Jacques's rugby team, and on the other, the photograph of Jacques's mother or the photograph (itself a still from a film) of the imprisoned inhabitants of Theresienstadt. As Roland Barthes rightly says in his book *Camera Lucida* (1980), a book with which *Austerlitz* is in deep dialogue, photographs shock us because they so finally represent *what has been*. We look at most old photographs, and we think: 'That person is going to die, and is in fact now dead.' Barthes calls photographers 'agents of death', because they freeze the subject and the moment into finitude. Over photographs, he writes, we shudder as over a catastrophe that has already occurred: 'Whether or not the subject is already dead, every photograph is this catastrophe.'*This effect is surely heightened when we look at photographs of victims of the Nazis – whether being rounded up, or just walking along a street in a ghetto. In such cases, we think: 'They *know* they are going to die, and they are certainly already dead, and there is nothing we can do about it.' As the stolid rugby players do not, these victims seem to be looking at us (even when they are not directly looking at the camera), and asking us to *do* something. This is what gives the photograph of young Jacques (reproduced on the cover of this book) a particular intensity. The boy in his party cape, with the wedge of unruly fair hair, looks out at the camera not imploringly, but confidently, if a little sceptically. Yet understandably, Jacques Austerlitz, looking at this photograph of himself, from a time when he was still in Prague and still had parents and had not yet been put on the train to London, tells the narrator that he feels 'the piercing, inquiring gaze of the page boy who had come to demand his dues, who was waiting in the grey light of dawn on the empty field for me to

* Roland Barthes, *Camera Lucida*, trans. Richard Howard (New York: Hill and Wang, 1981).

accept the challenge and avert the misfortune lying ahead of him'. Jacques Austerlitz was rescued by the Kindertransport, and did indeed avert the misfortune lying ahead of him. But he could not avert the misfortune lying ahead of his parents, and so, even in middle age, he is forever frozen in the attitude of that picture, always waiting to avert misfortune. He thus resembles the little porcelain horseman that he saw in the window of the antiques shop in Terezín, a small statue of a man rescuing a young girl, arrested in a 'moment of rescue, perpetuated but forever just occurring'. Is Jacques Austerlitz the rescuer, or the one awaiting rescue? Both, surely.

There is, of course, a further dimension to Sebald's use of photographs: they are fictional. In the very area of historical writing and historical memory most pledged to the sanctity of accuracy, of testimony and fatal fact, Sebald launches his audacious campaign: his use of photographs relies on, and plays off, the tradition of verity and reportage. On the one hand, these photographs sear us with the promise of their accuracy – as Barthes says, photographs are astonishing because they 'attest that what I see has existed': 'In Photography, the presence of the thing (at a certain past moment) is never metaphoric.' We are lulled into staring at these photographs, and saying to ourselves: 'There is Jacques Austerlitz, dressed in his cape. And there is his mother!' We say this, in part because photographs make us want to say this, but also because Sebald mixes these photographs of people with his undeniably accurate and veridical photographs of buildings (for instance, the photograph of the Breendonk prison, in Belgium, where Jean Améry was tortured by the Nazis, and which the narrator visits, *is* a photograph of the actual building). On the other hand, we know, in our heart of hearts (and perhaps unwillingly?) that Jacques Austerlitz is a fictional character, and that therefore the photograph of the little boy cannot be a photograph of him.

Indeed, in this book, Sebald's photographs of humans can be said to be fictional twice over: they are photographs of invented characters; and they are often photographs of actual people who once lived but who are now lost to history. Take the photograph of the rugby team, with Jacques Auster-litz supposedly sitting on the front row, at the right. Who are these young men? Where did Sebald get hold of this faded group portrait? And is it likely that any of them are still alive? What is certain is that they have passed into obscurity: we don't look at the portrait and say to ourselves, 'There's the young Winston Churchill, in the middle row.' The faces are unknown, forgotten. They are, precisely, not Wittgenstein's famous eyes. The photograph of the little boy in his cape is even more acute in its poignancy. I have read reviews of this book that suggest it is a photograph of the young Sebald — such is our natural desire, I suppose, not to let the little boy pass into orphaned anonymity. But the photograph is not of the young Sebald; it can be found in Sebald's literary archive at Marbach, outside Stuttgart, and there the reader finds an ordinary photographic postcard, with, on the reverse side, 'Stockport: 30p', written in ink.*The boy's identity has disappeared (as has the woman whose photograph is shown as Agatá, the boy's

* Deutsches Literaturarchiv, Marbach am Neckar. Sebald once confided to me, in an interview, that about 30 per cent of the photographs in *The Emigrants* had an entirely fictitious relationship to their supposed subjects. Sebald, for instance, wrote the farewell note that Ambros Adelwarth writes to his family, and then took the photograph himself.

mother), and has disappeared — it might be said — even more thoroughly than Hitler's victims, since they at least belong to blessed memory, and their murders cry out for public memorial, while the boy has vanished into the private obscurity and ordinary silence that will befall most of us. In Sebald's work, then, and in this book especially, we experience a vertiginous relationship to a select number of photographs of humans — these pictures are explicitly part of the story that we are reading, which is about saving the dead (the story of Jacques Austerlitz); and they are also part of a larger story that is not found in the book (or only by implication), which is *also* about saving the dead. These people stare at us, as if imploring us to rescue them from the banal amnesia of existence. But if Jacques Austerlitz certainly cannot save his dead parents, then we certainly cannot save the little boy. To 'save' him would mean saving every person who dies, would mean saving everyone who has ever died in obscurity. *This*, I think, is the double meaning of Sebald's words about the boy: it is Jacques Austerlitz, but it is also the boy from Stockport (as it were) who stares out at us asking us to 'avert the misfortune' of his demise, which of course we cannot do.

If the little boy is lost to us, so is Austerlitz too. Like his photograph, he has also become a thing, and this is surely part of the enigma of his curious last name. He has a Jewish last name, which can be found in Czech and Austrian records; as Jacques correctly tells us, Fred Astaire's father was born with the last name of Austerlitz ('Fritz' Austerlitz was born in Austria, and had converted from Judaism to Catholicism). But Austerlitz is primarily not the name of a person but of a famous battle, and a well-known Parisian train station. The name is unfortunate for Jacques, because its historical resonance continually pulls us away from his Jewishness (from his individuality), and towards a world-historical reference that has nothing much to do with him. Imagine a novel in which almost every page featured the phrase 'Waterloo said' or 'Agincourt said'. Sebald plays with this oddity most obviously in the passage when the young Austerlitz first finds out his true surname, at school. 'What does it mean?' asks Jacques, and the headmaster tells him that it is a small place in Moravia, site of a famous battle. During the next school year, the battle of Austerlitz is indeed discussed, and it turns out to be one of the set pieces of Mr Hilary, the

romantic history teacher who makes such an impres-
sion on the young Jacques. 'Hilary told us, said
Austerlitz, how at seven in the morning the peaks
of the highest hills emerged from the mist . . .
The Russian and Austrian troops had come down
from the mountain sides like a slow avalanche . . .'
At this moment, when we encounter the familiar
'said Austerlitz', we are briefly unsure if the charac-
ter or the battle itself is speaking.

Go back, for a minute, to the headmaster's reply,
because it is one of the most quietly breathtaking
moments in the novel, and can stand as an emblem
of Sebald's great powers of reticence and understate-
ment. The headmaster, Mr Penrith-Smith (a nice
joke, because Penrith-Smith combines both an
English place-name and the most anonymous, least
curious surname in English) has told Jacques that
he is not called Dafydd Elias but Jacques Austerlitz.
Jacques asks, with the enforced politeness of the
English schoolboy, 'Excuse me, sir, but what does
it mean?' To which Mr Penrith-Smith replies: 'I
think you will find it is a small place in Moravia,
site of a famous battle, you know.' And that is all!
And it is 1949. Jacques asks the question that could
be said to be the question of the entire novel, and

the headmaster refers him only to the famous battle of 1805 between the French and the Austrians. Consider everything that is omitted, or repressed, from this reply. The headmaster might have said that Austerlitz is a Jewish name, and that Jacques is a refugee from the Nazis. He might, with the help of Mr Hilary's expertise, have added that Austerlitz, near Brno in what was then Czechoslovakia, once had a thriving Jewish population, and that perhaps Jacques's name derived from that community. He might have mentioned that in 1941, the Germans established the ghetto of Theresienstadt, north of Prague (named after Queen Maria Theresa, who, in 1745, issued an edict limiting the number of Jewish families in Moravia), and that the remaining Jews of Austerlitz almost certainly perished there, or later in Auschwitz, to which place most of the inmates of Theresienstadt were eventually taken. He might have added that Jacques's parents were unlikely to be alive.

But Mr Penrith-Smith says none of it, and Jacques Austerlitz will spend the rest of the novel trying to find his own answer to his own question. Instead, the headmaster's bland reply turns Jacques into the public past, into a date. What does it mean? And the answer Jacques receives is, in effect: '1805, that's what it means.' Of all the rescues that the novel poses, the most difficult may be this one: to restore to Jacques Austerlitz the individuality of his name and experience, to rescue the living privacy of the surname 'Austerlitz' from the dead, irrelevant publicity of the place-name 'Austerlitz'. Jacques should not be a battle, nor a railway station, nor a thing. Ultimately, we cannot perform this rescue, and the novel does not let us. The private and the public names keep on intertwining, and herein lies the power of the novel's closing pages. We helplessly return to the Gare d'Austerlitz, from where Jacques's father may have left Paris. In the new Bibliothèque Nationale, Jacques learns that the building rests on the ruins of a huge wartime warehouse, where the Germans 'brought all the loot they had taken from the homes of the Jews of Paris'. It was known as the Austerlitz-Tolbiac storage depot. Everything our civilization produced was brought here, says the library official, and often pilfered by German officers – ending up in, say, a 'Grunewald villa' in Berlin. This knowledge is like a literalization of the well-known dictum of Walter Benjamin, that there is no document of civilization which is not at the same time a document of barbarism. Standing on the ruins of history, standing both in and on top of history's depository, Jacques Austerlitz is joined by his name to these ruins: and again, at the end of the book, as at the beginning, he threatens to become simply part of the rubble of history, a thing, a depository of facts and dates, not a human being. And throughout the novel, present but never spoken, never written – it is the most beautiful act of Sebald's withholding – is the other historical name that shadows the name Austerlitz, the name that begins and ends with the same letters, the name which we sometimes misread Austerlitz as, the place that Agatá Austerlitz was almost certainly 'sent east' to in 1944, and the place that Maximilian Aychenwald was almost certainly sent to from the French camp in Gurs in 1942: Auschwitz.

James Wood
Grunewald, Berlin, 2011

# Austerlitz

In the second half of the 1960s I travelled repeatedly from England to Belgium, partly for study purposes, partly for other reasons which were never entirely clear to me, staying sometimes for just one or two days, sometimes for several weeks. On one of these Belgian excursions which, as it seemed to me, always took me further and further abroad, I came on a glorious early summer's day to the city of Antwerp, known to me previously only by name. Even on my arrival, as the train rolled slowly over the viaduct with its curious pointed turrets on both sides and into the dark station concourse, I had begun to feel unwell, and this sense of indisposition persisted for the whole of my visit to Belgium on that occasion. I still remember the uncertainty of my footsteps as I walked all round the inner city, down Jeruzalemstraat, Nachtegaalstraat, Pelikaanstraat, Paradijsstraat, Immerseelstraat and many other streets and alleyways, until at last, plagued by a headache and my uneasy thoughts, I took refuge in the zoo by the Astridplein, next to the Centraal Station, waiting for the pain to subside. I sat there on a bench in dappled shade, beside an aviary full of brightly feathered finches and siskins fluttering about. As the afternoon drew to a close I walked through the park, and finally went to see the Nocturama, which had first been opened only a few months earlier. It was some time before my eyes became used to its artificial dusk, and I could make out the different animals leading their sombrous lives behind the glass by the light of a pale moon. I cannot now recall exactly what creatures I saw on that visit to the Antwerp Nocturama, but there were probably bats and jerboas from Egypt and the Gobi Desert, native European hedgehogs and owls, Australian opossums, pine martens, dormice and lemurs, leaping from branch to branch, darting back and forth over the greyish-yellow sandy ground, or disappearing into a bamboo thicket. The only animal which has remained lingering in my memory is the racoon. I watched it for a long time as it sat beside a little stream with a serious expression on its face, washing the same piece of apple over and over again, as if it hoped that all this washing, which went far beyond any reasonable thoroughness, would help it to escape the unreal world in which it had arrived, so to speak, through no fault of its own. Otherwise, all I remember of the denizens of the Nocturama is that several of them had strikingly large eyes, and the fixed,

inquiring gaze found in certain painters and philosophers who seek to penetrate the darkness

which surrounds us purely by means of looking and thinking. I believe that my mind also dwelt on the question of whether the electric light was turned on for the creatures in the Nocturama when real night fell and the zoo was closed to the public, so that as day dawned over their topsy-turvy miniature universe they could fall asleep with some degree of reassurance. Over the years, images of the interior of the Nocturama have become confused in my mind with my memories of the *Salle des pas perdus*, as it is called, in Antwerp Centraal Station. If I try to conjure up a picture of that waiting-room today I immediately see the Nocturama, and if I think of the Nocturama the waiting-room springs to my mind, probably because when I left the zoo that afternoon I went straight into the station, or rather first stood in the square outside it for some time to look up at the façade of that fantastical building, which I had taken in only vaguely when I arrived in the morning. Now, however, I saw how far the station constructed under the patronage of King Leopold II exceeded its purely utilitarian function, and I marvelled at the verdigris-covered negro boy who, for a century now, has sat upon his dromedary on top of an oriel turret to the left of the station façade, a monument to the world of the animals and native peoples of the African continent, alone against the Flemish sky. When I entered the great hall of the Centraal Station with its dome arching sixty metres high above it, my first thought, perhaps triggered by my visit to the zoo and the sight of the dromedary, was that this magnificent although then severely dilapidated foyer ought to have cages for lions and leopards let into its marble niches, and aquaria for sharks, octopuses and crocodiles, just as some zoos, conversely, have little railway trains in which you can, so to speak, travel to the farthest corners of the earth. It was probably because of ideas like these, occurring to me almost of their own accord there in Antwerp, that the waiting-room which, I know, has now been turned into a staff canteen struck me as another Nocturama, a curious confusion which may of course have been the result of the sun's sinking behind the city rooftops just as I entered the room. The gleam of gold and silver on the huge, half-obscured mirrors on the wall facing the windows was not yet entirely extinguished before a subterranean twilight filled the waiting-room, where a few travellers sat far apart, silent and motionless. Like the creatures in the Nocturama, which had included a strikingly large number of dwarf species — tiny fennec foxes, springhares, hamsters — the railway passengers seemed to me somehow miniaturized, whether by the unusual height of the ceiling or because of the gathering dusk, and it was this, I suppose, which prompted the passing thought, nonsensical in itself, that they were the last members of a diminutive race which had perished or had been expelled from its homeland, and that because they alone survived they wore the same sorrowful expression as the creatures in the zoo. One of the people waiting in the *Salle des pas perdus* was Austerlitz, a man who then, in 1967, appeared almost youthful, with fair, curiously wavy hair of a kind I had seen elsewhere only on the German hero Siegfried in Fritz Lang's *Nibelungen* film. That day in Antwerp, as on all our later meetings, Austerlitz wore heavy walking boots and workman's trousers made of faded blue calico, together with a tailor-made but long outdated suit jacket. Apart from these externals he also differed from the other travellers in being the only one who was not staring apathetically into space, but instead was occupied in making notes and sketches obviously relating to the room where we were both sitting — a magnificent hall more suitable, to my mind, for a state ceremony than as a place to wait for the next connection to Paris or Oostende — for when he was not actually writing something down his glance often dwelt on the row of windows, the fluted pilasters, and other structural details of the waiting-room. Once Austerlitz took a camera out of his rucksack, an old Ensign with telescopic bellows, and took several pictures of the mirrors, which were now quite dark, but so far I have been unable to find them among the many hundreds of pictures, most of them unsorted, that he entrusted to me soon after we met again in the winter of 1996. When I finally went over to Austerlitz with a question about his obvious interest in the waiting-room, he was not at all surprised by my direct approach but answered me at once, without the slightest hesitation, as I have variously found since that solitary travellers, who so often pass days on end in uninterrupted silence, are glad to be spoken to. Now and then they are even ready to open up to a stranger unreservedly on such occasions, although that was not the case with Austerlitz in the *Salle des pas perdus*, nor did he subsequently tell me very much about his origins and his own life. Our Antwerp conversations, as he sometimes called them later, turned primarily on architectural history, in accordance with his own astonishing professional expertise, and it was the subject we discussed that evening as we sat together until nearly midnight in the restaurant facing the waiting-room on the other side of the great domed hall. The few guests still lingering at that late hour one by one deserted the buffet, which was constructed like a mirror image of the waiting-room, until we were left alone with a solitary man drinking Fernet and the barmaid, who sat enthroned on a stool behind the counter, legs crossed, filing her nails with complete devotion and concentration. Austerlitz commented in passing of this lady, whose peroxide-blonde hair was piled up into a sort of bird's nest, that she was the goddess of time past. And on the wall behind her, under the lion crest of the kingdom of Belgium, there was indeed a mighty clock, the dominating feature of the buffet, with a hand some six feet long travelling round a dial which had once been gilded, but was now blackened by railway soot and tobacco smoke. During the pauses in our conversation we both noticed what an endless length of time went by before another minute had passed, and how alarming seemed the movement of that hand, which resembled a sword of justice, even though we were expecting it every time it jerked forward, slicing off the next one-sixtieth of an hour from the future and coming to a halt with such a menacing quiver that one's heart almost stopped. Towards the end of the nineteenth century, Austerlitz began, in reply to my questions about the history of the building of Antwerp station, when Belgium, a little patch of yellowish grey barely visible on the map of the world, spread its sphere of influence to the African continent with its colonial enterprises, when deals of huge proportions were done on the capital markets and raw-materials exchanges of Brussels, and the citizens of Belgium, full of boundless optimism, believed that their country, which had been subject so long to foreign rule and was divided and disunited in itself, was about to become a great new economic power — at that time, now so long ago although it determines our lives to this day, it was the personal wish of King Leopold, under whose auspices such apparently inexorable progress was being made, that the money suddenly and abundantly available should be used to erect public buildings which would bring international renown to his aspiring state. One of the projects thus initiated by the highest authority in the land was the central station of the Flemish metropolis where we were sitting now, said Austerlitz; designed by Louis Delacenserie, it was inaugurated in the summer of 1905, after ten years of planning and building, in the presence of the King himself. The model Leopold had recommended to his architects was the new railway station of Lucerne, where he had been particularly struck by the concept of the dome, so dramatically exceeding the usual modest height of railway buildings,* a concept realized by Delacenserie in his own design, which was inspired by the Pantheon in Rome, in such

* On looking through these notes I remember that in February 1971, during a short visit to Switzerland, one of the places I visited was Lucerne. After seeing the Glacier Museum I spent some time standing on the bridge over the lake on my way back to the station, because the view of its dome and the snow-white heights of the Pilatus massif rising in the clear winter sky behind it had reminded me of my conversation with Austerlitz in Antwerp four and a half years earlier. A few hours later, on the night of 4 February, long after I was fast asleep in my hotel room in Zurich,

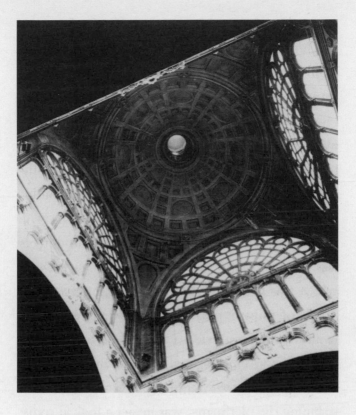

a fire broke out in Lucerne Station, spread very rapidly and entirely destroyed the domed building. I could not get the pictures I saw next day in the newspapers and on television out of my head for several weeks, and they gave me an uneasy, anxious feeling which crystallized into the idea that I had been

stupendous fashion that even today, said Auster-
litz, exactly as the architect intended, when we
step into the entrance hall we are seized by a
sense of being beyond the profane, in a cathedral
consecrated to international traffic and trade.
Delacenserie borrowed the main elements of his
monumental structure from the palaces of the
Italian Renaissance, but he also struck Byzantine
and Moorish notes, and perhaps when I arrived,
said Austerlitz, I myself had noticed the round grey
and white granite turrets, the sole purpose of
which was to arouse medieval associations in the
minds of railway passengers. However laughable
in itself, Delacenserie's eclecticism, uniting past
and future in the Centraal Station with its marble
stairway in the foyer and the steel and glass roof
spanning the platforms, was in fact a logical stylis-
tic approach to the new epoch, said Austerlitz,
and it was also appropriate, he continued, that
in Antwerp Station the elevated level from which
the gods looked down on visitors to the Roman

to blame, or at least one of those to blame, for the Lucerne
fire. In my dreams, even years later, I sometimes saw the
flames leaping from the dome and lighting up the entire
panorama of the snow-covered Alps.

Pantheon should display, in hierarchical order, the deities of the nineteenth century – mining, industry, transport, trade and capital. For halfway up the walls of the entrance hall, as I must have noticed, there were stone escutcheons bearing symbolic sheaves of corn, crossed hammers, winged wheels and so on, with the heraldic motif of the beehive standing not, as one might at first think, for nature made serviceable to mankind, or even industrious labour as a social good, but symbolizing the principle of capital accumulation. And time, said Austerlitz, represented by the hands and dial of the clock, reigns supreme among these emblems. The clock is placed some twenty metres above the only baroque element in the entire ensemble, the cruciform stairway which leads from the foyer to the platforms, just where the image of the emperor stood in the Pantheon in a line directly prolonged from the portal; as governor of a new omnipotence it was set even above the royal coat of arms and the motto *Eendracht maakt macht*. The movements of all travellers could be surveyed from the central position occupied by the clock in Antwerp Station, and conversely all travellers had to look up at the clock and were obliged to adjust their activities to its demands. In fact, said Austerlitz, until the railway timetables were synchronized the clocks of Lille and Liège did not keep the same time as the clocks of Ghent and Antwerp, and not until they were all standardized around the middle of the nineteenth century did time truly reign supreme. It was only by following the course time prescribed that we could hasten through the gigantic spaces separating us from each other. And indeed, said Austerlitz after a while, to this day there is something illusionistic and illusory about the relationship of time and space as we experience it in travelling, which is why whenever we come home from elsewhere we never feel quite sure if we have really been abroad. From the first I was astonished by the way Austerlitz put his ideas together as he talked, forming perfectly balanced sentences out of whatever occurred to him, so to speak, and the way in which, in his mind, the passing on of his knowledge seemed to become a gradual approach to a kind of historical metaphysic, bringing remembered events back to life. I shall never forget how he concluded his comments on the manufacture of the tall waiting-room mirrors by wondering, glancing up once more at their dimly shimmering surfaces as he left, *combien des ouvriers périrent, lors de la manufacture de tels miroirs, de malignes et funestes affectations à la suite de l'inhalation de vapeurs de mercure et de cyanide.* And just as Austerlitz had broken off with these words that first evening, so he continued his observations the following day, for which we had arranged a meeting on the promenade beside the Schelde. Pointing to the broad river sparkling in the morning sun, he spoke of a picture painted by Lucas van Valckenborch towards the end of the sixteenth century during what is now called the Little Ice Age, showing the frozen Schelde from the opposite bank, with the city of Antwerp very dark beyond it and a strip of flat countryside stretching towards the sea. A shower of snow is falling from the lowering sky above the tower of the cathedral of Our Lady, and out on the river now before us some four hundred years later, said Austerlitz, the people of Antwerp are amusing themselves on the ice, the common folk in coats of earthy brown colours, persons of greater distinction in black cloaks with white lace ruffs round their necks. In the foreground, close to the right-hand edge of the picture, a lady has just fallen. She wears a canary-yellow dress, and the cavalier bending over her in concern is clad in red breeches, very conspicuous in the pallid light. Looking at the river now, thinking of that painting and its tiny figures, said Austerlitz, I feel as if the moment depicted by Lucas van Valckenborch had never come to an end, as if the canary-yellow lady had only just fallen over or swooned, as if the black velvet hood had only this moment dropped away from her head, as if the little accident, which no doubt goes unnoticed by most viewers, were always happening over and over again, and nothing and no one could ever remedy it. On that day, after we had left our viewing point on the promenade to stroll through the inner city, Austerlitz spoke at length about the marks of pain which, as he said he well knew, trace countless fine lines through history. In his studies of railway architecture, he said when we were sitting in a bistro in the Glove Market later that afternoon, tired from our wandering through the city, he could never quite shake off thoughts of the agony of leave-taking and the fear of foreign places, although such ideas were not part of architectural history proper. Yet, he said, it is often our mightiest projects that most obviously betray the degree of our insecurity. The construction of fortifications, for instance – and Antwerp was an outstanding example of that craft – clearly showed how we feel obliged to keep surrounding ourselves with defences, built in successive phases as a precaution against any incursion by enemy powers, until the idea of concentric rings making their way steadily outward comes up against its natural limits. If we study the development of fortifications from Floriani, da Capri and San Micheli, by way of Rusenstein, Burgsdorff, Coehoorn and Klengel, and so to Vauban and Montalembert, it is amazing, said Austerlitz, to see the persistence with which generations of masters of the art of military architecture, for all their undoubtedly outstanding gifts, clung to what we can easily see today was a fundamentally wrong-headed idea: the notion that by designing an ideal tracé with blunt bastions and ravelins projecting well beyond it, allowing the cannon of the fortress to cover the entire operational area outside the walls, you could make a city as secure as anything in the world can ever be. No one today, said Austerlitz, has the faintest idea of the boundless amount of theoretical writings on

the building of fortifications, of the fantastic nature
of the geometric, trigonometric and logistical
calculations they record, of the inflated excesses
of the professional vocabulary of fortification and
siegecraft, no one now understands its simplest
terms, *escarpe* and *courtine*, *faussebraie*, *réduit* and
*glacis*, yet even from our present standpoint we
can see that towards the end of the seventeenth
century the star-shaped dodecagon behind

Saarlouis
Vauban, 1680

trenches had finally crystallized, out of the various
available systems, as the preferred ground-plan:
a kind of ideal typical pattern derived from the

Golden Section, which indeed, as study of the intricately sketched plans of such fortified complexes as those of Coevorden, Neuf-Brisach and Saarlouis will show, immediately strikes the layman as an emblem both of absolute power and of the ingenuity the engineers put to the service of that power. In the practice of warfare, however, the star-shaped fortresses which were being built and improved everywhere during the eighteenth century did not answer their purpose, for intent as everyone was on that pattern, it had been forgotten that the largest fortifications will naturally attract the largest enemy forces, and that the more you entrench yourself the more you must remain on the defensive, so that in the end you might find yourself in a place fortified in every possible way, watching helplessly while the enemy troops, moving on to their own choice of terrain elsewhere, simply ignored their adversaries' fortresses, which had become positive arsenals of weaponry, bristling with cannon and overcrowded with men. The frequent result, said Austerlitz, of resorting to measures of fortification marked in general by a tendency towards paranoid elaboration was that you drew attention to your weakest point, practically inviting the enemy to attack it, not to mention the fact that as architectural plans for fortifications became increasingly complex, the time it took to build them increased as well, and with it the probability that as soon as they were finished, if not before, they would have been overtaken by further developments, both in artillery and in strategic planning, which took account of the growing realization that everything was decided in movement, not in a state of rest. And if the defensive power of a fortress really was put to the test, then as a rule, and after the squandering of enormous quantities of war material, the outcome remained more or less undecided. There could not be a clearer illustration of this anywhere, said Austerlitz, than here in Antwerp, where in 1832, as haggling over parts of Belgian territory went on even after the new kingdom had been founded, the citadel, built by Pacciolo and further fortified with a ring of outworks by the Duke of Wellington, was besieged for three weeks by a French army of fifty thousand men. In mid-December, from their base in the fort of Montebello which they had already taken, the French succeeded in storming the half-ruined outwork of the St Laurent lunette and advancing to a position immediately beneath the walls with their breaching batteries. The siege of Antwerp, which was unsurpassed in the history of warfare, at least for some years, both in terms of expenditure and vehemence, said Austerlitz, reached its memorable culmination when some seventy thousand thousand-pound shells were fired at the citadel from the huge mortars invented by Colonel Pairhans, destroying everything without trace except for a couple of casemates. The old Dutch general Baron de Chassé, commander of the pile of rubble which was all that remained of the fortress, had already had the mines laid to blow himself up, along with that monument to his loyalty and heroic courage, when word from his king with permission to surrender reached him just in time. Although the whole insanity of fortification and siegecraft was clearly revealed in the taking of Antwerp, said Austerlitz, the only conclusion anyone drew from it, incredibly, was that the defences surrounding the city must be rebuilt even more strongly than before, and moved further out. In 1859, accordingly, the old citadel and most of the outer forts were levelled and work began on

the construction of a new *enceinte* ten miles long,
with eight forts situated over half an hour's march
away from it, a project which proved inadequate
after less than twenty years because of the longer
range of modern guns and the increasingly
destructive power of explosives, so that, in obedi-
ence to the same old logic, construction now
began on yet another ring of fifteen heavily forti-
fied outworks six to nine miles away from the
*enceinte*. During the thirty years or more it took to
build this complex the question arose, as was only
to be expected, said Austerlitz, of whether the
expansion of Antwerp beyond the old city bound-
aries through its rapid industrial and commercial
development did not mean that the line of forts
ought to be moved yet another three miles further
out, which would actually have made it over thirty
miles long, bringing it within sight of the outskirts
of Mechelen, with the result that the entire Belgian
army would have been insufficient to garrison the
fortifications. So, said Austerlitz, they just went
on working to complete the system already under
construction, although they knew it was now far
from being able to meet the actual requirements.
The last link in the chain was the fortress of

Breendonk, said Austerlitz, a fort completed just before the outbreak of the First World War in which, within a few months, it proved completely useless for the defence of the city and the country. Such complexes of fortifications, said Austerlitz, concluding his remarks that day in the Antwerp Glove Market as he rose from the table and slung his rucksack over his shoulder, show us how, unlike birds, for instance, who keep building the same nest over thousands of years, we tend to forge ahead with our projects far beyond any reasonable bounds. Someone, he added, ought to draw up a catalogue of types of buildings, listed in order of size, and it would be immediately obvious that domestic buildings of *less* than normal size — the little cottage in the fields, the hermitage, the lock-keeper's lodge, the pavilion for viewing the landscape, the children's bothy in the garden — are those that offer us at least a semblance of peace, whereas no one in his right mind could truthfully say that he liked a vast edifice such as the Palace of Justice on the old Gallows Hill in Brussels. At the most we gaze at it in wonder, a kind of wonder which in itself is a form of dawning horror, for somehow we know by instinct that outsize buildings cast the shadow of their own destruction before them, and are designed from the first with an eye to their later existence as ruins. These remarks, made by Austerlitz as he was leaving, were still in my mind next morning when I was sitting over a coffee in the Glove Market which he had left so abruptly the day before, and was hoping that he might reappear. And as I was glancing through the newspapers while I waited, I came upon an article – I don't remember now if it was in the *Gazet van Antwerpen* or *La libre Belgique* – about the fortress of Breendonk, from which it emerged that in 1940, when for the second time in its history the fort had to be surrendered to the Germans, it was made into a reception and penal camp which remained in existence until August 1944, and that since 1947, preserved unchanged as far as possible, it had been a national memorial and a museum of the Belgian Resistance. If the name of Breendonk had not come up in my conversation with Austerlitz the previous evening, this mention of it in the paper, even supposing I had noticed it at all, would hardly have made me go to see the fort that very day. The passenger train I boarded later that morning took a good half-hour to travel the short distance to Mechelen, where a bus runs from outside the station to the small town of Willebroek; it is on the outskirts of this town that the fort stands in its grounds of some ten hectares, set among the fields rather like an island in the sea and surrounded by an embankment, a barbed-wire fence and a wide moat. It was unusually hot for the time of year, and large cumulus clouds were piling up on the south-west horizon as I crossed the bridge over the dark water. After the previous day's conversation, I still had an image in my head of a star-shaped bastion with walls towering above a precise geometrical ground-plan, but what I now saw before me was a low-built concrete mass, rounded at all its outer edges and giving the gruesome impression of something hunched and misshapen: the broad back of a monster, I thought, risen from this Flemish soil like a whale from the deep. I felt reluctant to pass through the black gateway into the fortress itself, and instead began by walking round it on the outside, through the unnaturally deep green, almost blue-tinged grass growing on the island. From whatever viewpoint I tried to form a picture of the complex I could make out no architectural plan, for its projections and indentations kept shifting, so far exceeding my comprehension that in the end I found myself unable to connect it with anything shaped by human civilization, or even with the silent relics of our prehistory and early history. And the longer I

looked at it, the more often it forced me, as I felt, to lower my eyes, the less comprehensible it seemed to become. Covered in places by open ulcers with the raw crushed stone erupting from them, encrusted by guano-like droppings and calcareous streaks, the fort was a monolithic, monstrous incarnation of ugliness and blind violence. Even later, when I studied the symmetrical ground-plan with its outgrowths of limbs and claws, with the semi-circular bastions standing out from the front of the main building like eyes, and the stumpy projection at the back of its body, I could not, despite its now evident rational structure, recognize anything designed by the human mind but saw it, rather, as the anatomical blue-print of some alien and crab-like creature. The path round the fort led past the tarred black posts of the execution ground, and the labour site where the prisoners had to clear away the earth-works around the walls, moving over a quarter of a million tons of soil and rubble with only shovels and wheelbarrows to help them. These wheel-barrows, one of which can still be seen in the anteroom of the fort, must have seemed terrify-ingly primitive even then. They consisted of a kind of stretcher with two crude handles at one end and an iron-shod wooden wheel at the other. A container with sloping sides, roughly cobbled together from unplaned planks, stood on the crossbars of the stretcher, the whole clumsy con-traption resembling the handcarts used by farmers where I lived as a child for clearing muck out of the stables, except that the wheelbarrows in Breendonk were twice as large, and even when they were empty must have reached around a hundredweight. I could not imagine how the prisoners, very few of whom had probably ever done hard physical labour before their arrest and internment, could have pushed these barrows full

of heavy detritus over the sun-baked clay of the
ground, furrowed by ruts as hard as stone, or
through the mire that was churned up after a
single day's rain; it was impossible to picture
them bracing themselves against the weight until
their hearts nearly burst, or think of the overseer
beating them about the head with the handle of
a shovel when they could not move forward.
However, if I could not envisage the drudgery
performed day after day, year after year, at
Breendonk and all the other main and branch
camps, when I finally entered the fort itself and
glanced through the glass panes of a door on the
right into the so-called mess of the SS guards with
its scrubbed tables and benches, its bulging stove
and the various adages neatly painted on its wall in
Gothic lettering, I could well imagine the sight of
the good fathers and dutiful sons from Vilsbiburg
and Fuhlsbüttel, from the Black Forest and the
Bavarian Alps, sitting here when they came off
duty to play cards or write letters to their loved
ones at home. After all, I had lived among them
until my twentieth year. My memory of the
fourteen stations which the visitor to Breendonk
passes between the entrance and the exit has

clouded over in the course of time, or perhaps I could say it was clouding over even on the day when I was in the fort, whether because I did not really want to see what it had to show or because all the outlines seemed to merge in a world illuminated only by a few dim electric bulbs, and cut

off for ever from the light of nature. Even now, when I try to remember them, when I look back at the crab-like plan of Breendonk and read the words of the captions — *Former Office*, *Printing Works*, *Huts*, *Jacques Ochs Hall*, *Solitary Confinement Cell*, *Mortuary*, *Relics Store* and *Museum* — the darkness does not lift but becomes yet heavier as I think how little we can hold in mind, how everything is constantly lapsing into oblivion with every extinguished life, how the world is, as it were, draining itself, in that the history of countless places and objects which themselves have no power of memory is never heard, never described or passed on. Histories, for instance, like those of the straw mattresses which lay, shadow-like, on the stacked plank beds and which had become thinner and shorter because the chaff in them disintegrated over the years, shrunken – and now, in writing this, I do remember that such an idea occurred to me at the time – as if they were the mortal frames of those who once lay there in that darkness. I also recollect now that as I went on down the tunnel which could be said to form the backbone of the fort, I had to resist the feeling taking root in my heart, one which to this day often comes over me in macabre places, a sense that with every forward step the air was growing thinner and the weight above me heavier. At the time, anyway, in that silent noonday hour in the early summer of 1967 which I spent inside the fort of Breendonk, encountering no other visitors, I hardly dared to go on to the point where, at the end of a second long tunnel, a corridor not much more than the height of a man, and (as I think I remember) somewhat sloping, leads down to one of the casemates. This casemate, in which you sense immediately that there

is a layer of concrete several metres thick overhead, is a narrow room with walls converging at a sharp angle on one side, rounded on the other, and with its floor at least a foot lower than the passage giving access to it, so that it is less like an oubliette than a pit. As I stared at the smooth, grey floor of this pit, which seemed to me to be sinking further and further down, the grating over the drain in the middle of it and the metal pail standing beside the drain, a picture of our laundry room at home in W. rose from the abyss and with it, suggested perhaps by the iron hook hanging on a cord from the ceiling, the image of the butcher's shop I always had to pass on my way to school, where at noon Benedikt was often to be seen in a rubber apron washing down the tiles with a thick hose. No one can explain exactly what happens within us when the doors behind which our childhood terrors lurk are flung open. But I do remember that there in the casemate at Breendonk a nauseating smell of soft soap rose to my nostrils, and that this smell, in some strange place in my head, was linked to the bizarre German word for scrubbing-brush, *Wurzelbürste*, which was a favourite of my father's and which I had always disliked. Black striations began to quiver before my eyes, and I had to rest my forehead against the wall, which was gritty, covered with bluish spots, and seemed to me to be perspiring with cold beads of sweat. It was not that as the nausea rose in me I guessed at the kind of third-degree interrogations which were being conducted here around the time I was born, since it was only a few years later that I read Jean Améry's description of the dreadful physical closeness between torturers and their victims, and of the tortures he himself suffered in Breendonk when he was hoisted aloft by his hands, tied behind his back, so that with a crack and a splintering sound which, as he says, he had not yet forgotten when he came to write his account, his arms dislocated from the sockets in his shoulder joints, and he was left dangling as they were wrenched up behind him and twisted together above his head: *la pendaison par les mains liées dans le dos jusqu'à évanouissement* – this is how it is described in the book *Le Jardin des Plantes*, in which Claude Simon descends once more into the storehouse of his memories, and on page 235 begins to tell the fragmentary tale of a certain Gastone Novelli who, like Améry, was subjected to this particular form of torture. The passage opens with an entry of 26 October 1943 from General Rommel's diary, in which Rommel comments that in view of the total powerlessness of the police in Italy one must now take charge oneself. As a result of the measures thereupon introduced by the Germans, says Simon, Novelli was arrested and taken to Dachau. Novelli, Simon continues, never mentioned what happened to him there except on one occasion, when he said that after his liberation from the camp he found the sight of a German, or indeed any so-called civilized being, male or female, so intolerable that, hardly recovered, he embarked on the first ship he could find, to make his living prospecting for diamonds and gold in South America. For some time Novelli lived in the green jungle with a tribe of small people who had gleaming, coppery skins and had emerged beside him as if out of nowhere one day, without moving so much as a leaf. He adopted their customs, and to the best of his ability compiled a dictionary of their language, consisting almost entirely of vowels, particularly the sound A in countless variations of intonation and emphasis, not a word of which, Simon writes, had yet been recorded by the Linguistic Institute in São Paulo. Later Novelli returned to his native land and began to paint pictures. His main sub-ject, depicted again and again in different forms and compositions — *filiforme, gras, soudain plus épais ou plus grand, puis de nouveau mince, boiteux* — was the letter A, which he traced on the coloured ground he had applied sometimes with the point of a pencil, sometimes with the stem of his brush or an even blunter instrument, in ranks of scarcely legible ciphers crowding closely together and above one another, always the same and yet never repeating themselves, rising and falling in waves like a long-drawn-out scream.

AAAAAAAAAAAAAAAAAAAAAAAAAAAAAAAA
AAAAAAAAAAAAAAAAAAAAAAAAAAAAAAAA
AAAAAAAAAAAAAAAAAAAAAAAAAAAAAAAA

Although Austerlitz did not reappear in the Glove Market in Antwerp that June day in 1967 on which, in the end, I went out to Breendonk, our paths kept crossing, in a way that I still find hard to understand, on all my Belgian excursions of that time, none of them planned in advance. A few days after our first encounter in the *Salle des pas perdus* of the Centraal Station, I met him again in an industrial quarter on the south-western outskirts of the city of Liège, which I had reached towards evening, coming on foot from St Georges-sur-Meuse and Flémalle. The sun was just breaking once again through the inky blue wall of cloud heralding a storm, and the factory buildings and yards, the long rows of terraced housing for the labourers, the brick walls, the slate roofs and the window panes shone as if a fire were glowing within them. When the rain began lashing down on the streets I took refuge in a tiny bar called, as I remember, the Café des Espérances, where to my considerable surprise I found Austerlitz bent over his notes at one of the Formica tables. On this second meeting, as on all subsequent occasions, we simply went on with our conversation, wasting no time in commenting on the improbability of our meeting again in a place like this, which no sensible person would have sought out. From where we sat until late that evening in the Café des Espérances, you could look through a back window down into a valley, perhaps a place of water meadows in the past, where now the reflected light from the blast furnaces of a gigantic iron foundry glared against the dark sky, and I remember clearly how, as we both gazed intently at this spectacle, Austerlitz launched into a discourse of over two hours on the way in which, during the nineteenth century, the vision of model towns for workers entertained by philanthropic entrepreneurs had inadvertently changed into the practice of accommodating them in barracks — just as our best-laid plans, said Austerlitz, as I still remember, always turn into the exact opposite when they are put into practice. It was several months after this meeting in Liège that I came upon Austerlitz, again entirely by chance, on the old Gallows Hill in Brussels, on the steps of the Palace of Justice which, as he immediately told me, is the largest accumulation of stone blocks anywhere in Europe. The building of this singular architectural monstrosity, on which Austerlitz was planning to write a study at the time, began in the 1880s at the urging of the bourgeoisie of Brussels, over-hastily and before the details of the grandiose scheme submitted by a certain Joseph Poelaert had been properly worked out, as a result of which, said Austerlitz, this huge pile of over seven hundred thousand cubic metres contains corridors and stairways leading nowhere, and doorless rooms and halls where no one would ever set foot, empty spaces surrounded by walls and representing the innermost secret of all sanctioned authority. Austerlitz went on to tell me that he himself, looking for a labyrinth used in the initiation ceremonies of the freemasons, which he had heard was in either the basement or the attic storey of the palace, had wandered for hours through this mountain range of stone, through forests of columns, past colossal statues, upstairs and downstairs, and no one ever asked him what he wanted. During these wanderings, feeling tired or wishing to get his bearings from the sky, he had stopped at one of the windows set deep in the walls to look out over the leaden grey roofs of the palace, crammed together like pack ice, and down into ravines and shaft-like interior courtyards never penetrated by any ray of light. He had gone on and on down the corridors, said

Austerlitz, sometimes turning left and then right again, then walking straight ahead and passing through many tall doorways, and once or twice he had climbed flights of creaking wooden stairs which gave the impression of being temporary structures, branching off from the main corridors here and there and leading half a storey up or down, only to end in dark cul-de-sacs with roll-top cupboards, lecterns, writing desks, office chairs and other items of furniture stacked up at the end of them, as if someone had been obliged to hold out there in a state of siege. He had even heard, said Austerlitz, of people who, over the years, had managed to start up a small business in one or other of the empty rooms and remote corridors of that great warren: a tobacconist's, a bookie's, a bar, and it was rumoured, Austerlitz added, that a man called Achterbos had once turned a gentlemen's lavatory down in the basement into a public convenience for, among others, passers-by in the street, installing himself at the entrance with a small table and a plate to take the money, and that later, when he engaged an assistant who was handy with a comb and a pair of scissors, it was a barber's shop for a while.

I heard several such apocryphal stories from Austerlitz, anecdotes in curious contrast to his usual rigorous objectivity, not only that day but on our later encounters, for instance one quiet November afternoon when we spent some time sitting in a café with a billiards room in Terneuzen – I still remember the proprietress, a woman with thick-lensed spectacles who was knitting a grass-green sock, the glowing nuggets of coke in the hearth, the damp sawdust on the floor, the bitter smell of chicory – and looked out through the panoramic window, which was framed by the tentacles of an ancient rubber plant, at the vast expanse of the misty grey mouth of the Schelde. Then, not long before Christmas, I saw Auster-litz coming towards me on the promenade at Zeebrugge when evening was falling and there was not another living soul in sight. It turned out that we had both booked on the same ferry, so we slowly walked back to the harbour together, with the emptiness of the North Sea on our right and on our right the tall façades of the apartment blocks set among the dunes, with the bluish light of tele-vision screens flickering behind their windows, curiously unsteady and ghostly. It was night by the time the ferry sailed. We stood together on the stern deck. The white wake vanished into the darkness, and I remember that we once thought we saw a few snowflakes swirling in the lamplight. Only on this night crossing of the Channel, in fact, did I discover from a chance remark dropped by Austerlitz that he was a lecturer at a London institute of art history. As it was almost impossible to talk to him about anything personal, and as neither of us knew where the other came from, we had always spoken in French since our first conversation in Antwerp, I with lamentable awkwardness, but Austerlitz with such natural perfection that for a long time I thought he had been brought up in France. When we switched to English, in which I was better versed, I was strangely touched to notice in him an insecurity which had been entirely concealed from me before, expressing itself in a slight speech impediment and occasional fits of stammering, during which he clutched the worn spectacle case he always held in his left hand so tightly that you could see the white of his knuckles beneath the skin.

*

Almost every time I went to London in the years that followed I visited Austerlitz where he worked in Bloomsbury, not far from the British Museum. I would usually spend an hour or so sitting with him in his crowded study, which was like a stockroom of books and papers with hardly any space left for himself, let alone his students, among the

stacks piled high on the floor and the overloaded shelves. When I began my own studies in Germany I had learnt almost nothing from the scholars then lecturing in the humanities there, most of them academics who had built their careers in the 1930s and 1940s and still nurtured delusions of power, and I found Austerlitz the first teacher I could listen to since my time in primary school. I remember to this day how easily I could grasp what he called his tentative ideas when he talked about the architectural style of the capitalist era, a subject which he said had fascinated him since his own student days, speaking in particular of the compulsive sense of order and the tendency towards monumentalism evident in lawcourts and penal institutions, railway stations and stock exchanges, opera houses and lunatic asylums, and the dwellings built to rectangular grid patterns for the labour force. His investigations, so Austerlitz once told me, had long outstripped their original purpose as a project for a dissertation, proliferating in his hands into endless preliminary sketches for a study, based entirely on his own views, of the family likeness between all these buildings. Why he had embarked on such a wide field, said Austerlitz, he did not know; very likely he had been poorly advised when he first began his research work. But then again, it was also true that he was still obeying an impulse which he himself, to this day, did not really understand, but which was somehow linked to his early fascination with the idea of a network such as that of the entire railway system. At the very beginning of his studies, said Austerlitz, and later, when he was first living in Paris, he used to visit one of the main railway stations almost daily, usually the Gare du Nord or the Gare de l'Est and especially in the morning or evening, to see the steam locomotives moving into the soot-blackened, glass-roofed halls, or to watch the brightly illuminated, mysterious Pullman trains slide gently out into the night like ships on the endless expanse of the sea. He had quite often found himself in the grip of dangerous and entirely incomprehensible currents of emotion in the Parisian railway stations, which, he said, he regarded as places marked by both blissful happiness and profound misfortune. I can still see Austerlitz one afternoon in the London institute making this comment on what he once later described as his obsession with railway stations, speaking not so much to me as to himself, and it was the only hint of his personal life he allowed himself to give me before I returned to Germany at the end of 1975, intending to settle permanently in my native country, to which I felt I had become a stranger after nine years of absence. As far as I remember I wrote to Austerlitz from Munich a couple of times, but I never had any reply to my letters, either because, as I thought at the time, Austerlitz was away somewhere, or as I now think because he did not like writing to Germany. Whatever the reason for his silence, the link between us was broken, and I did not renew it when, scarcely a year later, I decided to return to the United Kingdom. It would now of course have been up to me to let Austerlitz know of the unforeseen change to my plans, and my failure to do so may have resulted from the fact that soon after my return I went through a difficult period which dulled my sense of other people's existence, and from which I only very gradually emerged by turning back to the writing I had long neglected. At any rate, I did not often think of Austerlitz in all those years, and when the thought of him did cross my mind I always forgot him again next moment, so that we did not in fact resume our old relationship, which had been both a close and a distant one, until two decades later in December 1996, and through a curious chain of circumstances. I was in some anxiety at the time because I had noticed, looking up an address in the telephone book, that the sight in my right eye had almost entirely disappeared overnight, so to speak. Even when I glanced up from the page open in front of me and turned my gaze on the framed photographs on the wall, all my right eye could see was a row of dark shapes curiously distorted above and below – the figures and landscapes familiar to me in every detail having resolved indiscriminately into a black and menacing cross-hatching. At the same time I kept feeling as if I could see as clearly as ever on the edge of my field of vision, and had only to look sideways to rid myself of what I took at first for a merely hysterical weakness in my eyesight. Although I tried several times, I did not succeed. Instead, the grey areas seemed to be spreading, and now and then, opening and closing my eyes alternately to compare their degrees of clarity, I thought that I had suffered some impairment on the left as well. Considerably alarmed by what I feared was the progressive decline of my eyesight, I remembered reading once that until well into the nineteenth century a few drops of liquid distilled from belladonna, a plant of the nightshade family, used to be applied to the retinas of operatic divas before they went on stage, and those of young women about to be introduced to a suitor, with the result that their eyes shone with a rapt and almost supernatural radiance, but they themselves could see almost nothing. I no longer know how I connected this memory with my own condition that dark December morning, except that in my mind it had something to do with the deceptiveness of that star-like, beautiful gleam and the danger of its premature extinction, an idea which filled me with concern for my ability to continue working and at the same time, if I may so put it, with a vision of release in which I saw myself, free of the constant compulsion to read and write, sitting in a wicker chair in a garden, surrounded by a world of indistinct shapes recognizable only by their faint colours. Since there was no improvement in my condition over the next few days, I went to London just before Christmas to see a Czech ophthalmologist who had been recommended to me. As usual when I go down to London on my own, a kind of dull despair stirred within me on that December morning. I looked out at the flat, almost treeless landscape, the vast brown expanse of the ploughed fields, the railway stations where I would never get out, the flock of gulls which makes a habit of gathering on the football pitch on the outskirts of Ipswich, the allotments, the crippled bushes overgrown with dead traveller's joy on the embankments, the quicksilver mudflats and channels at Manningtree, the boats capsized on their sides, the Colchester water-tower, the Marconi factory in Chelmsford, the empty greyhound track at Romford, the ugly backs of the terraced houses past which the railway line runs in the suburbs of the metropolis, the Manor Park cemetery and the tower blocks of flats in Hackney, sights which are always the same and flit past me whenever I go to London, yet remain alien and incomprehensible in spite of all the years that have passed since my arrival in England. I always feel particularly apprehensive on the last stretch of the journey, where just before turning into Liverpool Street station the train must wind its way over several sets of points through a narrow defile, and where the brick walls rising above both sides of the track with their round arches, columns and niches, blackened with soot and diesel oil, put me in mind once again that morning of an underground columbarium. It was around three in the afternoon by the time I reached Harley Street and one of its mauve brick buildings, almost all of them occupied by dermatologists, urologists, gynaecologists, neurologists, psychiatrists, ear, nose and throat specialists and eye surgeons, and was standing by the window in the soft lamplight of Zděnek Gregor's slightly over-heated waiting-room. From the grey sky that lowered over the city outside a few isolated snowflakes were floating down, and disappeared into the dark chasms of the yards behind the buildings. I thought of the onset of winter in the mountains, the complete absence of sound, and my childhood wish for everything to be snowed over, the whole village and the valley all the way to the mountain peaks, and how I used to imagine what it would be like when we thawed out again and emerged from the ice in spring. And as I stood in the waiting-room remembering the snow of the Alps, the whitened panes of the bedroom window, the curved drifts around the porch, the softly capped insulators of the telegraph poles, and the trough of the well which was sometimes frozen over for months, the opening lines of one of my favourite poems came into my mind . . . *And so I long for snow to sweep across the low heights of London* . . . I imagined that out there in the gathering dusk I could see the districts of the city of London criss-crossed by innumerable streets and railway lines, crowding ever more closely together as they marched east and north, one reef of buildings above the next and then the next, and so on, far beyond Holloway and Highbury, and I saw the snow falling on this huge outcropping of stone slowly, steadily, until everything was covered up and buried . . . *London a lichen mapped on mild clays and its rough circle without purpose* . . . It was a circle of this kind with an indistinct outline that Zděnek Gregor drew on a piece of paper to illustrate the extent of the grey area in my right eye when he had examined it. Usually, he said, this was only a temporary disability, in which a bubble suffused by clear liquid formed on the macula, rather like a blister under wallpaper. There was considerable uncertainty, said Zděnek Gregor, about the causes of the disorder, described by the literature on the subject as central serous chorioretinopathy. All that was really known was that it occurred almost exclusively in middle-aged men who spent too much time reading and writing. After the consultation I must have a procedure called a fluorescing angiography carried out to determine the affected area of the retina more precisely – this would mean taking a series of photographs of my eyes or rather, if I understood him correctly, of the back of the eye through the iris, the pupil and the vitreous humour. The technician already waiting for me in a small room specially equipped for such purposes was a man of extraordinarily distinguished appearance who wore a white turban and looked, I foolishly thought, rather like the Prophet Muhammad. He carefully rolled up my shirt-sleeve, and inserted the tip of the needle into the prominent vein below the crook of my elbow without my feeling anything at all. While he was introducing the contrast medium into my bloodstream he said I might feel slightly unwell in a little while, and in any case my skin would be discoloured yellow for a few hours. After we had sat in silence for a moment or two, both in our respective places in the little room which, like a sleeping-car, was illuminated only by a dim bulb, he asked me to move closer to him and place my head in the framework fixed in a kind of stand on the table, with my chin in a shallow depression and my forehead against the iron band above it. As I write this I once again see the little points of light that shot into my widely opened eyes each time he pressed the shutter release. Half an hour later I was sitting in the saloon bar of the Great Eastern Hotel at Liverpool Street, waiting for the next train home. I had sought out a dark corner, since by now I did indeed feel rather qualmish inside my yellow skin. On the way to the station in the taxi we had seemed to be driving in a wide, loop-ing trajectory through some kind of Luna Park, so strangely did the city lights turn beyond the wind-screen, and now the dim globes of the sconces, the mirrors behind the bar and the colourful batteries of bottles of spirits were circling before my eyes as if I were on a roundabout. Leaning my head against the wall, and breathing deeply and slowly from time to time when I felt nausea rising, I had for a good while been watching the toilers in the City gold-mines as they came to meet at their usual watering hole early in the evening, all of them identical in their dark-blue suits, striped shirts and gaudy ties, and as I tried to grasp the mysterious habits of the members of this

species, which is not to be found in any bestiary
— their preference for crowding close together,
their semi-gregarious, semi-aggressive demean-
our, the way they put their throats back in empty-
ing their glasses, the increasingly excitable babble
of their voices, the sudden hasty departure of one
or another of them — as I was watching all of this I
suddenly noticed a solitary figure on the edge of
the agitated crowd, a figure who could only be
Austerlitz, whom I realized at that moment I had
not seen for nearly twenty years. He had not
changed at all in either his carriage or his clothing,
and even had the rucksack still slung over his
shoulder. Only his fair, wavy hair was paler,
although it still stuck out oddly from his head as it
used to. None the less, while I had always thought
he was about ten years older than I, he now
seemed ten years younger, whether because of my
own poor state of health or because he was one of
those bachelors who retain something boyish
about them all their days. As far as I remember, I
was overcome for a considerable time by my
amazement at the unexpected return of Auster-
litz. In any case, I recollect that before approach-
ing him I had been thinking at some length about

his personal similarity to Ludwig Wittgenstein, and the horror-stricken expressions on both their faces. I believe it was mainly the rucksack, which Austerlitz told me later he had bought for ten shillings from Swedish stock in an army surplus store in the Charing Cross Road just before he began his studies, describing it as the only truly reliable thing in his life, which put into my head what on the surface was the rather outlandish idea

of a certain physical likeness between him and the philosopher who died of the disease of cancer in Cambridge in 1951. Wittgenstein always carried a rucksack too, in Puchberg and in Otterthal, when he went to Norway, Ireland, or Kazakhstan, or home to his sisters to spend Christmas with them in the Alleegasse. That rucksack, which his sister Margarete once told him in a letter was almost as dear to her as himself, went everywhere with him, even, I believe, across the Atlantic on the liner *Queen Mary*, and then on from New York to Ithaca. And now, whenever I see a photograph of Wittgenstein somewhere or other, I feel more and more as if Austerlitz were gazing at me out of it, and when I look at Austerlitz it is as if I see in him the disconsolate philosopher, a man locked into the glaring clarity of his logical thinking as inextricably as into his confused emotions, so striking is the likeness between the two of them: in stature, in the way they study one as if across an invisible barrier, in the makeshift organization of their lives, in a wish to manage with as few possessions as possible, and in the inability, typical of Austerlitz as it was of Wittgenstein, to linger over any kind of preliminaries. Accordingly, and without wasting any words on the coincidence of our meeting again after all this time, Austerlitz took up the conversation that evening in the bar of the

Great Eastern Hotel more or less where it had last been broken off. He had spent the afternoon, he told me, looking round the Great Eastern, which was soon to be thoroughly renovated, concentrating mainly on the freemasons' temple incorporated into the hotel by the directors of the railway company at the turn of the century, when the building had only just been completed and furnished with the utmost luxury. Though I really gave up my architectural studies long ago, he said, I sometimes relapse into my old habits, even if I don't make notes and sketches any more, but simply marvel at the strange edifices we construct. That had been the case today, when his way led him past the Great Eastern and, obeying a sudden impulse, he had gone into the foyer where, as it turned out, he had been very courteously received by the business manager, a Portuguese called Pereira, despite my request, said Austerlitz, which can't be one he hears every day, and despite my odd appearance. Pereira, Austerlitz went on, took me up a broad staircase to the first floor, produced a large key and unlocked the portal of the temple, a hall with walls panelled in sand-coloured marble and red Moroccan onyx, a

black and white chequered floor, and a vaulted
ceiling with a single golden star at the centre
emitting its rays into the dark clouds all around it.
Then Pereira and I went all over the hotel, most
of it taken out of use already, through the great
dining hall which could accommodate more than
three hundred guests under its high glass dome,

through the smoking rooms and the billiards
saloons, through suites and up staircases to the
fourth floor where the kitchens used to be, and
then down to the basement and the floor below

the basement, once upon a time a cool labyrinth for the storage of Rhine wines, claret and champagne, for the making of thousands of items of pâtisserie and the preparation of vegetables, red meat and pale poultry. As for the fish section, where perch, pike, plaice, sole and eels lay heaped on black slate slabs with fresh water constantly running over them, Pereira described it as a whole underworld in itself, said Austerlitz, and if it hadn't been too late he, Austerlitz, would go round the place again with me. He added that he would particularly like to show me the temple, with its ornamental gold-painted picture of a three-storey ark floating beneath a rainbow, and the dove just returning to it carrying the olive branch in her beak. Oddly enough, said

Austerlitz, as he stood in front of this attractive motif with Pereira that afternoon he had been

thinking of our encounters in Belgium, so long ago now, and telling himself he must find someone to whom he could relate his own story, a story which he had learned only in the last few years and for which he needed the kind of listener I had once been in Antwerp, Liège and Zeebrugge. Contrary to all statistical probability, then, there was an astonishing, positively imperative internal logic to his meeting me here in the bar of the Great Eastern Hotel, a place he had never before entered in his life. Having said this, Austerlitz fell silent, and for a while, it seemed to me, he gazed into the farthest distance. Since my childhood and youth, he finally began, looking at me again, I have never known who I really was. From where I stand now, of course, I can see that my name alone, and the fact that it was kept from me until my fifteenth year, ought to have put me on the track of my origins, but it has also become clear to me of late why an agency greater than or superior to my own capacity for thought, which circumspectly directs operations somewhere in my brain, has always preserved me from my own secret, systematically preventing me from drawing the obvious conclusions and embarking on the inquiries they would have suggested to me. It hasn't been easy to make my way out of my own inhibitions, and it will not be easy now to put the story into anything like proper order. I grew up, began Austerlitz that evening in the bar of the Great Eastern Hotel, in the little country town of Bala in Wales, in the home of a Calvinist preacher and former missionary called Emyr Elias who was married to a timid-natured Englishwoman. I have never liked looking back at the time I spent in that unhappy house, which stood in isolation on a hill just outside the town and was much too large for two people and an only child. Several rooms on the top floor were kept shut up year in, year out. Even today I still sometimes dream that one of those locked doors opens and I step through it, into a friendlier, more familiar world. Several of the rooms that were not locked were unused too. Furnished sparsely with a bed or a chest of drawers, curtains drawn even during the day, they drowsed in a twilight that soon extinguished every sense of self-awareness in me. So I can recall almost nothing of my early days in Bala except how it hurt to be suddenly called by a new name, and how dreadful it was, once my own clothes had disappeared, to have to go around dressed in the English fashion in shorts, knee-length socks which were always slipping down, a string vest like a fish-net and a mouse-grey shirt, much too thin. I know that I often lay awake for hours in my narrow bed in the manse, trying to conjure up the faces of those whom I had left, I feared through my own fault, but not until I was numb with weariness and my eyelids sank in the darkness did I see my mother bending down to me just for a fleeting moment, or my father smiling as he put on his hat. Such comfort made it all the worse to wake up early in the morning and have to face the knowledge, new every day, that I was not at home now but very far away, in some kind of captivity. Only recently have I recalled how oppressed I felt, in all the time I spent with the Eliases, by the fact that they never opened a window, and perhaps that is why when I was out and about somewhere on a summer's day years later, and passed a house with all its windows thrown open, I felt an extraordinary sense of being carried away and out of myself. It was only a few days ago that, thinking over that experience of liberation, I remembered how one of the two windows of my bedroom was walled up on the inside while it remained unchanged on the outside, a circumstance which, as one is never both outside and inside a house at the same time, I did not register until I was thirteen or fourteen, although it must have been troubling me throughout my childhood in Bala. The manse was always freezing, Austerlitz continued, not just in winter, when the only fire was often in the kitchen stove and the stone floor in the hallway was frequently covered with hoar frost, but in autumn too, and well into spring and the infallibly wet summers. And just as cold reigned in the house in Bala, so did silence. The minister's wife was always busy with her housework, dusting, mopping the tiled floor, doing the laundry, polishing the brass door fittings and preparing the meagre meals which we usually ate without a word. Sometimes she merely walked round the house making sure that everything was in its proper place, from which she would never allow it to be moved. I once found her sitting on a chair in one of the half-empty rooms upstairs, with tears in her eyes and a crumpled wet handkerchief in her hand. When she saw me standing in the doorway she rose and said it was nothing, she had only caught a cold, and as she went out she ran her fingers through my hair, the one time, as far as I remember, she ever did such a thing. Meanwhile it was the minister's unalterable custom to sit in his study, which had a view of a dark corner of the garden, thinking about next Sunday's sermon. He never wrote any of these sermons down, but worked them out in his head, toiling over them for at least four days. He would always emerge from his study in the evening in a state of deep despondency, only to disappear into it again next morning. But on Sunday, when he stood up in chapel in front of his congregation and often addressed them for a full hour, he was a changed man; he spoke with a moving eloquence which I still feel I can hear, conjuring up before the eyes of his flock the Last Judgment awaiting them all, the lurid fires of purgatory, the torments of damnation and then, with the most wonderful stellar and celestial imagery, the entry of the righteous into eternal bliss. With apparent ease, as if he were making up the most appalling horrors as he went along, he always succeeded in filling the hearts of his congregation with such sentiments of remorse that at the end of the service quite a number of them went home looking white as a sheet. The minister himself, on the other hand, was in a comparatively jovial mood for the rest of Sunday. At midday dinner, which always began with tapioca soup, he would make a few informative and semi-jocular remarks to his wife, who was exhausted from cooking the meal, inquired after my welfare, generally by asking, 'And how is the boy?', and tried to draw me out a little. The meal always finished with the minister's favourite dish of rice pudding, and he usually fell silent as he enjoyed it. Once dinner was over he lay down on the sofa to rest for an hour, or in fine weather he would sit out under the apple tree in the front garden looking down the valley, as well satisfied with his week's work as the Lord God of Sabaoth after the creation of the world. Before evening prayers he went to his roll-top desk and took out the tin box in which he kept the calendar published by the Calvinist Methodists of Wales, a grey little book already worn rather threadbare and listing the Sundays and church festivals for the years 1928 to 1946, in which he had made regular entries against every date week by week, removing the thin solid-ink pencil from the back of the book, moistening its tip with his tongue, and very slowly and neatly, like a schoolboy under supervision, noting down the name of the chapel where he had preached that day and the biblical passage he had taken as his text, for instance, under 20 July 1939: The Tabernacle, Llandrillo – *Psalms* CLXVII, 4, 'He telleth the number of the stars: he calleth them all by their names'; under 3 August 1941: Chapel Uchaf, Gilboa – *Zephaniah* III, 6, 'I have cut off the nations: their towers are desolate; I made their streets waste, that none passeth by'; and under 21 May 1944: Chapel Bethesda, Corwen – *Isaiah* XLVIII, 18, 'O that thou hadst hearkened to my commandments! then had thy peace been as a river and thy righteousness as the waves of the sea!' The last entry in this little book, which is among those few of the minister's possessions to have passed into my hands after his death and through which I have often glanced recently, said Austerlitz, was made on one of the additional leaves inserted at the end and is dated 7 March 1952. It runs: Bala Chapel – *Psalms* CII, 6, 'I am like a pelican of the wilderness: I am like an owl of the desert.' For the most part, of course, these Sunday sermons, and I must have heard over five hundred of them, went over my head when I was a child, but even if the meaning of the various words and phrases was a mystery to me for a long time, and whether Elias delivered them in English or Welsh, I did understand that his subject was the sinfulness and punishment of mankind, fire and ashes and the approaching end of the world. However, said Austerlitz, in my memory Calvinist eschatology is linked not so much to these biblical images of destruction as to what I saw with my own eyes when I was out with Elias. Many of his younger colleagues in the ministry had been called up into the army soon after the beginning of the war, and consequently at least every other Sunday he had to go and preach to another congregation, often quite a long way off. At first we drove across country in a little two-seater trap drawn by an almost snow-white pony, and in accordance with Elias's usual custom he would sit hunched up in the blackest of moods on the outward journey. On the way back, however, his spirits rose, just as they did at home on Sunday afternoons; he sometimes even hummed to himself, and cracked the whip around the pony's ears now and then. And these light and dark sides of the minister Elias were reflected in the mountainous landscape around us. I remember, said Austerlitz, how we were once driving through the endless Tanat valley, with nothing on the hillsides to right and left of us but crooked bushes, ferns and rusty-hued vegetation, and then, for the last part of the way up to the col, only grey rock and drifting mist, so that I was afraid we were coming to the very ends of the earth. But on another day, when we had just reached the Pennant pass I saw a gap open up in the banked clouds towering high in the west, and the rays of the sun cast a narrow beam of light down to the valley floor lying at a dizzying depth below us. Where there had been nothing a moment ago but fathomless gloom, there now shone a little village with a few orchards, meadows and fields, surrounded by black shadows but sparkling green like the Islands of the Blest, and as we walked down the road from the pass beside the pony and trap everything grew lighter and lighter, the mountain sides emerged from the darkness shining brightly, the fine grasses bending in the wind shimmered with light, the silvery willows gleamed down on the banks of the stream; before long we had descended from the barren heights and found ourselves among trees and bushes again, beneath the softly rustling oaks and maples, and rowans already laden with red berries. Once, I think when I was nine, I went away with Elias to a place in South Wales where the flanks of the mountains had been ripped open on both sides of the road, and the woods mauled and cut down. I don't remember the name of the village we reached at nightfall. It was surrounded by pithead stocks of coal spilling down into the alleys here and there. We had been given a room in the house of one of the church elders, from which there was a view of a winding-tower with a gigantic wheel turning now this way and now that in the gathering dusk, and further down the valley tall flames and showers of sparks shot high into the sky from the smelting furnaces of an iron and steel works, at regular intervals of about three or four minutes. When I was in bed Elias sat on a stool by the window, looking out in silence for a long time. I think that it was the sight of the valley first illuminated by the firelight, then sinking back into darkness, which inspired him to preach on a text from Revelation next morning, delivering a sermon on the wrath of the Lord, on the war and the devastation of the dwellings of men, a diatribe in which, so the elder told him when we left, he had surpassed himself. If the congregation had been almost petrified by terror during the sermon, I myself could hardly have had the divine power invoked by Elias more permanently impressed on my mind than by the fact that a bomb had dropped in broad daylight that afternoon in the little town at the end of the valley, where Elias was to take evening prayers that same day. The ruins were still smouldering when we reached the centre of the town, and people were standing about in the road in small groups, some with their hands still raised to their mouths in horror. The fire engine had driven straight across a round flower-bed, and there on the grass, dressed in their Sunday best, lay the bodies of those who, as I hardly needed Elias to tell me, had sinned against the Lord's commandment to keep the Sabbath day holy. In this way a kind of Old Testament mythology of retribution gradually built up inside my head, and I always saw its supreme expression in the submersion of the village of Llanwddyn beneath the waters of the

Vyrnwy reservoir. As far as I can remember it was on the way back from one of his journeys to preach away from home, at either Abertridwr or Pont Llogel, that Elias stopped the pony-trap on the banks of this lake and walked out with me to the middle of the dam, where he told me about his family home lying down there at a depth of about a hundred feet under the dark water, and not just his own family home but at least forty other houses and farms, together with the church of St John of Jerusalem, three chapels and three pubs, all of them drowned when the dam was finished in the autumn of 1888. In the years before its submersion, so Elias had told him, said Austerlitz, Llanwddyn had been particularly famous for its games of football on the village green when the full moon shone in summer, often lasting all night and played by over ten dozen youths and men of almost every age, some of them from neighbouring villages. The story of the football games of Llanwddyn occupied my imagi-nation for a long time, said Austerlitz, first and foremost, I am sure, because Elias never told me anything else about his own life either before or afterwards. At this one moment on the Vyrnwy dam when, intentionally or unintentionally, he allowed me a glimpse into his clerical heart, I felt for him so much that he, the righteous man, seemed to me like the only survivor of the deluge which had destroyed Llanwddyn, while I imagined all the others – his parents, his brothers and sisters, his relations, their neighbours, all the other villagers – still down in the depths, sitting in their houses and walking along the road, but unable to speak and with their eyes opened far too wide. This notion of mine about the sub-aquatic existence of the people of Llanwddyn also had something to do with the album which Elias first showed me on our return home that evening, containing several photographs of his birthplace, now sunk beneath the water. As there were no

other pictures of any kind in the manse, I leafed again and again though these few photographs, which came into my own possession only much later along with the Calvinist calendar, until the people looking out of them, the blacksmith in his leather apron, Elias's father the sub-postmaster, the shepherd walking along the village street with his sheep, and most of all the girl sitting in a chair in the garden with her little dog on her lap, became as familiar to me as if I were living with them down at the bottom of the lake. At night, before I fell asleep in my cold room, I often felt as if I too had been submerged in that dark water, and like the poor souls of Vyrnwy must keep my eyes wide open to catch a faint glimmer of light far above me, and see the reflection, broken by ripples, of the stone tower standing in such fearsome isolation on the wooded bank. Sometimes I even imagined that I had seen one or other of the people from the photographs in the album walking down the road in Bala, or out in the fields, particularly around noon on hot summer days, when there was no one else about and the air flickered hazily. Elias said I was not to speak of such things, so instead I spent every free moment I could with Evan the cobbler, whose workshop was not far from the manse and who had a reputation for seeing ghosts. I also learned Welsh from Evan, picking it up very quickly, because I liked his stories much better than the endless psalms and biblical verses I had to learn by heart for Sunday school. Unlike Elias, who always connected illness and death with tribulations, just punishment and guilt, Evan told tales of the dead who had been struck down by fate untimely, who knew they had been cheated of what was due to them and tried to return to life. If you had an eye for them they were to be seen quite often, said Evan. At first glance they seemed to be normal people, but when you looked more closely their faces would blur or flicker slightly at the edges. And they were usually a little shorter than they had been in life, for the experience of death, said Evan, diminishes us, just as a piece of linen shrinks when you first wash it. The dead almost always walked alone, but they did sometimes go around in small troops; they had been seen wearing brightly coloured uniforms or wrapped in grey cloaks, marching up the hill above the town to the soft beat of a drum, and only a little taller than the walls round the fields through which they went. Evan told me the story of how his grandfather once had to step aside on the road from Frongastell to Pyrsau to let one of these ghostly processions pass by when it caught up with him. It had consisted entirely of beings of dwarfish stature who strode on at a fast pace, leaning forward slightly and talking to each other in reedy voices. Hanging from a hook on the wall above Evan's low work-bench, said Austerlitz, was the black veil that his grandfather had taken from the bier when the small figures muffled in their cloaks carried it past him, and it was certainly Evan, said Austerlitz, who once told me that nothing but a piece of silk like that separates us from the next world. It is a fact that through all the years I spent at the manse in Bala I never shook off the feeling that something very obvious, very manifest in itself was hidden from me. Sometimes it was as if I were in a dream and trying to perceive reality; then again I felt as if an invisible twin brother were walking beside me, the reverse of a shadow, so to speak. And I suspected that some meaning relating to myself lay behind the Bible stories I was given to read in Sunday school from my sixth year onwards, a meaning quite different from the sense of the printed words as I ran my index finger along the lines. I can still see myself, said Austerlitz, muttering intently and spelling out the story of Moses again and again from the large-print children's edition of the Bible Miss Parry had given me when I had been set to learn by heart the chapter about the confounding of the languages of the earth, and succeeded in reciting it correctly and with good expression. I have only to turn a couple of pages of that book, said Austerlitz, to remember how anxious I felt at the time when I read the tale of the daughter of Levi, who made an ark of bulrushes and daubed it with slime and with pitch, placed the child in the ark and laid it among the reeds by the side of the water – *yn yr hesg ar fin yr afon*, I think that was how it ran. Further on in the story of Moses, said Austerlitz, I particularly liked the episode where the children of Israel cross a terrible wilderness, many days' journey long and wide, with nothing in sight but sky and sand as far as the eye can see. I tried to picture the pillar of cloud going before the people on their wanderings 'to lead them the way', as the Bible puts it, and I immersed myself, forgetting all around me, in a full-page illustration showing the desert of Sinai looking just like the part of Wales where I grew up, with bare mountains crowding close together and a grey-hatched background, which I took sometimes for the sea and sometimes for the air above it. And indeed, said Austerlitz on a later occasion when he showed me his Welsh children's Bible, I knew that my proper place was among the tiny figures populating the camp. I examined every square inch of the

illustration, which seemed to me uncannily famil-
iar. I thought I could make out a stone quarry in a
rather lighter patch on the steep slope of the
mountain over to the right, and I seemed to see a
railway track in the regular curve of the lines
below it. But my mind dwelt chiefly on the fenced
square in the middle and the tent-like building at
the far end, with a cloud of white smoke above it.
Whatever may have been going on inside me at
the time, the children of Israel's camp in the
wilderness was closer to me than life in Bala,
which I found more incomprehensible every day,
or at least, said Austerlitz, that is how it strikes me
now. That evening in the bar of the Great Eastern
Hotel Austerlitz also told me that there was no
wireless set or newspaper in the manse in Bala. I
don't know that Elias and his wife Gwendolyn
ever mentioned the fighting on the continent of
Europe, he said. I couldn't imagine any world
outside Wales. Only after the end of the war did
this state of affairs begin to change. A new epoch
seemed to dawn with the victory celebrations,
when even in Bala there was dancing in the streets,
which were decked with brightly coloured bunt-
ing. For me, it began when I first broke the ban on

going to the cinema, and after that I used to watch the newsreel from the cubby-hole occupied by the film projectionist Owen, one of the three sons of the visionary Evan. Around the same time Gwendolyn's state of health deteriorated, almost imperceptibly at first but then with increasing speed. She, who had always kept everything in the most painfully neat order, began to neglect first the house and then herself. She simply stood in the kitchen, looking helpless, and when Elias prepared a meal as best he could she would eat almost nothing. Her illness was certainly the reason why I was sent to a private school near Oswestry in the autumn term of 1946, when I was twelve years old. Like most such educational establishments, Stower Grange was the most unsuitable place imaginable for an adolescent. The headmaster, a man called Penrith-Smith, who wandered aimlessly about the school buildings in his dusty gown all day from early morning until late at night, was hopelessly forgetful and absent-minded, and the rest of the teaching staff in that immediate post-war period were also a curious collection of oddities, most of them over sixty or suffering from some affliction. School life ran more or less of its own accord, not so much thanks to the masters who taught us at Stower Grange as in spite of them, and certainly not by virtue of any particular ethos but through customs and traditions, a number of them positively oriental in character, going back over many generations of pupils. There were all kinds of forms of major tyranny and minor despotism, forced labour, enslavement, serfdom, the bestowal and withdrawal of privileges, hero-worship, ostracism, the imposition of penalties and the granting of reprieves, and by dint of these the pupils, without any supervision, governed themselves and indeed the entire school, not excluding the masters. Even when Penrith-Smith, a remarkably kindly man, did have to chastise one of us in his office for some reason which had been brought to his notice, you could easily have gained the impression that the victim was temporarily granting the headmaster who inflicted the punishment a privilege due in fact only to him, the boy who had reported to take it. Sometimes, particularly at weekends, it seemed as if all the masters had gone away leaving the pupils in their care to their own devices in the school, which was at least two miles outside town. Then some of us would wander about at our own sweet will, while others hatched plots to extend their power bases, or went to the laboratory furnished only with a few rickety benches and stools at the end of the dark basement corridor known, for some inexplicable reason, as the Red Sea, to toast bread and make scrambled eggs from a sulphur-yellow powdered egg substitute, a large supply of which was kept in one of the wall cupboards, along with other substances intended for chemistry lessons. Given the conditions at Stower Grange, of course, quite a number of boys spent all their schooldays there in a state of misery. For instance, said Austerlitz, I remember a boy called Robinson, who was obviously so unable to reconcile himself to the harshness and idiosyncrasies of school life that at the age of nine or ten he tried, on several occasions, to run away in the middle of the night by climbing down a drainpipe and striking out across country. A policeman always brought him back next morning in the check dressing-gown which, curiously, he must have put on especially for his flight, and handed him over to the headmaster like a common criminal. However, unlike poor Robinson, said Austerlitz, I myself found my years at Stower Grange a time not of imprisonment but of liberation. While most of us, even those who tormented their contemporaries, crossed off the days on the calendar until they could go home, I would have preferred never to return to Bala at all. From the very first week I realized that for all the adversities of the school it was my only escape route, and I immediately did all I could to find my way around its strange jumble of countless unwritten rules, and the often almost carnivalesque lawlessness that prevailed. It was a great advantage that I soon began to distinguish myself on the rugby field, perhaps because a dull pain always present within me, although I was unaware of it at the time, enabled me to lower my head and make my way through ranks of opponents better than any of my fellow pupils. The fearlessness I displayed in rugger matches, as I remember them always played under a cold winter sky or in pouring rain, very soon gave me special status without my having to try for it by other means, such as recruiting vassals or enslaving weaker boys. Another crucial factor in my good progress at school was the fact that I never found reading and studying a burden.

Far from it, for confined as I had been until now to the Bible in Welsh and homiletic literature, it seemed as if a new door were opening whenever I turned a page. I read everything in the school library, which contained an entirely arbitrary selection of works, and everything I could borrow from my teachers – works on geography and history, travel writings, novels, biographies – and sat up until late in the evening over reference books and atlases. My mind thus gradually created a kind of ideal landscape in which the Arabian desert, the realm of the Aztecs, the continent of Antarctica, the snow-covered Alps, the North-West Passage, the river Congo and the Crimean peninsula formed a single panorama, populated by all the figures proper to those places. As I could move into that world at any time I liked – in a Latin lesson, during divine service, on the interminable weekends – I never fell into the depression from which so many of the boys at Stower Grange suffered. I felt miserable only when it was time to go home for the holidays. Even on my first return to Bala at half-term on All Saints' Day, I felt as if my life were once again under the unlucky star which had been my companion as long as I could remember. Gwendolyn had gone further downhill during my two months' absence. She now lay in bed all day looking fixedly up at the ceiling. Elias came in to see her for a while every morning and every evening, but neither he nor Gwendolyn spoke a single word. It seems to me now, looking back, said Austerlitz, as if they were slowly being killed by the chill in their hearts. I don't know what kind of illness Gwendolyn died of, and I suspect that she herself could not have said. At least, she had no weapon against it but the curious compulsion which came over her several times a day, and perhaps during the night too, to powder herself with a kind of cheap talc from a large container standing on the little table beside her bed. Gwendolyn used such quantities of this powder, fine as dust and slightly greasy, that the linoleum floor around her bed, and soon the whole room and the corridors of the upper storey as well, were covered with a white layer, slightly sticky because of the damp air. I only recently remembered this white pall over the manse, said Austerlitz, when I was reading the reminiscences of his childhood and youth by a Russian writer who describes a similar mania for powder in his grandmother, a lady who, although she spent most of her time lying on a sofa nourishing herself almost exclusively on wine gums and almond milk, enjoyed an iron constitution and always slept with her window wide open, so that once, after a night of stormy weather, she woke up in the morning under a blanket of snow without coming to the slightest harm. However, it was different in the manse. The sick-room windows were kept closed, and the white powder which had settled on everything, grain by grain, and through which visible paths had now been trodden, was not at all like glittering snow. Rather, it resembled the ectoplasm that, as Evan had once told me, clairvoyants can produce from their mouths in great bubbles which then fall to the ground, where they soon dry and fall to dust. No, it was not newly fallen snow wafting around the manse; what filled it was something unpleasant, and I did not know where it came from, only much later and in another book finding for it the completely incomprehensible but to me, said Austerlitz, immediately enlightening term 'arsanical horror'. It was during the coldest winter in human memory that I came home for the second time from the school in Oswestry, and found Gwendolyn barely alive. There was a coal fire smouldering on the hearth of her sick-room. The yellowish smoke that rose from the glowing coals and never entirely dispersed up the chimney mingled with the smell of carbolic pervading the whole house. I stood for hours at the window, studying the wonderful formations of icy mountain ranges two or three inches high formed above the crossbars by water running down the panes. Now and then solitary figures emerged from the snowy landscape outside. Wrapped in dark scarves and shawls, umbrellas open to keep off the flurry of snowflakes, they stumbled up the hill. I heard them knocking the snow off their boots down in the porch before they slowly climbed the stairs, escorted by the neighbour's daughter who was now keeping house for the minister. With a certain hesitancy, and as if they had to bend underneath something, they stepped over the threshold and put whatever they had brought – a jar of pickled red cabbage, a can of corned beef, a bottle of rhubarb wine – down on the chest of drawers. Gwendolyn took no notice of these visitors, and the visitors themselves dared not look at her. They usually stood at the window with me for a little while, looking out too, and sometimes cleared their throats slightly. When they had gone again, it was as quiet as before except for the shallow breathing I could hear behind me, and an eternity seemed to pass between each breath. On Christmas Day, making a great effort, Gwendolyn sat up in bed once more. Elias had brought her a cup of sweet tea, but she only moistened her lips with it. Then she said, so quietly that you could hardly hear her: What was it that so darkened our world? And Elias replied: I don't know, dear, I don't know. Gwendolyn lingered until the New Year. On Epiphany Day, however, she reached the final stage. The cold had grown stronger than ever outside, and it had become more and more silent. The whole country, so I heard later, came to a standstill that winter. Even Lake Bala, which I had thought as big as the ocean when I arrived in Wales, was covered by a thick sheet of ice. I thought of the roach and eels in its depths, and the birds which the visitors had told me were falling from the branches of the trees, frozen stiff. It was never really light in these days, and when at last, very far away, the sun shone faintly in the misty blue sky, the dying woman opened her eyes wide and would not move her glance from the weak light filtering through the window panes. Only when darkness fell did she lower her lids, and not long after that a gurgling sound began to emerge from her throat with every breath she took. I sat beside her all night, together with the minister. At dawn the stertorous breathing stopped. Gwendolyn's body arched slightly and then sank back again. It was a kind of tensing movement; I had felt it once before, when I picked up an injured rabbit from the headland of a field, and its heart stopped in my hand for fear. But directly after she had arched herself in death Gwendolyn's body seemed to shrink a little, reminding me of what Evan had told me. I saw her eyes sink back in their sockets, and her thin lips, now stretched tautly back, half-bared her crooked bottom teeth, while outside, for the first time in many days, the rose-coloured light of dawn touched the rooftops of Bala. I don't remember exactly how the rest of that day passed after she died, said Austerlitz. I think I was so exhausted that I lay down and slept very deeply for a very long time. When I got up again, Gwendolyn was already in her coffin, which stood on the four mahogany chairs in the front room. She was wearing her wedding dress, kept all these years in a trunk upstairs, and a pair of white gloves with a great many little mother of pearl buttons which I had never seen before. The sight of them brought tears into my eyes, the first tears I had ever shed in the manse. Elias was sitting beside the coffin keeping watch over the dead woman, while on his own out in the empty barn, which creaked with the frost, the young assistant minister who had ridden over from Corwen on a pony was rehearsing the sermon he would preach on the day of the funeral. Elias never recovered from his wife's death. Grief is not the right word for the condition into which he had fallen since she lay dying, said Austerlitz. Although I did not understand it at the time, as a boy of thirteen, I can see now that the unhappiness building up inside him had destroyed his faith just when he needed it most. When I came home again in the summer, it was weeks since he had been able to carry out his duties as a minister. He climbed into the pulpit once more, opened the Bible, and in a broken voice, as if reading to himself alone, announced his text from Lamentations: 'He has made me dwell in darkness as those who have been long dead.' Elias did not preach the sermon itself. He merely stood there for a while, looking out over the heads of his congregation, who were paralysed by alarm, with what seemed to me the motionless eyes of one blinded. Then he slowly climbed down from the pulpit and left the chapel. He was taken away to Denbigh before the end of that summer. I visited him there only once, just before Christmas, with one of the elders of the congregation. The patients were accommodated in a large stone building, and I remember, said Austerlitz, that we had to wait in a room painted green. After quarter of an hour or so, an attendant came and took us up to Elias, who was lying in a bed with railings, his face to the wall. The attendant said: Your son's here to see you, *parch*, but even when he was addressed a second and a third time Elias did not answer. When we left the ward again one of the other inmates, a grey little man with tangled hair, plucked my sleeve and whispered behind his hand: He's not the full shilling, you know — which at the time, curiously enough, said Austerlitz, I felt was a reassuring diagnosis and made the whole wretched situation tolerable. — More than a year after my visit to the Denbigh asylum, at the beginning of the summer term of 1949, when we were just preparing for the exams which would determine our subsequent careers, said Austerlitz, resuming his narrative after a certain time, the headmaster Penrith-Smith summoned me to his study one morning. I can still see him in his frayed gown, wreathed in the blue tobacco smoke from his pipe, standing in the sunlight that slanted in through the small panes of the lead-glazed window and repeating several times in various ways, in his typically confused manner, that in the circumstances my conduct had been exemplary, truly exemplary, given the events of the last two years, and if in the next few weeks I came up to my teachers' expectations of me, which were undoubtedly justified, the Stower Grange trustees would award me a sixth-form scholarship. First, however, it was his duty to tell me that I must put not Dafydd Elias but Jacques Austerlitz on my exam papers. It appears, said Penrith-Smith, that this is your real name. My foster parents, with whom he had discussed the matter at length when

I entered the school, had meant to tell me about my origins in good time before the examinations, and if possible adopt me, but as matters now stood, said Penrith-Smith, that was unfortunately out of the question. All he knew himself was that the Eliases had taken me into their house at the beginning of the war, when I was only a little boy, so he could tell me no more. He was sure it would all be settled once Elias's condition improved. As far as the other boys are concerned, said Penrith-Smith, you remain Dafydd Elias for the time being. There's no need to let anyone know. It's just that you will have to put Jacques Austerlitz on your examination papers or else your work may be considered invalid. Penrith-Smith had written the name on a piece of paper, and when he handed it to me I could think of nothing to say, said Austerlitz, but 'Thank you, sir.' At first, what disconcerted me most was that I could connect no ideas at all with the word Austerlitz. If my new name had been Morgan or Jones, I could have related it to reality. I even knew the name Jacques from a French nursery rhyme. But I had never heard of an Austerlitz before, and from the first I was convinced that no one else bore that name, no one in Wales, or in the Isles, or anywhere else in the world. And since I began investigating my own history some years ago, I have never in fact come upon another Austerlitz, not in the telephone books of London or Paris, Amsterdam or Antwerp. But not long ago, turning on the wireless, I happened upon an announcer saying that Fred Astaire, of whom I had previously known nothing at all, was born with the surname of Austerlitz. Astaire's father, who according to this surprising radio programme came from Vienna, had worked as a master brewer in Omaha, Nebraska, where Astaire was born, and from the veranda of the Austerlitz family's house you could hear freight trains being shunted back and forth in the city's marshalling yard. Astaire is reported to have said later that this constant, uninterrupted shunting sound, and the ideas it suggested of going on a long railroad journey, were his only early childhood memories. And just a couple of days after I chanced in this way upon the story of a man entirely unknown to me, Austerlitz added, a neighbour who describes herself as a passionate reader told me that in Kafka's diaries she had found a small, bow-legged man of my own name who, as Kafka recorded, had been called in to circumcise his nephew. I feel it is unlikely that these trails lead anywhere, nor do I entertain any hopes of a note I found some time ago in a file on the practice of euthanasia, mentioning one Laura Austerlitz who made a statement to an Italian investigating judge on 28 June 1966 about the crimes committed in a rice mill on the peninsula of San Saba near Trieste in 1944. At least, said Austerlitz, I haven't yet succeeded in tracking down this namesake of mine. I don't even know if she is still alive, thirty years after making her statement. But personally, as I was saying, I had never heard the name Austerlitz before that April day in 1949 when Penrith-Smith handed me the piece of paper on which he had written it. I couldn't work out the spelling, and read the strange term which sounded to me like some password three or four times, syllable by syllable, before I looked up and said: Excuse me, sir, but what does it mean? To which Penrith-Smith replied: I think you will find it is a small place in Moravia, site of a famous battle, you know. And sure enough, the Moravian village of Austerlitz was discussed at great length during the next school year, for the curriculum in the Lower Sixth included European history, generally regarded as a complicated and not entirely safe subject, so that as a rule it was confined to the period from 1789 to 1814 which ended with a great English victory. The master who was to teach us this period – both glorious and terrible, as he often emphasized – was one André Hilary, who had only just taken up his post at Stower Grange after being demobbed and who, as it soon turned out, was familiar with every detail of the Napoleonic era. André Hilary had studied at Oriel College, but had grown up surrounded by an enthusiasm for Napoleon going back through several generations of his family. His father, so he once told me, said Austerlitz, had him baptized André in memory of Marshal Masséna, duke of Rivoli. Hilary could trace the orbit of the Corsican comet, as he put it, across the sky from its very beginning to its extinction in the South Atlantic Ocean, enumerating all the constellations through which it passed, and the events and characters on which it cast light at any point of its ascendancy or decline, speaking without any preparation and just as if he had been there himself. The Emperor's childhood in Ajaccio, his studies at the military academy of Brienne, the siege of Toulon, the stresses and strains of the Egyptian expedition and his return over a sea full of enemy ships, the crossing of the Great St Bernard, the battles of Marengo, Jena and Auerstedt, of Eylau and Friedland, of Wagram, Leipzig and Waterloo – Hilary brought it all vividly to life for us, partly by recounting the course of these events, often passing from plain narrative to dramatic descriptions and then on to a kind of impromptu performance distributed among several different roles, from one to another of which he switched back and forth with astonishing virtuosity, and partly by studying the gambits of Napoleon and his opponents with the cold intelligence of a non-partisan strategist, surveying the entire landscape of those years from above with an eagle eye, as he once and not without pride remarked. Most of us were deeply impressed by Hilary's history lessons, not least, said Austerlitz, because very often, probably owing to his suffering from slipped discs, he gave them while lying on his back on the floor, nor did we find this at all comic, for it was at such times that Hilary spoke with particular clarity and authority. His undoubted *pièce de résistance* was the battle of Austerlitz. He spoke on it at length, describing the terrain, the highway leading east from Brünn to Olmütz, with the hilly Moravian countryside on its left and the Pratzen heights on its right, the curious cone-shaped mountain which reminded the veterans in the Napoleonic army of the Egyptian pyramids, the villages of Bellwitz, Skolnitz and Kobelnitz, the game park and pheasant enclosure, the watercourse of the Goldbach and the pools and lakes to the south, the French encampment as well as that of the ninety thousand Allies, which extended over a length of nine miles. Hilary told us, said Austerlitz, how at seven in the morning the peaks of the highest hills emerged from the mist like islands in a sea and, as the day gradually grew brighter over the rounded hill-tops, the milky haze in the valleys became noticeably denser. The Russian and Austrian troops had come down from the mountain sides like a slow avalanche, and soon, increasingly unsure where they were going, were wandering around on the slopes and in the meadows below, while the French, in a single onslaught, captured the now half-abandoned positions on the Pratzen heights and then proceeded to attack the enemy in the rear from that vantage point. Hilary painted us a picture of the disposition of the regiments in their white and red, green and blue uniforms, constantly forming into new patterns in the course of the battle like crystals of glass in a kaleidoscope. Again and again we heard the names of Kolovrat and Bagration, Kutusov, Bernadotte, Miloradovich, Soult, Murat, Vandamme and Kellermann, we saw the black clouds of smoke hovering over the guns, the cannonballs flying past above the heads of the troops, the glint of bayonets as the first rays of the sun penetrated the mist; we even seemed to hear the heavy cavalry clashing, and felt (like a weakness sensed in our own bodies) whole ranks of men collapsing beneath the surge of the oncoming force. Hilary could talk for hours about the second of December 1805, but none the less it was his opinion that he had to cut his accounts far too short, because, as he several times told us, it would take an endless length of time to describe the events of such a day properly, in some inconceivably complex form recording who had perished, who survived, and exactly where and how, or simply saying what the battlefield was like at nightfall, with the screams and groans of the wounded and dying. In the end all anyone could ever do was sum up the unknown factors in the ridiculous phrase, 'The fortunes of battle swayed this way and that', or some similarly feeble and useless cliché. All of us, even when we think we have noted every tiny detail, resort to set pieces which have already been staged often enough by others. We try to reproduce the reality, but the harder we try, the more we find the pictures that make up the stock-in-trade of the spectacle of history forcing themselves upon us: the fallen drummer boy, the infantryman shown in the act of stabbing another, the horse's eye starting from its socket, the invulnerable Emperor surrounded by his generals, a moment frozen still amidst the turmoil of battle. Our concern with history, so Hilary's thesis ran, is a concern with pre-formed images already imprinted on our brains, images at which we keep staring while the truth lies elsewhere, away from it all, somewhere as yet undiscovered. I myself, added Austerlitz, in spite of all the accounts of it I have read, remember only the picture of the final defeat of the Allies in the battle of the Three Emperors. Every attempt to understand the course of events inevitably turns into that one scene where the hosts of Russian and Austrian soldiers are fleeing on foot and horseback on to the frozen Satschen ponds. I see cannonballs suspended for an eternity in the air, I see others crashing into the ice, I see the unfortunate victims flinging up their arms as they slide from the toppling floes, and I see them, strangely, not with my own eyes but with those of short-sighted Marshal Davout, who has made a forced march with his regiments from Vienna and, glasses tied firmly behind his head with two laces, looks like an early motorist or aviator. When I look back at André Hilary's performances today, said Austerlitz, I remember once again the idea I developed at the time of being linked in some mysterious way to the glorious past of the people of France. The more often Hilary mentioned the word Austerlitz in front of the class, the more it really did become my own name, and the more clearly I thought I saw that what had at first seemed like an ignominious flaw was changing into a bright light always hovering before me, as promising as the sun of Austerlitz itself when it rose above the December mists. All that school year I felt as if I had been chosen, and although, as I also knew, such a belief in no way matched my uncertain status, I have held fast to it almost my whole life. I don't think that any of my fellow pupils at Stower Grange knew my new name, and the masters, who had been informed of my double identity by Penrith-Smith, went on calling me Elias too. André Hilary was the only one to whom I myself told my real name. It was soon after we had handed in an essay on the concepts of empire and nation that Hilary summoned me to his study outside regular school hours to return my work, which he had marked with a triple-starred A, giving it back in person and not, as he put it, along with everyone else's pathetic efforts. He himself had published various articles in historical journals, and he said he could not have written such a perceptive piece in so comparatively short a space of time; he wondered whether I had perhaps been initiated into historical studies at home by my father or an elder brother. When I answered Hilary's question I had some difficulty in not losing my command over myself, and it was in this situation, which I felt I could no longer endure, that I told him the secret of my real name. It was some time before he was able to calm down. He struck his forehead again and again, breaking into exclamations of astonishment, as if Providence had finally sent him the pupil he had always wanted. For the rest of my time at Stower Grange, Hilary supported and encouraged me in every possible way. I owe it to him first and foremost, said Austerlitz, that I far outstripped the rest of my year in our final examinations in history, Latin, German and French, and could go on my own way into freedom, as I confidently thought at the time, provided with a generous scholarship. When we said goodbye André Hilary gave me a present from his collection of Napoleonic memorabilia, a gold-framed piece of dark card on which, behind shining glass, were fixed three rather fragile willow leaves from a tree on the island of St Helena, along with a scrap of lichen resembling a pale sprig of coral taken by one of Hilary's forebears, as the tiny caption said, from the heavy granite tombstone of Marshal Ney on 31 July 1830. This memento, worth nothing in itself, is still in my possession, said Austerlitz. It means more to me than almost any other picture, first because despite their fragility the relics preserved in it, the lichen and the dried lanceolate willow leaves, have remained intact for more than a century, but also because it reminds me daily of Hilary, without whom I would surely never have been able to emerge from the shadows of the manse in Bala. Moreover, it was Hilary who, after my foster-father's death in the Denbigh asylum early in 1954, undertook the task of winding up his meagre estate and then set on foot the process of my naturalization, which in view of the fact that Elias had obliterated every indication of my origin involved a good deal of difficulty. When I was studying at Oriel, like Hilary himself before me, he visited me regularly, and we took every opportunity of making excursions to the deserted and dilapidated country houses to be found all around Oxford, as elsewhere, in the post-war years. While I was still at school, said Austerlitz, as well as Hilary's support my friendship with Gerald Fitzpatrick in particular helped me to overcome the self-doubts that sometimes oppressed me. In line with the usual practice at public schools, Gerald was assigned to me as a fag when I entered the sixth form. It was his job to keep my room tidy, clean my boots, and bring the tray with the tea things. From the first day, when he asked me for one of the new photographs of the rugger team where I featured to the extreme right of the front row, I realized that Gerald felt as isolated as I did, said Austerlitz, who scarcely a week after our reunion at the Great Eastern Hotel sent me a postcard copy of the picture he had mentioned, without further comment. On that December

evening, however, in the hotel bar, which was quiet now, Austerlitz went on to tell me more about Gerald, and how he had suffered from awful homesickness ever since his arrival at Stower Grange, entirely against the grain of his naturally cheerful disposition. All the time, said

Austerlitz, in every free moment he had, he was rearranging the things he had brought from home in his tuck-box, and once, not long after he became my fag, I found him at the end of a corridor one dreary Saturday afternoon, with the autumn rain pouring down outside, trying to set fire to a pile of newspapers stacked on the stone floor beside the open door which led into a back yard. I saw his small, crouched figure in the grey light behind him, and the little flames licking around the edges of the newspaper, but the fire would not burn properly. When I asked what he thought he was doing, he said he wanted to make a huge blaze, and would not mind if the whole school were reduced to a pile of rubble and ashes. After that I kept an eye on Gerald. I let him off tidying my room and cleaning my boots, and I made the tea myself and shared it with him, a breach of regulations regarded with disapproval by most of my fellow pupils and my house-master himself, rather as if it were against the natural order of things. In the evenings Gerald often accompanied me to the dark-room where, at this time, I was making my first experiments with photography. This little cubby-hole behind the chemistry lab had not been used for years, but the wall cupboards and drawers still held several boxes with rolls of film, a large supply of photographic paper and a miscellaneous collection of cameras, including an Ensign such as I myself owned later. From the outset my main concern was with the shape and the self-contained nature of discrete things, the curve of banisters on a staircase, the moulding of a stone arch over a gateway, the tangled precision of the blades in a tussock of dried grass. I took hundreds of such photographs at Stower Grange, most of them in square format, but it never seemed to me right to turn the viewfinder of my camera on people. In my photographic work I was always especially entranced, said Austerlitz, by the moment when the shadows of reality, so to speak, emerge out of nothing on the exposed paper, as memories do in the middle of the night, darkening again if you try to cling to them, just like a photographic print left in the developing bath too long. Gerald enjoyed helping me, and I can still see him, a head shorter than I was, standing beside me in the dark-room, which was dimly illuminated only by the little reddish light, holding the photographs in tweezers and swishing them back and forth in a sink full of water. He often told me about his family on these occasions, and most of all he liked talking about the three homing pigeons who would be expecting his return, he thought, as eagerly as he usually awaited theirs. Gerald's Uncle Alphonso had given him these pigeons a year ago for his tenth birthday, said Austerlitz, two of them a slaty blue, one snow-white. Whenever possible, if someone was going to Bala or Aberystwyth by car, he would send his three pigeons to be freed at a distance, and they always infallibly found their way back to their loft. Once, towards the end of last summer, Tilly the white pigeon did stay away much longer than the homeward flight should have taken her, after being dispatched on a test flight from Dolgellau only a few miles up the valley, and it was not until the following day, when he was on the point of giving up hope, that she finally returned – on foot, walking up the gravel drive with a broken wing. I often thought later of this tale of the bird making her long journey home alone, wondering how she had managed to reach her destination over the steep terrain, circumventing numerous obstacles, and that question, said Austerlitz, a question which still exercises my mind today when I see a pigeon in flight, is one that, against all reason, seems to me connected with the way Gerald finally lost his life. — I believe, Austerlitz went on after some considerable time, it was on the second or third parents' visiting day that Gerald, proud of his privileged relationship with me, introduced me to his mother Adela. She can hardly have been thirty at the time, and she was very glad that after his initial difficulties her young son had found a protector in me. Gerald had already told me about his father Aldous, shot down over the Ardennes in the last winter of the war, and I had also heard how his mother was now living with only an old uncle and an even older great-uncle in a country house just outside the small seaside town of Barmouth. Gerald claimed that its position was the finest anywhere along the entire Welsh coast. Once Adela had discovered from Gerald that I had no parents or any family at all, I was invited to their house repeatedly, indeed constantly, even when I was doing my national service and when I was up at Oxford, and I could wish now, said Austerlitz, to have vanished without trace in the peace that always reigned there. At the very beginning of the school holidays, when we travelled westward up the Dee valley in the little steam train from Wrexham, I would feel my heart begin to lift. Bend after bend, our train followed the winding of the river, the green meadows looked in through the open carriage window, and so did the houses, stony grey or whitewashed, the gleaming slate roofs, the silver shades of the willows, the darker alder woods, the sheep-pastures climbing up beyond the trees, and higher still the mountains, sometimes tinged with blue, and the sky where the clouds, coming in from the sea, always drove eastwards. Scraps of steam vapour flew past outside; you could hear the engine whistling and feel the air cool on your forehead. Never have I travelled better, said Austerlitz, than on this journey of seventy miles at the most, which took us three and a half hours. When we stopped at Bala, the half way station, of course I could not help thinking back to my time in the manse, visible up there on its hill, yet it always seemed to me inconceivable that I had really been among its unhappy inhabitants for almost the whole of my life. And every time I set eyes on Lake Bala, particularly when its surface was churned up by the wind in winter, I remembered the story Evan the cobbler had told me, about the two headstreams of Dwy Fawr and Dwy Fach which are said to flow right through the lake, far down in its dark depths, never mingling their waters with its own. The two rivers, according to Evan, said Austerlitz, were called after the only human beings not drowned but saved from the biblical deluge in the distant past. At the far end of Lake Bala the railway line passed over a low anticline into the Afon Mawddach valley. The mountains were higher now, coming down closer and closer to the tracks until you reached Dolgellau, where they retreated again, and gentler slopes fell to the estuary of the Mawddach, which reaches far inland like a fjord. Finally, when we left the southern bank and crawled to the opposite side over the bridge, almost a mile long and supported on mighty posts of oak, on our right the river bed, inundated by the sea at high tide and looking like a mountain lake, and on our left Barmouth Bay stretching to the bright horizon, I felt so joyful that I often scarcely knew where to look first. Adela used to fetch us from Barmouth station, usually in the little black-painted pony-trap, and then it was only half an hour before the gravel of the drive up to Andromeda Lodge was crunching under our wheels, the bay pony stopped, and we could get down and enter into our holiday refuge. The two-storey house, built of pale-grey brick, was protected to the north and north-east by the Llawr Llech hills, which fall steeply away at this point. To the south-west the terrain lay open in a wide semi-circle, so that from the forecourt of the house you had a view of the full length of the estuary from Dolgellau to

Barmouth, while these places themselves were excluded from the panorama, which was almost devoid of human habitations, by a rocky outcrop on one side and a laurel-grown hill on the other. Only on the far side of the river could the little village of Arthog be seen – in certain atmospheric conditions, said Austerlitz, you might have thought it an eternity away – infinitesimally small, with the shadowy side of Cader Idris rising behind it to a height of almost three thousand feet above the shimmering sea. While the climate of the entire area was remarkably mild, temperatures in this especially favoured place were a couple of degrees higher even than the Barmouth average. The garden, which had run completely wild during the war years and went up the slope at the back of the house, contained plants and shrubs that I had never seen in Wales before: giant rhubarb and New Zealand ferns taller than a grown man, water lettuce and camellias, thickets of bamboo and palms. And a brook tumbled down over a rocky wall to the valley, its white spray constantly pervading the dappled twilight under the leafy canopy of the tall trees. But it was not only the plants, natives of warmer climates, that made you feel you were living in another world: the greatest exotic attractions of Andromeda Lodge were the white cockatoos which flew all around the house within a radius of up to two or three miles, calling from the bushes, bathing and luxuriating in the fine spray from the cascading brook until evening fell. Gerald's great-grandfather had brought several pairs home from the Moluccas and established them in the orangery, where they soon increased and multiplied, forming a large colony. They lived in small sherry casks that had been stacked on top of each other in a pyramid against one of the side walls, and departing from their native custom, said Austerlitz, they had lined these casks themselves with wood-shavings from a sawmill down beside the river. Most of them even survived the hard winter of 1947, since Adela kept the old orangery stove heated for them through the two icy months of January and February. It was wonderful, said Austerlitz, to see the dexterity with which the birds clambered around the trelliswork, hanging on by their beaks, and performing all kinds of acrobatic feats as they came down; to watch them flying in and out of the open windows or hopping and walking along the ground, always active and always, or that was the impression they gave, intent upon some purpose or other. In fact they were very like human beings in many ways. You might hear them sigh, laugh, sneeze and yawn. They cleared their throats before beginning to converse in their own cockatoo language, they showed themselves alert, scheming, mischievous and sly, deceitful, malicious, vindictive and quarrelsome. They liked certain people, particularly Adela and Gerald, and persecuted others with downright malice, for instance the Welsh housekeeper who seldom showed her face out of doors. They seemed to know exactly when she would be going to chapel, always wearing a black hat and carrying a black umbrella, and on these occasions they lay in wait to screech at her in the most obnoxious way. They also reflected human society in the way they ganged up together in ever-changing groups, or then again paired off in couples sitting side by side as if they knew nothing but harmony and were forever inseparable. They even had their own cemetery, with a long row of graves in a clearing surrounded by strawberry trees, and one of the rooms on the upper floor of

Andromeda Lodge had in it what was obviously a purpose-built wall cupboard, full of dark-green cardboard boxes containing a number of dead birds of species related to the cockatoos, their red-chested or yellow-headed brothers, Hyacinth and Scarlet Macaws, Ruby Lorikeets and Blue-winged Parrotlets, Horned Parakeets and Ground Parrots, all brought back by Gerald's great-grandfather or great-great-grandfather from his circumnavigation of the globe, or alternatively ordered from a trader called Théodore Grace in Le Havre for a few guineas or louis d'or, as noted on the provenances placed inside the boxes. The finest of all these birds, in a collection which also included some native woodpeckers, wrynecks, kites and orioles, was the African Grey Parrot. I can still see the inscription on his green cardboard sarcophagus: Jaco, *Ps. erithacus L.* He came from the Congo and had reached the great age of sixty-six in his Welsh exile, as his obituary recounted, adding that he had been very tame and trusting, was a quick learner, chattered away to himself and others, could whistle entire songs and had composed some too, but best of all he liked to mimic the voices of children and to have them teach him new words. His one bad habit was that if no one gave him any apricot kernels and hard nuts, which he could crack open with the greatest ease, he went about in a bad temper chewing and shredding the furniture. Gerald often took this special parrot out of his box. He was about nine inches long, and as his name suggests had ash-grey plumage, as well as a carmine tail, a black beak, and a pale face that you might have thought was marked by deep grief. Indeed, Austerlitz went on, there was some kind of cabinet of natural curiosities in almost every room at Andromeda Lodge: cases with multiple drawers, some of them glass-fronted, where the roundish eggs of parrots were arranged in their hundreds; collections of shells, minerals, beetles and butterflies; slowworms, adders and lizards preserved in formaldehyde; snail shells and sea urchins, crabs and shrimps, and large herbaria containing leaves, flowers and grasses. Adela had once told him, said Austerlitz, that the transformation of Andromeda Lodge into a kind of natural-history museum had begun in 1869, when Gerald's parrot-collecting ancestor made the acquaintance of Charles Darwin, then working on his study of the Descent of Man in a rented house not far from Dolgellau. Darwin had paid frequent visits to the Fitzpatricks of Andromeda Lodge in those days, and according to a family tradition he always praised the wonderful view from the house. It was from the same period, according to Adela, said Austerlitz, that the schism in the Fitzpatrick clan dated, a schism continuing to the present day, whereby one of the two sons in every generation abandoned the Catholic faith and became a natural scientist. For instance Aldous, Gerald's father, had been a botanist, while his brother Evelyn, over twenty years his senior, clung to the traditional Papist creed regarded in Wales as the worst of all per-versions. In fact the Catholic line of the family had always been represented by its crazier and more

eccentric members, as the case of Uncle Evelyn clearly illustrated. At the time when I was spending many weeks every year with the Fitzpatricks as Gerald's guest, said Austerlitz, Evelyn was perhaps in his mid-fifties, but was so crippled by Bechterew's disease that he looked like an old man, and could walk only with the greatest difficulty, bending right over. For that very reason, however, and to prevent his joints from seizing up entirely, he was always on the move in his rooms on the top floor, where a kind of handrail had been fitted along the walls, like the barre in a ballet school. He held on to this handrail as he inched his way forward, moaning quietly, his head and bent torso scarcely higher than his hand on the rail. It took him a good hour to make the rounds of his quarters, from the bedroom into the living-room, out of the living-room into the corridor, and from the corridor back to the bedroom. Gerald, who had already developed an aversion to the Roman faith, once claimed, said Austerlitz, that Uncle Evelyn had grown so crooked out of sheer miserliness, which he justified to himself by reflecting that he sent the money he did not spend in any given week, usually amounting to twelve or thirteen shillings, as a donation to the Mission to the Congo for the salvation of black souls still languishing in unbelief. There were no curtains or other furnishings in Evelyn's rooms, since he did not want to make unnecessary use of anything, even if it had been acquired long ago and simply had to be brought from another part of the house. Years before, he had had a narrow strip of lino leum laid on the wooden floor where he walked beside the walls, to spare the wood, and his dragging footsteps had worn the linoleum so thin that you could make out almost nothing of its original flower pattern. Not until the temperature on the thermometer beside the window had dropped to below fifty degrees Fahrenheit for several days running was the housekeeper allowed to light a tiny fire in the hearth, a fire burning almost no fuel at all. To save electricity, Evelyn always went to bed when darkness fell, which meant around four in the afternoon in winter, although lying down was perhaps even more painful for him than walking, so that as a rule, despite his exhausted state after his constant perambulations, it was a long time before he could get to sleep. Then, through the grille of a ventilation shaft that linked his bedchamber to one of the ground-floor living-rooms and inadvertently functioned as a kind of communication channel, he could be heard calling on numerous different saints for hours on end, in particular, if I remember correctly, Saints Catherine and Elizabeth, who suffered the most cruel of martyrdoms, begging them to intercede for him in the contingency, as he put it, of his imminent appearance before the judgment seat of his Heavenly Lord. Unlike Uncle Evelyn, said Austerlitz after a while, taking from his jacket pocket a kind of folder containing several post-card-sized photographs, Great-Uncle Alphonso, who was about ten years older and continued the line of the naturalist Fitzpatricks, looked posi-tively youthful. Always even-tempered, he spent most of his time out of doors, going on long expe-ditions even in the worst of weather, or when it was fine sitting on a camp stool somewhere near the house in his white smock, a straw hat on his head, painting watercolours. When he was thus engaged he generally wore glasses with grey silk tissue instead of lenses in the frames, so that the landscape appeared through a fine veil that muted its colours, and the weight of the world dissolved

before your eyes. The faint images that Alphonso transferred on to paper, said Austerlitz, were barely sketches of pictures – here a rocky slope, there a small bosky thicket or a cumulus cloud – fragments, almost without colour, fixed with a tint made of a few drops of water and a grain of malachite green or ash blue. I remember, said Austerlitz, how Alphonso once told his great-nephew and me that everything was fading before our eyes, and that many of the loveliest of colours had already disappeared, or existed only where no one saw them, in the submarine gardens fathoms deep below the surface of the sea. In his child-hood, he said, he used to walk beside the chalk cliffs of Devon and Cornwall, where hollows and basins have been carved and cut out of the rock by the breakers over millions of years, admiring the endless diversity of the semi-sentient marvels oscillating between the vegetable, animal and mineral kingdoms, the zooids and corallines, sea anemones, sea fans and sea feathers, the antho-zoans and crustaceans over which the tide washed twice a day while long fronds of seaweed swayed around them, and which then, as the water went out, revealed their wonderfully iridescent life in the rock pools exposed once more to the light and the air, showing all the colours of the rainbow — emerald, scarlet and rosy red, sulphur yellow, velvety black. At that time the whole south-west coast of the island was surrounded by a colourful fringe ebbing and flowing with the tides, and now, said Uncle Alphonso, barely half a century later, those glories had been almost entirely destroyed by our passion for collecting and by other imponderable disturbances and disruptions. On another occasion, said Austerlitz, Great-Uncle Alphonso took us up the hill behind the house on a still, moonless night to spend a few hours looking into the mysterious world of moths. Most of us, said Austerlitz, know nothing about moths except that they eat holes in carpets and clothes and have to be kept at bay by the use of camphor and naphthalene, although in truth their lineage is among the most ancient and most remarkable in the whole history of nature. Soon after darkness fell we were sitting on a promontory far above Andromeda Lodge, behind us the higher slopes and before us the immense darkness out at sea, and no sooner had Alphonso placed his incandescent lamp in a shallow hollow surrounded by heather and lit it than the moths, not one of which we had seen during our climb, came flying in as if from nowhere, describing thousands of different arcs and spirals and loops, until like snowflakes they formed a silent storm around the light, while others, wings whirring, crawled over the sheet spread under the lamp or else, exhausted by their wild circling, settled in the grey recesses of the egg boxes stacked in a crate by Alphonso to provide shelter for them. I do remember, said Austerlitz, that the two of us, Gerald and I, could not get over our amazement at the endless variety of these invertebrates, which are usually hidden from our sight, and that Alphonso let us simply gaze at their wonderful display for a long time, but I don't recollect now exactly what kinds of night-winged creatures landed there beside us, perhaps they were China-Marks, Dark Porcelains and Marbled Beauties, Scarce Silverlines or Burnished Brass, Green Foresters and Green Adelas, White Plumes, Light Arches, Old Ladies and Ghost Moths, but at any rate we counted dozens of them, so different in structure and appearance that neither Gerald nor I could grasp it all. Some had collars and cloaks, like elegant gentlemen on their way to the opera, said Gerald; some had a plain basic hue, but when they moved their wings showed a fantastic lining underneath, with oblique and wavy lines, shadows, crescent markings and lighter patches, freckles, zigzag bands, fringes and veining and colours you could never have imagined, moss green shot with blue, fox brown, saffron, lime yellow, satiny white, and a metallic gleam as of powdered brass or gold. Many of them were still resplendent in immaculate garments, others, their short lives almost over, had torn and ragged wings. Alphonso told us how each of these extravagant creatures had its own character, and that many of them lived only among alders, or on hot, stony slopes, in pastures on poor soil, or on moors. Describing their previous existence as larvae, he said that almost all caterpillars ate only one kind of food – the roots of couch grass, the leaves of sallow or barberry, withered bramble foliage – and they stuffed themselves with that chosen food, said Alphonso, until they became well-nigh senseless, whereas the moths ate nothing more at all for the rest of their lives, and were bent solely on the business of reproduction. They did sometimes seem to suffer thirst, and in periods of drought, when no dew had fallen at night for a long time, it was apparently known for them to set out together in a kind of cloud in search of the nearest river or stream, where they drowned in large numbers as they tried to settle on the flowing water. And I also remember what Alphonso said about the extraordinarily keen hearing of moths, said Austerlitz. They can make out the squeaking of bats from a great distance, and he, Alphonso, had himself noticed that in the evening, when the housekeeper came out into the yard to call her cat Enid in that shrill voice of hers, they always rose from the bushes and flew away into the darker trees. During the day, said Alphonso, they slept safely hidden under stones, or in cracks in the rock, in leaf litter on the ground or among foliage. Most of them are in a death-like state when you find them, and have to coax and quiver themselves back to life, crawling over the ground and jerkily moving their wings and legs before they are ready for flight. Their body temperature will then be thirty-six degrees, like that of mammals, and of dolphins and tunny fish swimming at full speed. Thirty-six degrees, according to Alphonso, has always proved the best natural level, a kind of magical threshold, and it had sometimes occurred to him, Alphonso, said Austerlitz, that all mankind's misfortunes were connected with its departure at some point in time from that norm, and with the slightly feverish, overheated condition in which we constantly found ourselves. On that summer night, said Austerlitz, we sat high above the estuary of the Mawddach in our hollow in the hills until daybreak, watching the moths fly to us, perhaps some ten thousand of them by Alphonso's estimate. The trails of light which they seemed to leave behind them in all kinds of curlicues and streamers and spirals, and which Gerald in particular admired, did not really exist, explained Alphonso, but were merely phantom traces created by the sluggish reaction of the human eye, appearing to see a certain afterglow in the place from which the insect itself, shining for only the fraction of a second in the lamplight, had already gone. It was such unreal phenomena, said Alphonso, the sudden incursion of unreality into the real world, certain effects of light in the landscape spread out before us, or in the eye of a beloved person, that kindled our deepest feelings, or at least what we took for them. Although I did not study natural history later, said Austerlitz, many of Great-Uncle Alphonso's botanical and zoological disquisitions have remained in my mind. Only a few days ago I was re-reading that passage in Darwin he once showed me, describing a flock of butterflies flying uninterruptedly for several hours ten miles out from the South American coast, when even with a telescope it was impossible to find a patch of empty sky visible between their whirling wings. But I always found what Alphonso told us at that time about the life and death of moths especially memorable, and of all creatures I still feel the greatest awe for them. In the warmer months of the year one or other of those nocturnal insects quite often strays indoors from the small garden behind my house. When I get up early in the morning, I find them clinging to the wall, motionless. I believe, said Austerlitz, they know they have lost their way, since if you do not put them out again carefully they will stay where they are, never moving, until the last breath is out of their bodies, and indeed they will remain in the place where they came to grief even after death, held fast by the tiny claws that stiffened in their last agony, until a draught of air detaches them and blows them into a dusty corner. Sometimes, seeing one of these moths that have met their end in my house, I wonder what kind of fear and pain they feel while they are lost. As Alphonso had told him, said Austerlitz, there is really no reason to suppose that lesser beings are devoid of sentient life. We are not alone in dreaming at night for, quite apart from dogs and other domestic creatures whose emotions have been bound up with ours for many thousands of years, the smaller mammals such as mice and moles also live in a world that exists only in their minds whilst they are asleep, as we can detect from their eye movements, and who knows, said Austerlitz, perhaps moths dream as well, perhaps a lettuce in the garden dreams as it looks up at the moon by night. I myself often felt as if I were dreaming during those weeks and months I spent at the Fitzpatricks' house, said Austerlitz, even in daylight. The view from the room with the blue ceiling which Adela always called mine did indeed verge on the unreal. I looked down from above on the treetops, mainly of cedars and parasol pines and resembling a green, hilly landscape going down from the road below the house to the river bank, I saw the dark folds of the mountain range on the other side of the river, and I spent hours looking out at the Irish Sea that was always changing with the time of day and the weather. How often I stood by the open window, unable to think coherently in the face of this spectacle, which was never the same twice. In the morning you saw the shadowy half of the world outside, the grey of the air lying in layers above the water. In the afternoon cumulus clouds often rose on the southwest horizon, their snow-white slopes and steep precipices displacing one another, towering above each other, reaching higher and higher, as high, Gerald once commented, said Austerlitz, as the peaks of the Andes or the Karakorum Mountains. Or you might see rain falling in the distance, drawn inland from the sea like heavy curtains drawn in a theatre, and on autumn evenings mist would roll on to the beach, accumulating by the mountain sides and forcing its way up the valley. But on bright summer days, in particular, so evenly disposed a lustre lay over the whole of Barmouth Bay that the separate surfaces of sand and water, sea and land, earth and sky could no longer be distinguished. All forms and colours were dissolved in a pearl-grey haze; there were no contrasts, no shading any more, only flowing transitions with the light throbbing through them, a single blur from which only the most fleeting of visions emerged, and strangely – I remember this well – it was the very evanescence of those visions that gave me, at the time, something like a sense of eternity. One evening, after we had done some shopping in Barmouth, Adela, Gerald, the dog Toby and I went out on the long footbridge running beside the railway line which, as I mentioned before, said Austerlitz, crosses the estuary of the Mawddach at this point, where it is over a mile wide. For a halfpenny each you could sit there on one of the seats protected on three sides, like little cabins, from wind and weather, with your back to the land and looking out to sea. It was the end of a fine day in late summer, the fresh salty air blew around us, and in the evening light the tide came in, gleaming like a dense shoal of mackerel, flowing under the bridge and up the river, so swift and strong that you might have thought you were going the other way, out to the open sea in a boat. We all four sat there together in silence until the sun had set. Even the usually restless Toby, who had the same odd ruff of hair around his face as the little dog belonging to the girl in the Vyrnwy photograph, did not move at our feet, but looked up, rapt, at the heights where the light still lingered and large numbers of swallows were swooping through the air. After a while, when the dark dots had become tinier and tinier in their arching flight, Gerald asked whether we knew that these voyagers never slept on the earth. Once they had left their nests, he said, picking up Toby and tickling him under the chin, they never touched the ground again. As night fell they would rise two or three miles in the air and glide there, banking now to one side, now to the other, and moving their outspread wings only occasionally, until they came back down to us at break of day. — Austerlitz had been so deeply immersed in his Welsh tale, and I in listening to him, that we did not notice how late it had grown. The last rounds had long since been poured, the last guests were gone except for the two of us. The barman had collected the glasses and ashtrays, wiped the tables with a cloth, and was now waiting to lock up after us with his hand on the light switch by the door. The way in which he wished us *Good night, gentlemen*, with his eyes clouded by weariness and his head tilted slightly to one side, struck me as an extraordinary mark of distinction, almost like an absolution or a blessing. And Pereira, the business manager of the Great Eastern, was equally civil and courteous when we entered the hotel foyer directly afterwards. He seemed positively expectant as he stood behind the reception desk in his starched white shirt and grey cloth waistcoat, with his hair immaculately parted, one of those rare and often rather mysterious people, as I thought on seeing him, who are infallibly to be found at their posts, and whom one cannot imagine ever feeling any need to go to bed. After I had made an appointment to meet Austerlitz the next day Pereira, having inquired after my wishes, led me upstairs to the first floor and showed me into a room containing a great deal of wine-red velvet, brocade, and dark mahogany furniture, where I sat until almost three in the morning at a secretaire faintly illuminated by the street lighting – the cast-iron radiator clicked quietly, and only occasionally did a black cab drive past outside in Liverpool Street – writing down, in the form of notes and disconnected sentences, as much as possible of what Austerlitz had told me that evening. Next morning I woke late, and after breakfast I sat for some time reading the newspapers, where I found not only the usual home and international news, but also the story of an ordinary man who was overcome by such deep grief after the death of his wife, for whom he had cared devotedly during her long and severe illness, that he decided to end his own life by means of a guillotine which he had built himself in the square concrete area containing the basement steps at the back of his house in Halifax. As a craftsman, and having taken careful stock of other possible methods, he thought the guillotine the most reliable way of carrying out his plan, and sure enough, as the short report said, he had finally been found lying with his head cut off by such an instrument of decapitation. It was of uncommonly sturdy construction, with every tiny detail neatly finished, and a slanting blade which, as the reporter remarked, two strong men could scarcely have lifted. The pincers with which he had cut through the wire operating it were still in his rigid hand. Austerlitz had come to fetch me around eleven, and when I told him this story as we walked down to the river through Whitechapel and Shoreditch he said nothing for quite a long time, perhaps, I told myself reproachfully afterwards, because he felt it was tasteless of me to dwell on the absurd aspects of the case. Only on the river bank, where we stood for a while looking down at the grey-brown water rolling inland, did he say, looking straight at me as he sometimes did with wide and frightened eyes, that he could understand the Halifax carpenter very well, for what could be worse than to bungle even the end of an unhappy life? Then we walked the rest of the way in silence, going on downstream from Wapping and Shadwell to the quiet basins which reflect the towering office blocks of the Docklands area, and so to the foot tunnel running under the bend in the river. Over on the other side we climbed up through Greenwich Park to the Royal Observatory, which had scarcely any visitors apart from us on this cold day not long before Christmas. At least, I do not remember meeting anyone during the hours we spent there, both of us separately studying the ingenious observational instruments and measuring devices, quadrants and sextants, chronometers and regulators, displayed in the glass cases.

Only in the octagonal observation room above the quarters of the former Astronomers Royal, where Austerlitz and I gradually resumed the conversation we had broken off, did a solitary Japanese tourist appear in the doorway. He hovered there for a while before he went all round the octagon once and then quietly vanished again, following the green arrow pointing the way. In this room, which as Austerlitz commented was ideal for its purpose, I was surprised by the simple beauty of the wooden flooring, made of planks of different widths, and by the unusually tall windows, each divided into a hundred and twenty-two lead-framed square glass panes, through which long telescopes were once turned on eclipses of the sun and the moon, on the intersection of the orbits of the stars with the line of the meridian, on the Leonid meteorite showers and the long-tailed comets flying through space. In accordance with his usual custom, Austerlitz took a few photographs, some of them of the snow-white stucco roses in the frieze of flowers running round the ceiling, others of the panorama of the city to the north and north-west on the far side of the park, shot through the leaded window panes, and while he was still busy with his camera he embarked on a disquisition of some length on time, much of which has remained clear in my memory. Time, said Austerlitz in the observation room in Greenwich, was by far the most artificial of all our inventions, and in being bound to the planet turning on its own axis was no less arbitrary than would be, say, a calculation based on the growth of trees or the duration required for a piece of limestone to disintegrate, quite apart from the fact that the solar day which we take as our guideline does not provide any precise measurement, so that in order to reckon time we have to devise an imaginary, average sun which has an invariable speed of movement and does not incline towards the equator in its orbit. If Newton thought, said Austerlitz, pointing through the window and down to the curve of the water around the Isle of Dogs glistening in the last of the daylight, if Newton really thought that time was a river like the Thames, then where is its source and into what sea does it finally flow? Every river, as we know, must have banks on both sides, so where, seen in those terms, where are the banks of time? What would be this river's qualities, qualities perhaps corresponding to those of water, which is fluid, rather heavy, and translucent? In what way do objects immersed in time differ from those left untouched by it? Why do we show the hours of light and darkness in the same circle? Why does time stand eternally still and motionless in one

— 142 —

place, and rush headlong by in another? Could we not claim, said Austerlitz, that time itself has been non-concurrent over the centuries and the millennia? It is not so long ago, after all, that it began spreading out over everything. And is not human life in many parts of the earth governed to this day less by time than by the weather, and thus by an unquantifiable dimension which disregards linear regularity, does not progress constantly forward but moves in eddies, is marked by episodes of congestion and irruption, recurs in ever-changing form, and evolves in no one knows what direction? Even in a metropolis ruled by time like London, said Austerlitz, it is still possible to be outside time, a state of affairs which until recently was almost as common in backward and forgotten areas of our own country as it used to be in the undiscovered continents overseas. The dead are outside time, the dying and all the sick at home or in hospitals, and they are not the only ones, for a certain degree of personal misfortune is enough to cut us off from the past and the future. In fact, said Austerlitz, I have never owned a clock of any kind, a bedside alarm or a pocket watch, let alone a wristwatch. A clock has always struck me as something ridiculous, a thoroughly mendacious object, perhaps because I have always resisted the power of time out of some internal compulsion which I myself have never understood, keeping myself apart from so-called current events in the hope, as I now think, said Austerlitz, that time will not pass away, has not passed away, that I can turn back and go behind it, and there I shall find everything as it once was, or more precisely I shall find that all moments of time have co-existed simultaneously, in which case none of what history tells us would be true, past events have not yet occurred but are waiting to do so at the moment when we think of them, although that, of course, opens up the bleak prospect of ever-lasting misery and never-ending anguish. — It was around three-thirty in the afternoon and dusk was gathering as I left the Observatory with Austerlitz. We lingered for a while in the walled forecourt. Far away, we could hear the hollow grinding of the city, and the air was full of the drone of the great planes flying low and as it seemed to me incredibly slowly over Greenwich from the north-east, at intervals of scarcely more than a minute, and then disappearing again westwards towards Heathrow. Like strange monsters going home to their dens to sleep in the evening, they hovered above us in the darkening air, rigid wings extended from their bodies. The leafless trees on the slopes of the park were already deep in the shadows rising from the earth; before us, at the foot of the hill, was the broad square of turf, black as night and crossed diagonally by two pale sandy paths and the white façades and colonnades of the National Maritime Museum, and on the Isle of Dogs on the far side of the river the sparkling glass towers rose above the rapidly gathering darkness into the last of the daylight. As we walked down to Greenwich, Austerlitz told me that a number of artists had painted the park in past centuries. Their pictures showed the green lawns and the canopies of the trees, usually with very small, isolated human figures in the foreground, generally ladies in brightly coloured hooped skirts carrying parasols, and a few of the white, half-tame deer kept in the park at that time. In the background of these paintings, however, behind the trees and the twin domes of the Royal Naval College, you saw the bend in the river and, like a faint line drawn out, as it were, towards the rim of the world, the city of uncounted souls, an indefinable shape, hunched and grey or plaster-coloured, a kind of excrescence or crust on the surface of the earth, and above the city the sky occupying half or more of the entire picture, perhaps with rain hanging down from the clouds in the far distance. I believe I first saw an example of these panoramas of Greenwich in one of the dilapidated country houses which, as I mentioned yesterday, I often visited with Hilary when I was studying at Oxford. I clearly remember, said Austerlitz, how on such an excursion, after walking for a long time in a park densely overgrown with young sycamore and birch trees, we came to a silent house of this kind, one of which on average, according to a calculation I made then, was being demolished every two or three days in the 1950s. We saw quite a number of houses at that time from which almost everything had been ripped out – the bookshelves, the panelling and banisters, the brass central-heating pipes and the marble fireplaces; houses with their roofs falling in, houses knee-deep in rubble, refuse and detritus, houses full of sheep and bird droppings and great lumps of plaster come down from the ceilings. Iver Grove, however, said Austerlitz, a house which stood in the middle of its wilderness of a park at the foot of a gentle south-facing slope, seemed largely intact, at least from the outside. None the less, as we paused on the broad stone steps which had been colonized by hart's-tongue ferns and other weeds and looked up at the blind windows, it seemed to us as if silent horror had seized upon the house at the prospect of its imminent and shameful end. Inside we found heaps of grain in one of the large ground-floor reception rooms, as if the place were a barn. In a second great hall, ornamented with baroque stucco work, hundreds of sacks of potatoes leaned against each other. We stood gazing at this sight for some time,

until — just as I was about to take some photographs — the owner of Iver Grove, who turned out to be a certain James Mallord Ashman, came towards the house along the western terrace. Fully understanding our interest in the buildings now everywhere falling into decay, he told us during a long conversation that after the family seat had been requisitioned for use as a convalescent home during the war years, the expense of putting it back into any kind of order, however makeshift, had been far beyond his means, so that he had been obliged to move to Grove Farm, which belonged to the estate and lay at the other end of the park, and to work the land himself. Hence, so Ashman told us, said Austerlitz, the sacks of potatoes and the grain on the floor. Iver Grove had been built around 1780 by one of Ashman's ancestors, said Austerlitz, a man who suffered from insomnia and withdrew into the observatory he had built at the top of the house to devote himself to various astronomical studies, particularly selenography or the delineation of the moon, and consequently, as Ashman told us, he had also been in frequent contact with John Russell of Guildford, a miniaturist and artist in pastels famous beyond the frontiers of England, who for several decades at this period was working on a map of the moon laid out over an area measuring five feet by five feet, and easily surpassing all earlier depictions of the earth's satellite in its precision and beauty, those of Riccioli and Cassini and those of Tobias Mayer and Hevelius alike. On nights when the moon did not rise or was veiled by cloud, said Ashman, when he had finished showing us round his house and we entered the billiards room, on such nights his ancestor used to play frame after frame of billiards against himself in this retreat, which he had equipped specially for the purpose, often until the dawn of day. Since his death on New Year's Eve 1813, no one had ever picked up a cue in the games room, said Ashman, not his grandfather or his father or himself, Ashman, let alone one of the women, of course. And indeed, said Austerlitz, everything was exactly as it must have been a hundred and fifty years before. The mighty mahogany table, weighted down by the slate slabs embedded in it, stood in its place unmoved; the scoring apparatus, the gold-framed looking-glass on the wall, the stands for the cues and their extension shafts, the cabinet full of drawers containing the ivory balls, the chalks, brushes, polishing cloths and everything else the billiard player requires, had never been touched again or changed in any way. Over the mantelpiece hung an engraving after Turner's *View from Greenwich Park*, and the records book in which the

selenographer, under the rubric Ashman vs. Ashman, had entered all games won or lost against himself in his fine curving hand still lay open on a tall desk. The inside shutters had always been kept closed, and the light of day never entered the room. Evidently, said Austerlitz, this place had always remained so secluded from the rest of the house that for a century and a half scarcely so much as a gossamer-thin layer of dust had been able to settle on the cornices, the black and white square stone flags of the floor, and the green baize cloth stretched over the table, which seemed like a self-contained universe. It was as if time, which usually runs so irrevocably away, had stood still here, as if the years behind us were still to come, and I remember, said Austerlitz, that when we were standing in the billiards room of Iver Grove with Ashman, Hilary remarked on the curious confusion of emotions affecting even a historian in a room like this, sealed away so long from the flow of the hours and days and the succession of the generations. Ashman replied that in 1941, when the house was requisitioned, he himself had hidden the doors to the billiards room and the nurseries on the top floor of the house by putting in false walls and pushing large wardrobes in front of them, and when these partitions were taken down in the autumn of 1951 or 1952, and he entered the nursery again for the first time in ten years, it wouldn't have taken much, said Ashman, to overset his reason altogether. The mere sight of the model train with the green Great Western Railway carriages, and the Noah's Ark with the pairs of well-behaved animals saved from the Flood looking out of it, had made him feel as if the chasm of time were opening up before him, and as he ran his finger over the long row of notches he had carved in silent fury at the age of eight on the edge of his little bedside table, the day before he was sent off to preparatory school, Ashman remembered, the same rage had flared up in him again, and before he knew what he was about he found himself standing in the yard behind the house, firing his rifle several times at the little clock-tower on the coach-house, where the marks he made are visible on the clock-face to this day. Ashman and Hilary, Iver Grove and Andromeda Lodge, whatever my thoughts turn to, said Austerlitz as we descended the darkening grassy slopes of the park to the city lights which had now come on in a wide semi-circle before us, it all arouses in me a sense of disjunction, of having no ground beneath my feet. I think it was in early October 1957, he continued abruptly after some time, when I was on the point of going to Paris to pursue the studies of architectural history on which I had embarked the previous year at the Courtauld Institute, that I last visited the Fitzpatricks in Barmouth for the double funeral of Uncle Evelyn and Great-Uncle Alphonso. They had died almost within a day of each other, Alphonso of a stroke as he was picking up his favourite apples out in the garden, Evelyn in his icy bed, cramped with pain and anguish. Autumn mists filled the whole valley on the morning of the burial of these two very different men, Evelyn always at odds with himself and the world, Alphonso animated by a cheerfully equable temperament. Just as the funeral procession began moving towards Cutiau cemetery, the sun broke through the hazy veils above the Mawddach, and a breeze blew along its banks. The few dark figures, the group of poplars, the flood of light over the water, the massif of Cader Idris on the far side of the river, these were the elements in a farewell scene which, curiously enough, I rediscovered a few weeks ago in one of the rapid watercolour sketches Turner often made, noting down what he saw either from life or looking back at the past later. This almost insubstantial picture, bearing the title of *Funeral at Lausanne*, dates from 1841, and thus from a time when Turner could hardly travel any more and dwelt increasingly on ideas of his own mortality, and perhaps for that very reason, when something like this little cortège in Lausanne emerged from his memory, he swiftly set down a

few brush-strokes in an attempt to capture visions which would melt away again the next moment. What particularly attracted me to Turner's water-colour, said Austerlitz, was not merely the similarity of the scene in Lausanne to the funeral at Cutiau, but the memory it prompted in me of my last walk with Gerald in the early summer of 1966, through the vineyards above Morges on the banks of Lake Geneva. During my subsequent studies of Turner's life and his sketchbooks I discovered the fact, entirely insignificant in itself but none the less one I found curiously moving, that in 1798 he, Turner, had himself visited the estuary of the Mawddach on a journey through Wales, and that at the time he was exactly the same age as I was at the funeral in Cutiau. As I speak of it now, said Austerlitz, it is as if I had been sitting in the south-facing drawing-room of Andromeda Lodge among the mourners only yesterday, as if I could still hear their quiet murmuring, and Adela saying she didn't know what she would do with herself now, all alone in that big house. Gerald, who was then in his last year of school and had come over from Oswestry especially for the funeral, told me about the lack of any improvement in conditions at Stower Grange, which he described as a horrible inkblot disfiguring the souls of its pupils for ever. He was kept from going mad, said Gerald, only by the fact that since joining the Air Cadet Corps he had been able to fly over the whole wretched place in a Chipmunk and get right away from it once a week. The further you can rise above the earth the better, he said, and for that same reason he had decided to study astronomy. About four o'clock I went down to Barmouth station with Gerald. When I returned — dusk was already falling, said Austerlitz, and fine rain hung suspended in the air, apparently without sinking to the ground — Adela came to meet me from the misty depths of the garden, muffled up in greenish-brown tweed with millions of tiny drops of water clinging to the fine fuzz of its outline and forming a kind of silvery radiance around her. She was carrying a large bunch of rust-coloured chrysanthemums in the crook of her right arm, and when we had walked side by side across the yard without a word and were standing in the doorway, she raised her free hand and put the hair back from my forehead, as if she knew, in this one gesture, that she had the gift of being remembered. Yes, I can still see Adela, said Austerlitz; in my mind she has remained unchanged, as beautiful as she was then. At the end of those long summer days we quite often played badminton together in the ballroom of Andromeda Lodge, which had been empty since the war, while Gerald fed and watered his pigeons before night fell. The feathered shuttle-cock flew between us as we struck it back and forth.

The trajectory it followed, always turning on its way although you could not have said how, was a streak of white drawn through the evening hour, and I could have sworn that Adela often hovered in the air just above the parquet floor for much longer than the force of gravity allowed. After our game we usually stayed in the ballroom for a little while, looking at the images cast on the wall opposite the tall, arched window by the last rays of the sun shining low through the moving branches of a hawthorn, until at last they were extinguished. There was something fleeting, evanescent about those sparse patterns appearing in constant succession on the pale surface, something which never went beyond the moment of its generation, so to speak, yet here, in this intertwining of sunlight and shadow always forming and re-forming, you could see mountainous landscapes with glaciers and ice-fields, high plateaux, steppes, deserts, fields full of flowers, islands in the sea, coral reefs, archipelagos and atolls, forests bending to the storm, quaking grass and drifting smoke. And once, I remember, said Austerlitz, as we gazed together at this slowly fading world, Adela leaned towards me and asked: Do you see the fronds of the palm trees, do you see the caravan coming through the dunes over there? By the time Austerlitz repeated this question of Adela's, a question still imprinted on his memory, we were on our way back into the city from Greenwich. Our taxi made slow progress in the dense evening traffic. It had begun to rain; the beams of headlights gleamed on the asphalt, cutting through the windscreen covered with silvery beads. It took us nearly an hour to travel a distance of not much more than three miles to Tower Bridge by way of Greek Street, Evelyn Street, Lower Road and Jamaica Road. Austerlitz leaned back with his arms round his rucksack, staring ahead in silence. Perhaps he had closed his eyes, I thought, but I did not venture to glance sideways at him. Only at Liverpool Street station, where he waited with me in McDonald's until my train left, and after a casual remark about the glaring light which, so he said, allowed not even the hint of a shadow and perpetuated the momentary terror of a lightning flash — only at Liverpool Street did he resume his story. I never saw Adela again after the day of the funeral, he began, which was my own fault, because I did not once return to England all the time I was in Paris. And then, he continued, when I had taken up my appointment in London and went to Cambridge to see Gerald, who had now finished his studies and was beginning his research work, Andromeda Lodge had been sold and Adela had gone to North Carolina with an entomologist called Willoughby. Gerald, who at the time had rented a cottage in the tiny village of Quy not far from Cambridge airfield and had bought a Cessna with his share of the proceeds from the sale of the property, kept coming back to his passion for flying in all our conversations, whatever their ostensible subjects. I remember, for instance, said Austerlitz, that once, when we were discussing our schooldays at Stower Grange, he told me at length how after I had gone up to Oxford he spent many of the endless hours of study at the school working out an ornithological system based, as its principal criterion, on the degree of a bird's aptitude for flight, and according to Gerald, said Austerlitz, whatever way he modified this system pigeons always led the field, not just for their speed in travelling very long distances but for their navigational abilities, which set them apart from all other living creatures. You can dispatch a pigeon from shipboard in the middle of a snow-storm over the North Sea, and if its strength holds out it will infallibly find its way home. To this day no one knows how these birds, sent off on their journey into so menacing a void, their hearts surely almost breaking with fear in their presentiment of the vast distances they must cover, make straight for their place of origin. At least, Gerald had said, the scientific explanations known to him claiming that pigeons take their bearings from the constellations, or air currents, or magnetic fields are not much more conclusive than the various theories he worked out himself as a boy of twelve, hoping that once he had solved this problem he would be able to make the pigeons fly the other way, for instance from their home in Barmouth to his place of exile in Oswestry, and he kept imagining them suddenly sailing down to him out of the sky, with sunlight filtered through the feathers of their motionless, outstretched wings, and landing with a faint coo in their throats on the sill of the window where, as he said, he often stood for hours on end. The sense of liberation he had felt when he first became aware of the lifting capacity of the air beneath him in one of the Cadet Corps planes, Gerald said, was indescribable, and he himself still remembered, added Austerlitz, how proud, indeed positively radiant Gerald had been when once, in the late summer of 1962 or 1963, they took off together from the runway of Cambridge airfield for an evening flight. The sun had set not long before we started, but as soon as we gained altitude we were surrounded once again by a glittering brightness which did not fade until we were going south, following the white strip of the Suffolk coast, when shadows emerged from the depths of the sea, gradually rising and inclining towards us, until the last gleam of light was extinguished on the horizons of the western world. Soon the shapes of the landscape below, the woods and the pale stubble fields, could be distinguished only as shadowy outlines, and I shall never forget, said Austerlitz, how the curving estuary of the Thames emerged before us as if out of nothing, a dragon's tail, black as cart-grease, winding its way through the falling night, while the lights of Canvey Island, Sheerness and Southend-on-Sea came on beside it. Later, as we described a wide arc over Picardy in the darkness and then turned back on course for England, if we raised our eyes from the illuminated board instruments to look through the glazed cockpit we could see the whole vault of heaven as I had never seen it before, apparently at a standstill but in truth turning slowly, with the constellations of the Swan, Cassiopeia, the Pleiades, the Charioteer, the Corona Borealis and all the rest almost lost in the shimmering dust of the myriads of nameless stars sprinkled over the sky. It was in the autumn of 1965, continued Austerlitz, who had drifted for some time in his memories, that Gerald began developing what we now know was his trail-blazing hypothesis on the so-called Eagle Nebula in the constellation of the Serpent. He spoke of huge regions of interstellar gas which, not unlike storm clouds, became concentrated into vast, billowing forms projecting several light years into the void, where new stars were born in a process of conden-sation steadily intensifying under the influence of gravity. I remember Gerald's saying that there were positive nurseries of stars out there, a claim which I recently found confirmed in a newspaper report accompanying one of the spectacular photographs sent back to earth from the Hubble telescope on its further journey into space. At any rate, said Austerlitz, Gerald then moved from Cambridge to continue his work at an astrophysics research institute in Geneva, where I visited him several times, and as we walked out of the city together and along the banks of the lake I observed the way his ideas, like the stars themselves, gradually emerged from the whirling nebulae of his astrophysical fantasies. On one of these occasions Gerald also told me about the flights he had made over the gleaming, snow-covered mountains in his Cessna, over the volcanic peaks of the Puy-de-Dôme region, down the beautiful Garonne and on to Bordeaux. I suppose it was inevitable that he would fail to come home from one of these flights, said Austerlitz. It was a bad day when I heard that he had crashed in the Savoy Alps, and perhaps that was the beginning of my own decline, a withdrawal into myself which became increasingly morbid and intractable with the passage of time.

*

Almost quarter of a year had passed before I next went to London and visited Austerlitz in his house in Alderney Street. On our parting in December we had agreed that I would wait to receive news from him. As the weeks went by I had felt less and less sure whether I would ever hear from him again, fearing at various times that I might have made a thoughtless remark, or offended him in some other way. It also occurred to me that, following his old custom, he might simply have gone away with some unknown purpose in mind and for an indefinite period. Had I realized at the time that for Austerlitz certain moments had no beginning or end, while on the other hand his whole life had sometimes seemed to him a blank point without duration, I would probably have waited more patiently. But at any rate, one day my mail included a picture postcard from the 1920s or 1930s showing a camp of white tents in the Egyptian desert, a picture taken during a campaign now remembered by no one, the message on the back saying merely

*Saturday 19 March, Alderney Street*, followed by a question mark and a capital *A* for Austerlitz. Alderney Street is quite a long way out in the East End of London. It is a remarkably quiet street running parallel to the main road not far from the Mile End junction, where there are always traffic jams and, on such Saturdays, market traders set up their stalls of clothes and fabrics on the pavements. Thinking back now, I see again a low block of flats like a fortress standing on the corner of the street; a garish green kiosk with its wares openly laid out,

though there was never anyone behind the counter; a cast-iron fence round a patch of grass on which you might think no one had ever trodden; and the brick wall on the right, about fifty yards long and as tall as a man. At the end of it I found the house where Austerlitz lived, the first in a row of six or seven. The interior, which appeared to be very spacious, contained only the most essential furniture and no curtains or carpets. The walls were painted a pale shade of matt grey, and the floorboards were also grey, but of a rather darker hue. Apart from what seemed to me a curiously elongated, old-fashioned ottoman, the front room, into which Austerlitz took me first, had nothing in it but a large table, also varnished matt grey, with several dozen photographs lying on it, most of them dating quite a long way back and rather worn at the edges. Some of the pictures were already familiar to me, so to speak: pictures of empty Belgian landscapes, stations and métro viaducts in Paris, the palm house in the Jardin des Plantes, various moths and other night-flying insects, ornate dovecotes, Gerald Fitzpatrick on the airfield near Quy, and a number of heavy doors and gateways. Austerlitz told me that he sometimes sat here for hours, laying out these photographs or others from his collection the wrong way up, as if playing a game of patience, and that then, one by one, he turned them over, always with a new sense of surprise at what he saw, pushing the pictures back and forth and over each other, arranging them in an order depending on their family resemblances, or withdrawing them from the game until either there was nothing left but the grey table top, or he felt exhausted by the constant effort of thinking and remembering and had to rest on the ottoman. I often lie here until late in the evening, feeling time roll back, said Austerlitz, as we passed into the sitting-room at the rear, where he lit the little gas fire and invited me to sit down on one of the chairs standing on either side of the hearth. This room too contained hardly any furniture; there were just the grey floorboards and the walls on which the light of the flickering blue flames was now cast in the gathering dusk. I can still hear the faint hiss of the gas, and I remember that while Austerlitz was making tea in the kitchen I sat entranced by the reflection of the little fire, which looked as if it were burning at some distance from the house on the other side of the glazed veranda doors, among the now almost pitch-black bushes in the garden. When Austerlitz had brought the tea tray in and was holding slices of white bread on a toasting-fork in front of the blue gas flames, I said something about the incomprehensibility of mirror images, to which he replied that he often sat in this room after nightfall, staring at the apparently motionless spot of light reflected out there in the darkness, and when he did so he inevitably thought of a Rembrandt exhibition he had seen once, many years ago, in the Rijksmuseum in Amsterdam, where he had not felt inclined to linger before any of the large-scale masterpieces which have been reproduced over and over again, but instead stood for a long time looking at a small painting measuring at most nine by twelve inches, from the Dublin collection, as far as he remembered, which according to its label showed the Flight into Egypt, although he could make out neither Mary and Joseph, nor the child Jesus, nor the ass, but only a tiny flicker of fire in the middle of the gleaming black varnish of the darkness which, said Austerlitz, he could see in his mind's eye to this day. — But where, he continued, shall I take up my story? When I came back from France I bought this house for what today is the positively ridiculous sum of

nine hundred and fifty pounds, and then I taught for
almost thirty years until I took early retirement in
1991, partly, said Austerlitz, because of the in-
exorable spread of ignorance even to the univer-
sities, and partly because I hoped to set out on
paper my investigations into the history of architec-
ture and civilization, as had long been my intention.
I might perhaps, Austerlitz said to me, have had
some idea since our first conversations in Antwerp
of the extent of his interests, the drift of his ideas
and the nature of his observations and comments,
always made extempore or first recorded in provi-
sional form, but eventually covering thousands of
pages. Even in Paris, said Austerlitz, I had thought
of collecting my fragmentary studies in a book,
although I constantly postponed writing it. The
various ideas I entertained at different times of this
book I was to write ranged from the concept of a
systematically descriptive work in several volumes
to a series of essays on such subjects as hygiene and
sanitation, the architecture of the penal system,
secular temples, hydrotherapy, zoological gardens,
departure and arrival, light and shade, steam and
gas, and so forth. However, even a first glance at
the papers I had brought here from the Institute to

Alderney Street showed that they consisted largely of sketches which now seemed misguided, distorted, and of little use. I began to assemble and recast anything that still passed muster in order to re-create before my own eyes, as if in the pages of an album, the picture of the landscape, now almost immersed in oblivion, through which my journey had taken me. But the more I laboured on this

project over several months, the more pitiful did the results seem. I was increasingly overcome by a sense of aversion and distaste, said Austerlitz, at the mere thought of opening the bundles of papers and looking through the endless reams I had written in the course of the years. Yet reading and writing, he added, had always been his favourite occupation.

How happily, said Austerlitz, have I sat over a book in the deepening twilight until I could no longer make out the words and my mind began to wander, and how secure have I felt seated at the desk in my house in the dark night, just watching the tip of my pencil in the lamplight following its shadow, as if of its own accord and with perfect fidelity, while that shadow moved regularly from left to right, line by line, over the ruled paper. But now I found writing such hard going that it often took me a whole day to compose a single sentence, and no sooner had I thought such a sentence out, with the greatest effort, and written it down, than I saw the awkward falsity of my constructions and the inadequacy of all the words I had employed. If at times some kind of self-deception none the less made me feel that I had done a good day's work, then as soon as I glanced at the page next morning I was sure to find the most appalling mistakes, inconsistencies and lapses staring at me from the paper. However much or little I had written, on a subsequent reading it always seemed so fundamentally flawed that I had to destroy it immediately and begin again. Soon I could not even venture on the first step. Like a tightrope walker who has forgotten how to put one foot in front of the other, all I felt was the swaying of the precarious structure on which I stood, stricken with terror at the realization that the ends of the balancing pole gleaming far out on the edges of my field of vision were no longer my guiding lights, as before, but malignant enticements to me to cast myself into the depths. Now and then a train of thought did succeed in emerging with wonderful clarity inside my head, but I knew even as it formed that I was in no position to record it, for as soon as I so much as picked up my pencil the endless possibilities of language, to which I could once safely abandon myself, became a conglomeration of the most inane phrases. There was not an expression in the sentence but it proved to be a miserable crutch, not a word but it sounded false and hollow. And in this dreadful state of mind I sat for hours, for days on end with my face to the wall, tormenting myself and gradually discovering the horror of finding that even the smallest task or duty, for instance arranging assorted objects in a drawer, can be beyond one's power. It was as if an illness that had been latent in me for a long time were now threatening to erupt, as if some soul-destroying and inexorable force had fastened upon me and would gradually paralyse my entire system. I already felt in my head the dreadful torpor that heralds disintegration of the personality, I sensed that in truth I had neither memory nor the power of thought, nor even any existence, that all my life had been a constant process of obliteration, a turning away from myself and the world. If someone had come then to lead me away to a place of execution I would have gone meekly, without a word, without so much as opening my eyes, just as people who suffer from violent sea-sickness, if they are crossing the Caspian Sea on a steamer, for instance, will not offer the slightest resistance should someone tell them that they are about to be thrown overboard. Whatever was going on within me, said Austerlitz, the panic I felt on facing the start of any sentence that must be written, not knowing how I could begin it or indeed any other sentence, soon extended to what is in itself the simpler business of reading, until if I attempted to read a whole page I inevitably fell into a state of the greatest confusion. If language may be regarded as an old city full of streets and squares, nooks and crannies, with some quarters dating from far back in time while others have been torn down, cleaned up and rebuilt, and with suburbs reaching further and further into the surrounding country, then I was like a man who has been abroad a long time and cannot find his way through this urban sprawl any more, no longer knows what a bus stop is for, or what a back yard is, or a street junction, an avenue or a bridge. The entire structure of language, the syntactical arrangement of parts of speech, punctuation, conjunctions, and finally even the nouns denoting ordinary objects were all enveloped in impenetrable fog. I could not even understand what I myself had written in the past – perhaps I could understand that least of all. All I could think was that such a sentence only appears to mean something, but in truth is at best a makeshift expedient, a kind of unhealthy growth issuing from our ignorance, something which we use, in the same way as many sea plants and animals use their tentacles, to grope blindly through the darkness enveloping us. The very thing which may usually convey a sense of purposeful intelligence – the exposition of an idea by means of a certain stylistic facility – now seemed to me nothing but an entirely arbitrary or deluded enterprise. I could see no connections any more, the sentences resolved themselves into a series of separate words, the words into random sets of letters, the letters into disjointed signs, and those signs into a blue-grey trail gleaming silver here and there, excreted and left behind it by some crawling creature, and the sight of it increasingly filled me with feelings of horror and shame. One evening, said Austerlitz, I gathered up all my papers, bundled or loose, my notepads and exercise books, my files and lecture notes, anything with my writing on it, and carried the entire collection out of the house to the far end of the garden, where I threw it on the compost heap and buried it under layers of rotted leaves and spadefuls of earth. For several weeks afterwards, while I turned out the rooms of my house and repainted the floors and walls, I did think I felt some relief from the burden weighing down on my life, but I soon realized that the shadows were falling over me. Especially in the evening twilight, which had always been my favourite time of day, I was overcome by a sense of anxiety, dif-fuse at first and then growing ever denser, through which the lovely spectacle of fading colours turned to a malevolent and lightless pallor, my heart felt constricted in my chest to a quarter of its natural size, until at last there remained only one idea in my head: I must go to the third-floor landing of a certain building in Great Portland Street, where I had once had a strange turn after visiting a doctor's surgery, and throw myself over the banisters into the dark depths of the stairwell. It was impossible for me then to go and see any of my friends, who were not numerous in any case, or mix with other people in any normal way. The mere idea of listening to anyone brought on a wave of revulsion, while the thought of talking myself, said Austerlitz, was perhaps worse still, and as this state of affairs continued I came to realize how isolated I was and always have been, among the Welsh as much as among the English and French. It never occurred to me to wonder about my true origins, said Austerlitz, nor did I ever feel that I belonged to a certain social class, professional group, or religious confession. I was as ill at ease among artists and intellectuals as in bourgeois life, and it was a very long time since I had felt able to make personal friendships. No sooner did I become acquainted with someone than I feared I had come too close, no sooner did someone turn towards me than I began to retreat. In the end I was linked to other people only by certain forms of courtesy which I took to extremes and which I know today, said Austerlitz, I observed not so much for the sake of their recipients as because they allowed me to ignore the fact that my life has always, for as far back as I can remember, been clouded by unrelieved despair. It was then, after my work of destruction in the garden and when I had turned out my house, that I began my nocturnal wanderings through London, to escape the insomnia which increasingly tormented me. For over a year, I think, said Austerlitz, I would leave my house as darkness fell, walking on and on, down the Mile End Road and Bow Road to Stratford, then to Chigwell and Romford, right across Bethnal Green and Canonbury, through Holloway and Kentish Town and thus to Hampstead Heath, or else south over the river to Peckham and Dulwich or westward to Richmond Park. It is a fact that you can traverse this vast city almost from end to end on foot in a single night, said Austerlitz, and once you are used to walking alone and meeting only a few nocturnal spectres on your way, you soon begin to wonder why, apparently because of some agreement concluded long ago, Londoners of all ages lie in their beds in those countless buildings in

Greenwich, Bayswater or Kensington, under a safe roof, as they suppose, while really they are only stretched out with their faces turned to the earth in fear, like travellers of the past resting on their way through the desert. My wanderings took me to the most remote areas of London, into outlying parts of the metropolis which I would never otherwise have seen, and when dawn came I would go back to Whitechapel on the Underground, together with all the other poor souls who flow from the suburbs towards the centre at that time of day. As I passed through the stations, I thought several times that among the passengers coming towards me in the tiled passages, on the escalators plunging steeply into the depths, or behind the grey windows of a train just pulling out, I saw a face known to me from some much earlier part of my life, but I could never say whose it was. These familiar faces always had something different from the rest about them, something I might almost call indistinct, and on occasion they would haunt and disturb me for days on end. In fact at this time, usually when I came home from my nocturnal excursions, I began seeing what might be described as shapes and colours of diminished corporeality through a drifting veil or cloud of smoke, images from a faded world: a squadron of yachts putting out into the shadows over the sea from the glittering Thames estuary in the evening light, a horse-drawn cab in Spitalfields driven by a man in a top hat, a woman wearing the costume of the 1930s and casting her eyes down as she passed me by. It was at moments of particular weakness, when I thought I could not go on any longer, that my senses played these tricks on me. It sometimes seemed to me as if the noises of the city were dying down around me and the traffic was flowing silently down the street, or as if someone had plucked me by the sleeve. And I would hear people behind my back speaking in a foreign tongue, Lithuanian, Hungarian, or something else with a very alien note to it, or so I thought, said Austerlitz. I had several such experiences in Liverpool Street station, to which I was always irresistibly drawn back on my night journeys. Before work began to rebuild it at the end of the 1980s this station, with its main concourse fifteen to twenty feet below street level, was one of the darkest and most sinister places in London, a kind of entrance to the underworld, as it has often been described. The ballast between the tracks, the cracked sleepers, the brick walls with their stone bases, the cornices and panes of the tall windows, the wooden kiosks for the ticket inspectors, and the towering cast-iron columns with their palmate capitals were all covered in a greasy black layer formed, over the course of a century, by coke dust and soot, steam, sulphur and diesel oil. Even on sunny days only a faint greyness, scarcely illuminated at all by the globes of the station lights, came through the glass roof over the main hall, and in

this eternal dusk, which was full of a muffled babble of voices, a quiet scraping and trampling of feet, innumerable people passed in great tides, disembarking from the trains or boarding them, coming together, moving apart, and being held up at barriers and bottlenecks like water against a weir. Whenever I got out at Liverpool Street station on my way back to the East End, said Austerlitz, I would stay there at least a couple of hours, sitting on a bench with other passengers who were already tired in the early morning, or standing somewhere, leaning on a handrail and feeling that constant wrenching inside me, a kind of heartache which, as I was beginning to sense, was caused by the vortex of past time. I knew that on the site where the station stood marshy meadows had once extended to the city walls, meadows which froze over for months on end in the cold winters of the so-called Little Ice Age, and that Londoners used to strap bone runners under their shoes, skating there as the people of Antwerp skated on the Schelde, some- times going on until midnight in the flickering light of the bonfires burning here and there on the ice in heavy braziers. Later on, the marshes were pro- gressively drained, elm trees were planted, market gardens, fish ponds and white sandy paths were laid out to make a place where the citizens could walk in their leisure time, and soon pavilions and country houses were being built all the way out to Forest Park and Arden. Until the seventeenth century, Austerlitz continued, the priory of the order of St Mary of Bethlehem stood on the site of the present main station concourse and the Great Eastern Hotel. It had been founded by a certain Simon FitzMary in gratitude for his miraculous rescue from the hands of the Saracens when he was on a crusade, so that the pious brothers and sisters could pray henceforward for the salvation of the founder's soul and the souls of his ancestors, his descendants and all those related to him. The hospital for the insane and other destitute persons which has gone down in history under the name of Bedlam also belonged to the priory outside Bishopsgate. Whenever I was in the station, said Austerlitz, I kept almost obsessively trying to imagine — through the ever-changing maze of walls — the location in that huge space of the rooms where the asylum inmates were confined, and I often wondered whether the pain and suffering accumulated on this site over the centuries had ever really ebbed away, or whether they might not still, as I sometimes thought when I felt a cold breath of air on my forehead, be sensed as we pass through them on our way through the station halls and up and down the flights of steps. Or I imagined the bleachfields stretching westwards from Bedlam, saw the white lengths of linen spread out on the green grass and the diminutive figures of weavers and washerwomen, and on the far side of the bleachfields the places where the dead were buried once the churchyards of London could hold no more. When space becomes too cramped the dead, like the living, move out into less densely populated districts where they can rest at a decent distance from each other. But more and more keep coming, a never-ending succession of them, and in the end, when the space is entirely occupied, graves are dug through existing graves to accommodate them, until all the bones in the cemetery lie jumbled up together. At Broad Street station, built in 1865 on the site of the former burial grounds and bleachfields, excavations during the demolition work of 1984 brought to light over four hundred skeletons underneath a taxi rank. I went there quite often at the time, said Austerlitz, partly because of my interest in architectural history and partly for other reasons which I could not explain even to myself, and I took photographs of the remains of the dead. I remember falling into conversation with one of the archaeologists, who told me that on average the skeletons of eight people had been found in every cubic metre of earth removed from the trench. In the course of the seventeenth and

eighteenth centuries the city had grown above these strata of soil mingled with the dust and bones of decayed bodies into a warren of putrid streets and houses for the poorest Londoners, cobbled together out of beams, clods of clay, and any other building material that came to hand. Around 1860 and 1870, before work on the construction of the two north-east terminals began, these poverty-stricken quarters were forcibly cleared and vast quantities of soil, together with the bones buried in them, were dug up and removed, so that the railway lines, which on the engineers' plans looked like muscles and sinews in an anatomical atlas, could be brought to the outskirts of the City. Soon the site in front of Bishopsgate was nothing but a grey-brown morass, a no-man's-land where not a living soul stirred. The little river Wellbrook, the ditches and ponds, the crakes and snipe and herons, the elms and mulberry trees, Paul Pindar's deer park, the inmates of Bedlam and the starving paupers of Angel Alley, Peter Street, Sweet Apple Court and Swan Yard had all gone, and gone now too are the millions and millions of people who passed through Broadgate and Liverpool Street stations

day in, day out, for an entire century. As for me, said Austerlitz, I felt at this time as if the dead were returning from their exile and filling the twilight around me with their strangely slow but incessant to-ing and fro-ing. I remember, for instance, that one quiet Sunday morning I was sitting on a bench on the particularly gloomy platform where the boat trains from Harwich came in, watching a man who wore a snow-white turban with his shabby porter's uniform as he wielded a broom, sweeping up the rubbish scattered on the paving. In doing this job, which in its pointlessness reminded me of the eternal punishments that we are told, said Austerlitz, we must endure after death, the white-turbanned porter, oblivious of all around, per-formed the same movements over and over again using, instead of a proper dustpan, a cardboard box with one side removed, and nudging it along in front of him with his foot, first up the platform and then down again until he had returned to his point of departure, a low doorway in the builders' fence reaching up to the second storey of the inte-rior façade of the station. He had emerged from this doorway half an hour ago and now disappeared through it again, with an odd jerk, as it seemed to me. To this day I cannot explain what made me follow him, said Austerlitz. We take almost all the decisive steps in our lives as a result of slight inner adjustments of which we are barely conscious. But in any case, that Sunday morning I suddenly found myself on the other side of the tall fence, facing the entrance to the Ladies' Waiting-Room, the existence of which, in this remote part of the station, had been quite unknown to me. The man in the turban was nowhere to be seen, and there was no one on the scaffolding either. I hesitated to approach the swing doors, but as soon as I had taken hold of the brass handle I stepped past a heavy curtain hung on the inside to keep out draughts, and entered the large room, which had obviously been disused for years. I felt, said Austerlitz, like an actor who, upon making his entrance, has completely and irrevocably forgotten not only the lines he knew by heart but the very part he has so often played. Minutes or even hours may have passed while I stood in that empty space beneath a ceiling which seemed to float at a vertiginous height, unable to move from the spot, with my face raised to the icy grey light, like moonshine, which came through the windows in a gallery beneath the vaulted roof, and hung above me like a tight-meshed net or a piece of thin, fraying fabric. Although this light, a profusion of dusty glitter, one might almost say, was very bright near the ceiling, as it sank lower it looked as if it were being absorbed by the walls and the deeper reaches of the room, as if it merely added to the gloom and were running down in black streaks, rather like rainwater running down the smooth trunks of beech trees or over the cast-concrete façade of a building. When the blanket of cloud above the city parted for a moment or two, occasional rays of light fell into the waiting-room, but they were generally extinguished again halfway down. Other beams of light followed curious trajectories which violated the laws of physics, departing from the rectilinear and twisting in spirals and eddies before being swallowed up by the wavering shadows. From time to time, and just for a split second, I saw huge halls open up, with rows of pillars and colonnades leading far into the distance, with vaults and brickwork arches bearing on them many-storeyed structures, with flights of stone steps, wooden stairways and ladders, all leading the eye on and on. I saw viaducts and footbridges crossing deep chasms thronged with tiny figures who looked to me, said Austerlitz, like prisoners in search of some way of escape from their dungeon, and the longer I stared upwards with my head wrenched painfully back, the more I felt as if the room where I stood were expanding, going on for ever and ever in an improbably foreshortened perspective, at the same time turning back into itself in a way possible only in such a deranged universe. Once I thought that very far away I saw a dome of open-work masonry, with a parapet around it on which grew ferns, young willows and various other shrubs where herons had built their large, untidy nests, and I saw the birds spread their great wings and fly away through the blue air. I remember, said Austerlitz, that in the middle of this vision of imprisonment and liberation I could not stop wondering whether it was a ruin or a building in the process of construction that I had entered. Both ideas were right in a way at the time, since the new station was literally rising from the ruins of the old Liverpool Street; in any case, the crucial point was hardly this speculation in itself, which was really only a distraction, but the scraps of memory beginning to drift through the outlying regions of my mind: images, for instance, like the recollection of a late November afternoon in 1968 when I stood with Marie de Verneuil – whom I had met in Paris, and of whom I shall have more to say – when we stood in the nave of the wonderful church of Salle in Norfolk, which towers in isolation above the wide fields, and I could not bring out the words I should have spoken then. White mist had risen from the meadows outside, and we watched in silence as it crept slowly into the church porch, a rippling vapour rolling forward at ground level and gradually spreading over the entire stone floor, becoming denser and denser and rising visibly higher, until we ourselves emerged from it only above the waist and it seemed about to stifle us. Memories like this came back to me in the disused Ladies' Waiting-Room of Liverpool Street station, memories behind and within which many things much further back in the past seemed to lie, all interlocking like the labyrinthine vaults I saw in the dusty grey light, and which seemed to go on and on for ever. In fact I felt, said Austerlitz, that the waiting-room where I stood as if dazzled contained all the hours of my past life, all the suppressed and extinguished fears and wishes I had ever entertained, as if the black and white diamond pattern of the stone slabs beneath my feet were the board on which the end-game would be played, and it covered the entire plane of time. Perhaps that is why, in the gloomy light of the waiting-room, I also saw two middle-aged people dressed in the style of the thirties, a woman in a light gabardine coat with a hat at an angle on her head, and a thin man beside her wear-ing a dark suit and a dog-collar. And I not only saw the minister and his wife, said Austerlitz, I also saw the boy they had come to meet. He was sitting by himself on a bench over to one side. His legs, in white knee-length socks, did not reach the floor, and but for the small rucksack he was holding on his lap I don't think I would have known him, said Austerlitz. As it was, I recognized him by that rucksack of his, and for the first time in as far back as I can remember I recollected myself as a small child, at the moment when I realized that it must have been to this same waiting-room I had come on my arrival in England over half a century ago. As so often, said Austerlitz, I cannot give any pre-cise description of the state of mind this realization induced; I felt something rending within me, and a sense of shame and sorrow, or perhaps something quite different, something inexpressible because we have no words for it, just as I had no words all those years ago when the two strangers came over to me speaking a language I did not understand. All I do know is that when I saw the boy sitting on the bench I became aware, through my dull bemusement, of the destructive effect on me of my desolation through all those past years, and a terrible weariness overcame me at the idea that I had never really been alive, or was only now being born, almost on the eve of my death. I can only guess what reasons may have induced the minister Elias and his wan wife to take me to live with them in the summer of 1939, said Austerlitz. Childless as they were, perhaps they hoped to reverse the petrifaction of their emotions, which must have been becoming more unbearable to them every day, by devoting themselves together to bringing up a boy then aged four and a half, or perhaps they thought they owed it to a higher authority to perform some good work beyond the level of ordinary charity, a work entailing personal devotion and sacrifice. Or perhaps they thought they ought to save my soul, innocent as it was of the Christian faith. I myself cannot say what my first few days in Bala with the Eliases really felt like. I do remember new clothes which made me very unhappy, and the inexplicable disappearance of my little green ruck-sack, and recently I have even thought that I could still apprehend the dying away of my native tongue, the faltering and fading sounds which I think lingered on in me at least for a while, like something shut up and scratching or knocking, something which, out of fear, stops its noise and falls silent whenever one tries to listen to it. And certainly the words I had forgotten in a short space of time, and all that went with them, would have remained buried in the depths of my mind had I not, through a series of coincidences, entered the old waiting-room in Liverpool Street station that Sunday morning, a few weeks at the most before it vanished for ever in the rebuilding. I have no idea how long I stood in the waiting-room, said Austerlitz, nor how I got out again and which way I walked back, through Bethnal Green or Stepney, reaching home at last as dark began to fall. Ex-hausted as I was, I lay down in my drenched clothes and fell into a deep, uneasy sleep from which, as I discovered afterwards by making the calculation several times, I did not wake until the middle of the night after the next day. In that sleep, when my body feigned death while feverish thoughts whirled through my head, I was at the innermost heart of a star-shaped fortress, a dungeon entirely cut off from the outside world, and I had to try finding my way into the open, passing down long, low passages which led me through all the buildings I had ever visited and described. It was a nightmarish, never-ending dream, with its main plot interrupted several times by other episodes. One of them gave me a bird's-eye view of a lightless landscape through which a very small railway train was hurrying, twelve earth-coloured miniature carriages and a coal-black locomotive under a plume of smoke wafting horizontally backwards, with the far end of the plume constantly blown this way and that, like the tip of a large ostrich feather, by the speed of the journey. In another episode, looking out of the window of my train compartment, I saw dark forests of firs, a deeply carved river valley, mountain ranges of cloud on the horizon, and windmills towering above the roofs of the houses clustered around them, with their broad sails cutting rhythmically through the faint light of dawn. In the middle of these dreams, said Austerlitz, somewhere behind his eyes, he had felt these overwhelmingly immediate images forcing their way out of him, but once he had woken he could recall scarcely any of them even in outline. I realized then, he said, how little practice I had in using my memory, and conversely how hard I must always have tried to recollect as little as possible, avoiding everything which related in any way to my unknown past. Inconceivable as it seems to me today, I knew nothing about the conquest of Europe by the Germans and the slave state they set up, and nothing about the persecution I had escaped, or at least, what I did know was not much more than a salesgirl in a shop, for instance, knows about the plague or cholera. As far as I was concerned the world ended in the late nineteenth century. I dared go no further than that, although in fact the whole history of the architecture and civilization of the bourgeois age, the subject of my research, pointed in the direction of the catastrophic events already casting their shadows before them at the time. I did not read newspapers because, as I now know, I feared unwelcome revelations, I turned on the radio only at certain hours of the day, I was always refining my defensive reactions, creating a kind of quarantine or immune system which, as I maintained my existence in a smaller and smaller space, protected me from anything that could be connected in any way, however distant, with my own early history. Moreover, I had constantly been preoccupied by that accumulation of knowledge which I had pursued for decades, and which served as a substitute or compensatory memory. And if some dangerous piece of information came my way despite all my precautions, as it inevitably did, I was clearly capable of closing my eyes and ears to it, of simply forgetting it like any other unpleasantness. Yet this self-censorship of my mind, the constant suppression of the memories surfacing in me, Austerlitz continued, demanded ever greater efforts and finally, and unavoidably, led to the almost total paralysis of my linguistic faculties, the destruction of all my notes and sketches, my endless nocturnal peregrinations through London, and the hallucinations which plagued me with increasing frequency up to the point of my nervous breakdown in the summer of 1992. I cannot say exactly how I spent the rest of that year, said Austerlitz; all I know is that next spring, when there was some improvement in my state of health, on one of my first ventures into the city I visited an antiquarian bookshop near the British Museum where I regularly went in search of architectural engravings. Absentmindedly, I leafed through the various boxes and drawers, staring sometimes for minutes on end at a star-shaped vault or diamond frieze, a hermitage, a monopteros or a mausoleum, without knowing what I was looking at or why. The owner of the bookshop, Penelope Peacefull, a very beautiful woman whom I had admired for many years, was sitting where she always sat in the mornings, slightly to one side of her desk with its load of books and papers, solving the crossword puzzle on the back of the *Telegraph* with her left hand. She smiled at me from time to time and then looked out at the street again, deep in thought. It was quiet in the shop except for soft voices coming from the little radio which stood beside Penelope, as usual, and these voices, which at first I could hardly make out but which soon became almost too distinct, cast such a spell over me that I entirely forgot the engravings lying before me, and stood there as still as if on no account must I let a single syllable emerging from the rather scratchy radio set escape me. I was listening to two women talking to each other about the summer of 1939, when they were children and had been sent to England on a special transport. They mentioned a number of cities — Vienna, Munich, Danzig, Bratislava, Berlin — but only when one of the couple said that her own transport, after two days travelling through the German Reich and the Netherlands, where she could see the great sails of the windmills from the train, had finally left the Hook of Holland on the ferry *Prague* to cross the North Sea to Harwich, only then did I know beyond any doubt that these fragments of memory were part of my own life as well. I was too alarmed by this sudden revelation to be able to write down the addresses and phone numbers given at the end of the programme. I merely saw myself waiting on a quay in a long crocodile of children lined up two by two, most of them carrying rucksacks or small leather cases. I saw the great slabs of paving at my feet again, the mica in the stone, the grey-brown water in the harbour basin, the ropes and anchor chains slanting upwards, the bows of the ship, higher than a house, the seagulls fluttering over our heads and screeching wildly, the sun breaking through the clouds, and the red-haired girl in the tartan cape and velvet beret who had looked after the smaller children in our compartment during the train journey through the dark countryside. Years later, as I now recalled again, I still had recurrent dreams of this girl playing me a cheerful tune on a kind of bandoneon, in a place lit by a bluish nightlight. Are you all right? I heard a voice say suddenly, as if from very far away, and it took me some time to remember where I was and realize that Penelope might have felt concerned by my sudden seizure. I remember telling her that it was nothing, that my thoughts were elsewhere, in the Hook of Holland as a matter of fact, whereupon Penelope raised her face slightly with an understanding smile, as if she herself had often been obliged to wait in that cheerless harbour. One way to live cheaply and without tears? she then immediately asked, tapping the tip of her ballpoint pen on the crossword in her folded newspaper, but just as I was about to confess that I had never been able to solve even the simplest clues in these tortuous English puzzles she said, Oh, it's *rent free*! and scribbled the eight letters swiftly down in the last empty spaces on the grid. When we had parted I sat for an hour on a bench in Russell Square under the tall plane trees, which were still leafless. It was a sunny day. A number of starlings were marching up and down on the grass, pecking desultorily at the crocuses. I watched them, noticing how the green-gold hues in their dark plumage gleamed, depending which way they turned to catch the light, and came to the conclusion that although I did not know whether I had come to England on the *Prague* or on some other ferry, the mere mention of the city's name in the present context was enough to convince me that I would have to go there. I thought of the difficulties Hilary had encountered when, during my last months at Stower Grange, he began taking steps to have me naturalized, and how he had never been able to find out anything from any of the social-services offices in Wales, or the Foreign Office, or the Aid Committee under whose auspices the transports of refugee children had come to England and who had lost a number of files during their several moves and evacuations, carried out during the bombing of London in very difficult circumstances and almost entirely without trained staff. I got the addresses of authorities who might be consulted in a case like mine from the embassy of the Czech Republic, and then, immediately after arriving at Ruzyně airport on a day which was much too bright, almost over-exposed, a day, said Austerlitz, when people looked as ill and grey as if they were all chronic smokers not far from death, I took a taxi to the Karmelitská in the Lesser Quarter, where the state archives are housed in a very peculiar building going far back in time if not even, like so much in the city of Prague, standing outside time altogether. You go in through a narrow doorway let into the main portal, and find yourself first in a dim barrel-vaulted entrance through which coaches and carriages used to drive into the inner courtyard. This courtyard measures some twenty by fifty metres, is roofed by a glazed dome, and on three storeys has galleries running round it, giving access to

the rooms containing the archives, where the windows look out on the street. The entire building, from the outside more like a mansion house than anything else, therefore consists of four wings, each not much more than three metres deep, set around the courtyard in an almost Illusionist manner and without any corridors or passages in them. It is a style resembling the prison architecture of the bourgeois epoch, when it was decided that the most useful design for the penal system was to build wings of cells around a rectangular or circular courtyard, with catwalks running along the interior. And it was not just of a prison that the archives building in the Karmelitská reminded me, said Austerlitz; it also suggested a monastery, a riding school, an opera house and a lunatic asylum, and all these ideas mingled in my mind as I looked at the twilight coming in from above, and thought that on the rows of galleries I saw a dense crowd of people, some of them waving hats or handkerchiefs, as passengers on board a steamer used to do when it put out to sea. At any rate, it was a little while before I managed to bring myself back to the present, and turned to the lodge near the entrance, from which the porter had been keeping an eye on me ever since I had crossed the threshold and, attracted by the light of the interior courtyard, had passed by him without noticing his presence. If you wanted to speak to this porter you had to lean a long way down to his window, which was so low that he appeared to be kneeling on the floor of his lodge. Although I had soon adopted the right position, said Austerlitz, I could not make myself understood, with the result that after launching into a long verbal torrent in which I could make out nothing but the words *anglický* and *Angličan*, repeated several times with special emphasis, the porter eventually phoned to request assistance from one of the archive's officials, who did indeed, at practically the next moment, while I was still filling in a visitor's form at the desk opposite the

lodge, materialize beside me as if she had, as they say, sprung out of the ground. Tereza Ambrosová – so she introduced herself to me, immediately asking in her slightly hesitant but otherwise very correct English what I wanted to know – Tereza Ambrosová was a pale woman of almost transparent appearance, and about forty years old. As we went up to the third floor in the cramped lift, which scraped against one side of the shaft, in silence and with a sense of awkwardness because of the unnatural physical proximity into which one is forced in such a box, I saw a gentle pulsation in the curve of a blue vein beneath the skin of her right temple, almost as fast as the throbbing in a lizard's throat when it lies motionless on a rock in the sun. We reached Mrs Ambrosová's office by walking down one of the galleries encircling the courtyard. I hardly dared glance over the balustrade to the depths below where two or three cars were parked, looking curiously elongated from above, or at least much longer than they would appear in the street. The office which we entered straight from this gallery was full of stacks of papers tied up with string, not a few of them discoloured by sunlight and brittle at the edges, crammed into roll-front cupboards, deposited on shelves that sagged under their weight, piled high on a rickety little trolley which seemed to be specially intended for the transport of files, on an old-fashioned wing chair pushed against the wall, and on the two desks facing each other in the room. There were a good dozen houseplants among these mountains of paper, in plain clay flowerpots or brightly coloured majolica jardinières: mimosas and myrtles, thick-leaved aloes, gardenias, and a large hoya twining its way around a trelliswork frame. Mrs Ambrosová, who had very courteously pulled out a chair for me beside her desk, listened attentively with her head tilted slightly to one side as, for the first time in my life, I began explaining to someone else that because of certain circumstances my origins had been unknown to me, and for other reasons I had never inquired into them, but now felt compelled, because of a series of coincidental events, to conclude or at least to conjecture that I had left Prague at the age of four and a half, in the months just before the war broke out, on one of the so-called children's transports departing from the city at the time, and I had therefore come to consult the archives in the hope that people of my surname living here between 1934 and 1939, who could not have been very numerous, might be found in the registers, with details of their addresses. I fell into such a panic as I offered these explanations, which suddenly struck me as not just far too cursory but positively absurd, that I began to stammer and could hardly bring out a word. All at once I felt the heat from the stout radiator, which was encrusted with several layers of lumpy oil paint and stood under the wide-open window; I heard nothing but the noise rising from the Karmelitská, the heavy rumble of the trams, the wailing sirens of police cars and ambulances somewhere in the distance, and I calmed down only when Tereza Ambrosová, whose deep-set violet eyes had been gazing at me with some concern, gave me a glass of water. As I took a few sips from this glass, which I had to hold in both hands, she said that the registers of those living in Prague at the time in question had been preserved complete, that Austerlitz was indeed one of the more unusual surnames, so she thought there could be no particular difficulty in finding me the entries I wanted by tomorrow afternoon. She would see to it personally, she told me. I cannot remember, said Austerlitz, with what words I said goodbye to Mrs Ambrosová, how I got out of the archives building or where I went after that; all I know is that I took a room in a small hotel on Kampa Island not far from the Karmelitská and sat there by the window until darkness fell, looking out at the heavy, leaden grey waters of the Vltava, and over the river to the city, which I now feared was entirely alien to me, a place with which I had no connection at all. These thoughts went through my head with grinding slowness, each more confused and harder to grasp than the one that went before. I spent the whole night either lying awake or tormented by fearful dreams in which I had to climb up and down flights of steps ringing hundreds of doorbells in vain, until, in the outermost suburbs, I came upon a darkly looming building, from the dungeon-like basement of which there emerged a caretaker called Bartoloměj Smečka, a veteran, it seemed, of long-lost campaigns, clad in a crumpled redingote and a flowered fancy waistcoat with a gold watch-chain draped over it, who having studied the note I handed him shrugged his shoulders, saying that unfortunately the tribe of the Aztecs had died out years ago, and that at best an ancient perroquet which still remembered a few words of their language might survive here and there. Next day, Austerlitz continued, I went back to the state archives building in the Karmelitská, where, in order to compose myself a little, I first took some photographs of the great inner court and the stairway leading up to the galleries, which in its asymmetrical construction reminded me of the follies built by so many English noblemen in their parks and gardens. In the end I went up this stairway, pausing on each landing for a while to look through one of the irregular openings in the wall and down at the empty yard, which I saw traversed only once by one of the archive's grey-coated porters, whose right leg flexed slightly inward as he walked. When I entered Tereza Ambrosová's office she was just watering her geranium cuttings, which stood in an assortment of flowerpots on the sill between the inner and outer windows. They do better in this overheated atmosphere than in the cold springtime air at home, said Mrs Ambrosová. We haven't been able to regulate the steam heating for a long time, so it's often like a hothouse in here, particularly at this time of year. That may be why you felt unwell yesterday, she said, adding, I've already made a note of the addresses of all those named Austerlitz in the register. As I suspected, they didn't come to more than half a dozen. Mrs Ambrosová put her green watering-can down and gave me a sheet of paper from her desk. Austerlitz Leopold, Austerlitz Viktor, Austerlitz Tomáš, Austerlitz Jeroným, Austerlitz Edward and Austerlitz František were listed one beneath another, and at the end there was an Austerlitzová Agáta, evidently a single woman.

The names were followed by the professions of their bearers – dealer in textiles *en gros*, rabbi, bandages manufacturer, principal clerk, silversmith, printing works proprietor, and finally opera singer – together with the number of the city district and the street: VII U vozovky, II Betlemská, and so on. Mrs Ambrosová suggested that before crossing the river I might begin my inquiries in the Lesser Quarter, which wasn't ten minutes' walk away from here, she said. I could try the Šporkova, a small street a few paces uphill from the Schönborn Palace, where the register of inhabitants for 1938 said that Agáta Austerlitzová had been living at Number Twelve in that year. And so, said Austerlitz, no sooner had I arrived in Prague than I found myself back among the scenes of my early childhood, every trace of which had been expunged from my memory for as long as I could recollect. As I walked through the labyrinth of alleyways, thoroughfares and courtyards between the Vlašská and Nerudova, and still more so when I felt the uneven paving of the Šporkova underfoot as step by step I climbed uphill, it was as if I had already been this way before and memories were revealing themselves to me not by means of any mental effort but through my senses, so long numbed and now coming back to life. It was true that I could recognize nothing for certain, yet I had to keep stopping now and then because my glance was caught by a finely wrought window grating, the iron handle of a bell-pull, or the branches of an almond tree growing over a garden wall. Once I stood for a considerable time outside the vaulted entrance to a building, said Austerlitz, looking up at a half-relief set in the smooth plaster above the keystone of the arch. The cast was no more than a square foot in size, and showed, set against a spangled sea-green background, a blue dog carrying a small branch in its mouth, which I could tell, by the prickling of my scalp, it had brought back out of my past. Then there was the cool air as I entered the front hall of Number Twelve Šporkova, the metal box for the electrics built into the wall beside the entrance with its lightning symbol, the octofoil mosaic flower in shades of

dove grey and snow white set in the flecked
artificial-stone floor of the hall, the smell of damp
limewash, the gently rising flight of stairs, with

hazelnut-shaped iron knobs placed at intervals in
the handrail of the banisters – all of them signs and
characters from the type-case of forgotten things, I

thought, and was overcome by such a state of blissful yet anxious confusion that more than once I had to sit down on the steps in the quiet stairwell and lean my head against the wall. It may have been as much as an hour before I finally rang the bell of the right-hand flat on the top floor, and then half an eternity seemed to pass before I heard movement inside, the door was opened, and I found myself facing Věra Ryšanová, who — as she was soon to tell me — had been my mother Agáta's neighbour and my nurserymaid in the thirties when she, Věra, had been studying Romance languages at Prague University. I think that the reason why I did not immediately recognize her, said Austerlitz, although despite her fragility she seemed quite unchanged, was my agitated condition, in which I could hardly believe my eyes. So I merely stammered out the sentence I had laboriously learnt by heart the day before: *Promiňte, prosím, že Vás obtěžuji. Hledám paní Agátu Austerlitzovou, která zde možná v roce devatenáct set třicet osm bydlela.* I am looking for a Mrs Agáta Austerlitzová who may have been living here in 1938. With a gesture of alarm, Věra covered her face with both hands, hands which, it flashed through my mind, were endlessly familiar to me, stared at me over her spread fingertips, and very quietly but with what to me was a quite singular clarity spoke these words in French: *Jacquot*, she said, *dis, est-ce que c'est vraiment toi?* We embraced, we held each other's hands, we embraced again, I don't know how often, before Věra led me through the dark hall into a room where everything was just as it had been almost sixty years ago. The furniture she had inherited in May 1933 together with her great-aunt's flat, the display cabinet with a masked Meissen china Pulcinello on the left and his beloved Columbine on the right, the glass-fronted bookcase with the fifty-five small volumes of the *Comédie humaine* bound in carmine red, the writing desk, the long ottoman, the camel-hair rug lying folded at one end of it, the blue-tinged aquatint of the Bohemian mountains — throughout my entire life, which was now unravelling headlong before me, all this had stayed in the same place because as Věra told me, said Austerlitz, once she had lost me and my mother, who was almost a sister to her, she could not bear to alter anything. I don't remember in what order Věra and I told each other our stories that late March afternoon and evening, said Auster-litz, but I think that after I had given her a brief account of myself, leaving out all that had weighed on me so heavily over the years, we spoke first about my lost parents, Agáta and Maximilian. Maximilian Aychenwald, who had come to Prague from St Petersburg where his father traded in spices until the year of the revolution, soon established himself as one of the most prominent officials of the Czech Social Democratic Party, said Věra. He had met my mother, fifteen years younger than he was and then appearing in various provincial towns as she embarked on her stage career, in Nikolsburg on one of the many journeys he made to speak at public gatherings and shop-floor meetings. In May 1933, when I had only just settled in here, said Věra, they came back from a visit to Paris which, as they never tired of repeating, had been full of the most wonderful events and encounters, and perhaps that was why they decided, directly upon their return, to move into a flat in this house together, though they always remained unmarried. Agáta and Maximilian, said Věra, both had a special fondness for all things French. Maximilian was a life-long republican, and had dreamt of making Czechoslovakia an island of freedom in the midst of the tide of Fascism then inexorably spreading throughout Europe, a kind of second Switzerland, while Agáta's rather more colourful notion of the ideal world was inspired by the works of Jacques Offenbach, whom she admired enormously, which incidentally, said Věra, was the reason for my first name, not a usual one among Czechs. It was through an interest in every aspect of French civilization, she added, something which as an enthusiastic student of Romance culture I shared with both Agáta and Maximilian, that a friendship began to develop between us immediately after our first conversation on the day when they moved in, a friendship which led as if quite naturally, so Věra told me, said Austerlitz, to her offering, since unlike Agáta and Maximilian she had her time largely at her own disposal, to assume the duties of nanny for the few years until I started nursery school. It was an offer she had never once regretted later, said Věra, for even before I could talk it had always seemed to her as if no one understood her better than this small boy who, by the age of not quite three, entertained her in the most delightful way with his conversational gifts. By agreement with Agáta, when we walked over the meadow slopes of the Seminar Garden among the pear and cherry trees, or on hot days through the shadier grounds of the park of Schönborn Palace, we spoke French, and only when we came home late in the afternoon and Věra was making our supper did we revert to Czech, for the discussion of more domestic and childish matters, as it were. In the middle of her account Věra herself, quite involuntarily, had changed from one language to the other, and I, who had not for a moment thought that Czech could mean anything to me, not at the airport or in the state archives, or even while learning by heart the question which would have been of scant use to me addressed to the wrong quarters, now understood almost everything Věra said, like a deaf man whose hearing has been miraculously restored, so that all I wanted to do was close my eyes and listen for ever to her polysyllabic flood of words. In the warm season of the year in particular, said Věra, she had always had to move the geraniums on the sill aside as soon as we came back from our daily walk, so that I could take my favourite place on the window-seat and look down on the garden with its lilac trees and the low building opposite where the hunchbacked tailor Moravec had his workshop, and while she, so Věra said, cut bread and boiled the kettle, I used to give her a running commentary on whatever Moravec happened to be doing: mending the worn hem of a jacket, rummaging in his button box, or sewing a quilted lining into an overcoat. But I was particularly anxious, Věra told me, said Austerlitz, not to miss the moment when Moravec put down his needle and thread, his big scissors and the other tools of his trade, cleared the baize-covered table, spread a double sheet of newspaper on it, and laid out on this sheet blackened with print the supper he must have been looking forward to for some time, a supper which varied according to the season and might be curd cheese with chives, a long radish, a few tomatoes with onions, a smoked herring or boiled potatoes. He's putting the sleeve dummy in the wardrobe, he's going out into the kitchen, now he's bringing in his beer, now he's sharpening his knife, he's cutting a slice of sausage, taking a long drink from his glass, wiping the foam from his mouth with the back of his hand – it was in this or some similar fashion, always the same yet always slightly different, that I used to describe the tailor's supper to her almost every evening, said Věra, and I often had to be reminded not to forget my own bread-and-butter soldiers. As she told me about my curious love of such observations, Věra had risen and opened both the inner and the outer windows to let me look down into the garden next door, where the lilac happened to be in flower, its blossoms so thick and white that in the gathering dusk it looked as if there had been a snow-storm in the middle of spring. And the sweet fragrance wafting up from the walled garden, the waxing moon already in the sky above the rooftops, the sound of church bells ringing down in the city, and the yellow façade of the tailor's house with its green balcony where Moravec, who as Věra told me had died long ago, frequently used to be seen in his time, swinging his heavy iron filled with red hot coals through the air, these and other images, said Austerlitz, ranged themselves side by side, so that deeply buried and locked away within me as they had been, they now came luminously back to my mind as I looked out of the window. It was the same when Věra, without a word, opened the door to the room where the little couch on which I always slept when my parents were away still stood in its place, at the foot of the four-poster bed with its barley-sugar uprights and pillows piled high which, together with the rest of the furniture, she had inherited from her great-aunt. The crescent moon shone into the dark room, and there was a white blouse hanging from the catch of the half-open window just as it had always hung there in the past, I now remembered, said Austerlitz. I saw Věra as she had been then, sitting beside me on the divan telling me stories from the Riesengebirge and the Bohemian Forest, I saw her uncommonly beautiful eyes misting over in the twilight, so to speak, when after reaching the end of the story she took off her glasses and bent down to me. Later, I now remembered, while she sat in the next room over her books, I liked to lie awake for a while, safe as I knew myself to be in the care of my solicitous guardian and the pale glow of the circle of light where she sat reading. With only the slightest effort of will I could conjure it all up; the hunchbacked tailor, who would now be in his own bedchamber, the moon travelling round the building, the patterns of the carpet and wallpaper, even the course traced by the hairline cracks in the tiles of the tall stove. But when I got tired of this game and wanted to go to sleep I had only to wait to hear Věra lift the next leaf of her book in the other room, and I can still feel, said Austerlitz, or perhaps it is only now that I feel again, the sense of my consciousness dissolving among the poppies and leafy tendrils etched into the opaque glass of the door before I caught the slight rustle of the page turning. On our walks, Věra continued when we were sitting in the living-room again, and she had given me a cup of peppermint tea with her two now unsteady hands, on our walks we hardly ever went further than the Seminar Garden, the Khotek Gardens and the other green spaces in the Lesser Quarter. Only occasionally, in summer, did we make rather longer expeditions with my little pushchair, which as I might perhaps remember had a small coloured whirligig fastened to it, going as far as Sofia Island, the swimming school on the banks of the Vltava, or the observation platform on Petřín Hill, from which we may have spent an hour or more looking at the city spread out below us with its many towers, all of which I had known by heart, as well as the names of the seven bridges spanning the glittering river. Since I have been unable to go out of doors, so that I now see almost nothing new, said Věra, the pictures we enjoyed so much at the time come back to me with increasing clarity, like pure fantasies. I often feel, said Věra, as if I were gazing at a diorama as I once did when I was a child in Reichenberg, seeing the figures inside a case filled with some strangely translucent aura poised motionless in mid-movement, owing their lifelike appearance, oddly enough, to their extremely diminutive size. In later life I never set eyes on anything more magical than the yellow Syrian desert in the Reichenberg diorama, the peaks of the Zillertal Alps rising white and radiant above the dark pine forests, and that moment frozen in time when the young poet Goethe, wearing a short, light-brown coat fluttering in the wind, is about to climb into a post chaise to which his travelling bags are already strapped. These days, Věra continued, the pictures of our excursions together from the Šporkova through the Lesser Quarter tend to go hand in hand with such reminiscences of my own childhood. When memories come back to you, you sometimes feel as if you were looking at the past through a glass mountain, and now, as I tell you this, if I close my eyes I see the two of us as it were disembodied, or, more precisely, reduced to the unnaturally enlarged pupils of our eyes, looking down from the observation platform on the Petřín Hill at the green slopes below, with the funicular railway making its way upwards like a fat caterpillar, while further out, on the other side of the city, the railway train you always waited so eagerly to see is making its way past the row of houses at the foot of the Vyšehrad and slowly crossing the bridge over the river, trailing a white cloud of vapour. When the weather was bad, said Věra, we often visited my aunt Otýlie in the glove shop on the Šeríková which she had been running since before the Great War and in which, as in some consecrated shrine or temple, a muted atmosphere banishing all profane ideas reigned. Aunt Otýlie was a spinster lady of alarmingly fragile appearance. She always wore an outer garment of pleated black silk with a detachable white lace collar, and moved about in a little cloud of lily-of-the-valley perfume. If she was not busy serving one of the women she described as her honoured lady clients, she was constantly occupied in maintaining order among her stock of hundreds, if not thousands, of different pairs of gloves of all kinds, ranging from cotton for everyday wear to the most elegant velvet or kid creations from Paris and Milan, arranged in a hierarchy of her own devising which she had preserved for decades through all the vicissitudes of time, and which only she really understood. But when we went to see her, said Věra, she gave you her entire attention, showed you this and that, let you look at the shallow drawers which glided out with extraordinary ease, and allowed you not just to pick up glove after glove but even to try them on, explaining the niceties of every model to you patiently, just as if she saw you as heir presumptive to her business. And I remember, Věra told me, said Austerlitz, that it was Aunt Otýlie who taught you to count at the age of three and a half, using a row of small, shiny black malachite buttons sewn to an elbow-length velvet glove which you particularly liked — *jedna, dva, tři*, counted Věra, and I, said Austerlitz, went on counting - *čtyři, pět, šest, sedm* — feeling like someone taking uncertain steps out on to the ice. Deeply moved as I was on my first visit to the Šporkova, I do not remember all Věra's stories in precise detail today, said Austerlitz, but I think that by some turn or other in our conversation we went on from Aunt Otýlie's glove shop to the Estates Theatre, where Agáta made her début in Prague in the autumn of 1938 in the role of Olympia, a part she had dreamed of since the beginning of her career. In mid-October, said Věra, on the evening before the first night, we went to the dress rehearsal of the operetta together, and as soon as we entered the theatre by the stage door, she said, I fell into a reverent silence, although I had been chattering nineteen to the dozen on our way through the city. I had also been unusually quiet and lost in thought during the performance of the somewhat haphazard arrangement of scenes, and on our way home by tram as well. It was because of this more or less casual remark of Věra's, said Austerlitz, that I went to see the Estates Theatre next morning, and sat alone for a long time in the stalls directly under the top of the dome, having obtained permission from the porter, in exchange for a not inconsiderable tip, to take some photographs in the recently refurbished auditorium. Around me the tiers of seats with their gilded adornments shining through the dim light rose to the roof; before me the proscenium arch of the stage on which Agáta had once stood was like a blind eye. And the harder I tried to conjure up at least some faint recollection of her appearance, the more the theatre seemed to be shrinking, as if I myself had shrunk to the stature of a little Tom Thumb enclosed in a sort of velvet-lined casket. Only after a while, when someone or other walked quickly over the stage behind the drawn curtain, sending a ripple through the heavy folds of fabric with his rapid pace, only then, said Austerlitz, did the shadows begin to move, and I saw the conductor of the orchestra down in the pit like a beetle in his black tail-coat, and other black-clad figures busy with all kinds of instruments, I heard their music mingling with the voices, and all of a sudden I thought that in between one of the musicians' heads and the neck of a double bass, in the bright strip of light between the wooden floor-boards and the hem of the curtain, I caught sight of a sky-blue shoe embroidered with silver sequins. On the evening of that day, when I visited Věra for the second time in her flat in the Šporkova and she confirmed, in answer to my question, that Agáta had indeed worn sequinned sky-blue shoes with her costume as Olympia, I felt as if something were shattering inside my brain. Věra said that I had been deeply affected by the dress rehearsal in the Estates Theatre, first and foremost, she suspected, because I was afraid Agáta had genuinely changed into someone who, though she might now be a magical figure, was also a complete stranger to me, and I myself, Austerlitz continued, suddenly remembered that I had been filled by a grief previously unknown to me when, long past my usual bedtime, I lay with my eyes wide open in the dark on the divan in Věra's room, listening to the church clocks strike the quarter-hours and waiting for Agáta to come home, waiting to hear the car bringing her back from that other world stop outside the gate, waiting for her to come into the room at last and sit down beside me, enveloped by a strange theatrical odour in which dust and drifts of perfume mingled. I see her wearing an ashen-grey silk bodice laced up in front, but I cannot make out her face, only an iridescent veil of pale, cloudy milkiness wafting close to her skin, and then, said Austerlitz, I see the scarf slip from her right shoulder as she lays her hand on my forehead. On my third day in Prague, so Austerlitz continued his story, when he had recovered some degree of composure, I went up to the Seminar Garden early in the morning. The cherry and pear trees of Věra's story had now been grubbed up and replaced by young saplings, with thin branches which would not bear fruit for some time yet to come. The path wound uphill, describing wide curves through the grass, which was wet with dew. Halfway up I met an old lady with an overfed, reddish-brown dachshund which was not very good on its legs and stopped now and then, staring with its brow furrowed at the ground ahead of it. The sight of it reminded me that on my walks with Věra I often used to see old ladies of this kind with bad-tempered little dogs, almost always wearing wire muzzles, which may have been the reason for their mute ill-will. Then I sat on a bench in the sun until nearly midday, looking out over the buildings of the Lesser Quarter and the River Vltava at the panorama of the city, which seemed to be veined with the curving cracks and rifts of past time, like the varnish on a painting. A little later, said Austerlitz, I discovered another such pattern created by no discernible law in the entwined roots of a chestnut tree clinging to a steep slope, through which Věra had told me, said Austerlitz, I liked to climb as a child. And the dark-green yews growing under the taller trees were familiar to me too, as familiar as the cool air which enveloped me at the bottom of the ravine and the countless windflowers covering the woodland floor, faded now in April, and I understood why, on one of my visits to a Gloucestershire country house with Hilary years ago, my voice failed me when, in the park which was laid out very much like the Schönborn gardens, we unexpectedly came upon a north-facing slope covered by the finely cut leaves and snow-white blooms of the March-flowering *Anemone nemorosa*.

—— It was with the botanical name of these shade-loving anemones that Austerlitz concluded another section of his story on that evening in the late winter of 1997, when we sat in the Alderney Street house amidst what seemed to me a silence of unfathomable profundity. Quarter or half an hour may have gone by in the light of the blue, evenly flickering flames of the little gas fire, before Austerlitz rose and said it would probably be best if I spent the night under his roof. So saying, he went upstairs ahead of me, and led me into a room which, like those on the ground floor, was quite unfurnished except for a kind of camp bed standing unfolded against one wall, with handles at both ends so that it resembled a stretcher. Beside the bed there was a wine crate with a blackened coat of arms burnt into it which had once contained Château Gruaud-Larose, and on the crate, in the gentle light of a shaded lamp, stood a glass, a carafe of water, and an old-fashioned radio in a dark-brown Bakelite case. Austerlitz wished me good night and latched the door carefully behind him. I went over to the window, looked down at the empty street below, turned back to the room, sat down on the bed, undid my shoelaces, thought about Auster-litz, whom I could now hear moving about the room next door, and then, when I looked up again, saw in the faint light a small collection of seven variously shaped Bakelite jars on the mantelpiece. None of these containers was more than two or three inches high, and when I opened them one by one and held them in the light of the lamp, each proved to contain the mortal remains of one of the moths which – as Austerlitz had told me – had met its end here in this house. I tipped one of them, a weightless, ivory-coloured creature with folded wings that might have been woven of some immaterial fabric, out of its Bakelite box on to the palm of my right hand. Its legs, which it had drawn up under its silver-scaled body as if just clearing some final obstacle, were so delicate that I could scarcely make them out, while the antennae curving high above the whole body also trembled on the edge of visibility. However, the staring black eye projecting somewhat from the head was distinct enough. Spellbound by this nocturnal apparition, which although it might have died years ago bore no sign of decay, I studied it intently before replacing it in its narrow tomb. As I lay down I turned on the radio set standing on the wine crate beside the bed. The names of cities and radio stations with which I used to link the most exotic ideas in my childhood appeared on its round, illuminated dial — Monte Ceneri, Rome, Ljubljana, Stockholm, Beromünster, Hilversum, Prague, and others besides. I turned the volume down very low and listened to a language I did not understand drifting in the air from a great distance: a female voice, which was sometimes lost in the ether, but then emerged again and mingled with the performance of two careful hands moving, in some place unknown to me, over the keyboard of a Bösendorfer or Pleyel and playing certain musical passages, I think from the *Well-Tempered Clavier*, which accompanied me far into the realms of slumber. When I woke in the morning only a faint crackle and hiss was coming from the narrow brass mesh over the loudspeaker. Soon afterwards, when I mentioned the mysterious radio at breakfast, Austerlitz told me he had always imagined that the voices moving through the air after the onset of darkness, only a few of which we could catch, had a life of their own, like bats, and shunned the light of day. In the long, sleepless nights of recent years, he said, when I was listening to the women announcers in Budapest, Helsinki or La Coruña, I often saw them weaving their erratic way far out in the air, and wished I were already in their company.

But to come back to my story . . . It was when I had returned from the Schönborn Garden, as we were sitting in Věra's flat again, that she first told me about my parents at greater length: their origins so far as she knew of them, the course of their lives, and the annihilation, within the space of only a few years, of their entire existence. Despite her dark and rather melancholy appearance, so I think Věra began, said Austerlitz, your mother Agáta was a very genial, on occasion even light-hearted woman. In this she was just like her father, old Austerlitz, who owned a fez and slipper-making factory in Sternberg which he had founded while the country was still under Austrian rule, and who had the ability of simply ignoring any unpleasantness. Once, when he was visiting this house, I heard him speak of the considerable boom in his business since Mussolini's men had taken to wearing that semi-Oriental item of headgear the fez, saying that he could hardly manufacture and export enough of them to Italy. At the time, Agáta herself, secure as she felt in the recognition she had won much faster than she dared to hope in her career as an opera and operetta singer, thought that everything would turn out all right in the end, whereas Maximilian, in spite of the cheerful disposition which he shared with Agáta, had been convinced ever since I knew him, said Věra, so Austerlitz told me, that the parvenus who had come to power in Germany and the corporate bodies and other human swarms endlessly proliferating under the new regime, a spectacle which inspired him, as he often said, with a sense of positive horror, had abandoned themselves from the first to a blind lust for conquest and destruction, taking its cue from the magic word thousand which the Reichskanzler, as we could all hear on the wireless, repeated constantly in his speeches. A thousand, ten thousand, twenty thousand, thirty-seven thousand, two hundred and forty thousand, a thousand times a thousand, thousands upon thousands: such was the refrain he barked out in his hoarse voice, drumming into the Germans the notion that the promise of their own greatness was about to be fulfilled. None the less, said Věra, Austerlitz continued, Maximilian did not in any way believe that the German people had been driven into their misfortune; rather, in his view, they had entirely re-created themselves in this perverse form, engendered by every individual's wishful thinking and bound up with false family sentiment, and had then brought forth, as symbolic exponents of their innermost desires, so to speak, the Nazi grandees, whom Maximilian regarded without exception as muddle-headed and indolent. From time to time, so Věra recollected, said Austerlitz, Maximilian would tell the tale of how once, after a trade-union meeting in Teplitz in the early summer of 1933, he had gone a little way up into the Erzgebirge, where he came upon some day-trippers in a beer garden who had been buying all manner of things in a village on the German side of the border, including a new kind of boiled sweet which had, embedded in its sugary mass, a raspberry-coloured swastika that literally melted in the mouth. At the sight of these Nazi treats, Maximilian had said, he suddenly realized that the Germans had wholly reorganized their production lines, from heavy industry down to the manufacturing of items such as these vulgar sweets, not because they had been ordered to do so but each of his own accord, out of enthusiasm for the national resurgence. Věra went on, said Austerlitz, to tell me that Maximilian visited Austria and Germany several times in the 1930s, to gain a more accurate idea of general developments, and that she remembered precisely how, immediately after returning from

Nuremberg, he had described the Führer's prodigious reception at the Party rally. Hours before his arrival, the entire population of Nuremberg and indeed people from much further afield, crowds flocking in not just from Franconia and Bavaria but from the most remote parts of the country, Holstein and Pomerania, Silesia and the Black Forest, stood shoulder to shoulder all agog with excitement along the predetermined route, until at last, heralded by roars of acclamation, the motorcade of heavy Mercedes limousines came gliding at walking pace down the narrow alley which parted the sea of radiant uplifted faces and the arms outstretched in yearning. Maximilian had told her, said Věra, that in the middle of this crowd, which had merged into a single living organism racked by strange, convulsive contractions, he had felt like a foreign body about to be crushed and then excreted. From where he stood in the square outside the Lorenzkirche, he said, he saw the motorcade making its slow way through the swaying masses down to the Old Town, where the houses with their pointed and crooked gables, their occupants hanging out of the windows like bunches of grapes, resembled a hopelessly overcrowded ghetto into which, so Maximilian had said, the long-awaited saviour was now making his entry. It was in just the same vein, said Věra, that Maximilian later repeatedly described the spectacular film of the Party rally which he had seen in a Munich cinema, and which confirmed his suspicions that, out of the humiliation from which the Germans had never recovered, they were now developing an image of themselves as a people chosen to evangelize the world. Not only did the overawed spectators witness the Führer's aeroplane descending slowly to earth through towering mountain ranges of cloud; not only was the tragic history they all shared invoked in the ceremony honouring the war dead during which, as Maximilian described it to us, Hitler and Höss and Himmler strode down the broad avenue lined, in straight serried ranks, with columns and companies created by the power of the new state out of a host of immovable German bodies, to the accompaniment of a funeral march which stirred the innermost soul of the entire nation; not only might one see warriors pledging themselves to die for the Fatherland, and the huge forests of flags mysteriously swaying as they moved away by torchlight into the dark – no, said Věra, Maximilian told us that a bird's-eye view showed a city of white tents extending to the horizon, from which as day broke the Germans emerged singly, in couples or in small groups, forming a silent procession and pressing ever closer together as they all went in the same direction, following, so it seemed, some higher bidding, on their way to the Promised Land at last after long years in the wilderness. It was only a few months after this experience of Maximilian's in the Munich cinema that the Austrians were to be heard over the wireless, hundreds of thousands of them pouring into the Heldenplatz in Vienna, their shouts breaking over us like a flood tide for hours on end, said Věra. In Maximilian's opinion, she told me, this collective paroxysm on the part of the Viennese crowds marked the watershed. It was still a sinister echo in our ears when, with summer hardly over, the first refugees arrived here in Prague, expelled from the now so-called Ostmark region after being robbed by their former fellow citizens of everything but a few schillings. In what they probably knew was the false hope of keeping their heads above water in a foreign country, they went from door to door as itinerant pedlars, offering for sale hairpins and slides, pencils and writing paper, ties and other items of haberdashery, just as their ancestors had once walked the countryside of Galicia, Hungary and the Tyrol with packs on their backs. I remember, said Věra, Austerlitz added, one such hawker, a man called Saly Bleyberg, who had built up his own garage business in the Leopoldstadt district of Vienna not far from the Praterstern during the difficult inter-war years, and who when Agáta invited him in for a cup of coffee told us the most appalling tales of the despicable conduct of the Viennese: the methods used to force him to make over his business to a certain Herr Haselberger, the manner in which he was then cheated of the sale price, which was ridiculously low anyway, how he was robbed of his bank deposits and securities, how all his furniture and his Steyr car were appropriated, and how at last he, Saly Bleyberg and his family, sitting on their suitcases in the hall of the building where they lived, had been obliged to hear the drunken caretaker negotiating with the young couple, obviously just married, who had come to look at the now vacant flat. Although the story we heard from poor Bleyberg, who kept crumpling the handkerchief in his hand with helpless rage, was far worse than anything we had imagined, and although after the Munich Agreement the situation held out no hope at all, said

Věra, Maximilian stayed in Prague throughout the winter, whether because of his work for the Party, which was now a matter of particular urgency, or because he refused, for as long as was humanly possible, to give up his belief that the law would protect a man. For her part, Agáta was not prepared to go to France ahead of Maximilian, although he had repeatedly advised her to leave, and so it was that your father, Věra told me, said Austerlitz, then in the utmost danger, did not leave until it was almost too late, on the afternoon of the fourteenth of March, by plane from Ruzyně to Paris. I still remember, said Věra, that when he said goodbye he was wearing a wonderful plum-coloured double-breasted suit, and a black felt hat with a green band and a broad brim. Next morning, at first light, the Germans did indeed march into Prague in the middle of a heavy snowstorm which seemed to make them appear out of nowhere. When they crossed the bridge and their armoured cars were rolling up the Narodní a profound silence fell over the whole city. People turned away, and from that moment they walked more slowly, like somnambulists, as if they no longer knew where they were going. What particularly upset us, so Věra remarked, said Austerlitz, was the instant change to driving on the right. It often made my heart miss a beat, she said, when I saw a car racing down the road on the wrong side, since it inevitably made me think that from now on we must live in a world turned upside down. Of course, Věra continued, it was much harder for Agáta than for me to manage under the new regime. Since the Germans had issued their decrees on the Jewish population, she could go shopping only at certain times; she must not take a taxi, she could sit only in the last carriage of the tram, she could not visit a coffee-house or cinema, or attend a concert or any other event. Nor could she herself appear on stage any more, and access to the banks of the Vltava and the parks and gardens she had loved so much was barred to her. All my green places are lost to me, she once said, adding that only now did she truly understand how wonderful it is to stand by the rail of a river steamer without a care in the world. The ever-extended list of bans — before long it was forbidden for Jews to walk on the pavement on the side of the road next to the park, to go into a laundry or dry cleaner's, or to make a call from a public telephone — all of this, I still hear Věra telling me, said Austerlitz, soon brought Agáta to the brink of despair. I can see her now pacing up and down this room, said Věra, I can see her striking her forehead with the flat of her hand, and crying out, chanting the syllables one by one: I do not un der stand it! I do not un der stand it! I shall ne ver un der stand it!! None the less, she went into the city as often as she could, applying to I don't know how many or what authorities, she stood for hours in the sole post office which the forty thousand Jews in Prague were allowed to use, waiting to send a telegram; she made inquiries, pulled strings, left financial deposits, produced affidavits and guarantees, and when she came home she would sit up racking her brains until late into the night. But the more trouble she took, and the longer she went on trying, the further did any hope of her getting an emigration permit recede, so in the summer, when there was already talk of the forthcoming war and the likelihood of even harsher restrictions when it broke out, she finally decided, Věra told me, said Austerlitz, that she would send me at least to England, having succeeded through the good offices of one of her theatrical friends in getting my name put down for one of the few children's transports leaving Prague for London during those months. Věra remembered, said Austerlitz, that the happy excitement

Agáta felt at this first successful outcome of her efforts was overshadowed by her grief and anxiety as she imagined how I would feel, a boy not yet five years old who had always led a sheltered life, on my long railway journey and then among strangers in a foreign country. On the other hand, said Věra, Agáta hoped that now the first step had been taken, some way for her to leave too would surely be found quite quickly, and then you could all be together in Paris. So she was torn between wishful thinking and her fear that she was doing something irresponsible and unforgivable, and who knows, Věra said to me, whether she might not have kept you with her after all had there been just a few more days left before you were to set off from Prague. I have only an indistinct, rather blurred picture of the moment of farewell at the Wilsonova station, said Věra, adding, after a few moments' reflection, that I had my things with me in a little leather suitcase, and food for the journey in a rucksack – *un petit sac à dos avec quelques viatiques*, said Austerlitz, those had been Věra's exact words, summing up, as he now thought, the whole of his later life. Věra also remembered the twelve-year-old girl with the bandoneon to whose care they had entrusted me, a Charlie Chaplin comic bought at

the last minute, the fluttering of white handkerchiefs
like a flock of doves taking off into the air as the
parents who were staying behind waved to their
children, and her curious impression that the train,
after moving off very slowly, had not really left at
all, but in a kind of feint had rolled a little way out of
the glazed hall before sinking into the ground. But
from that day on Agáta was a changed woman, Věra
continued, said Austerlitz. What she had preserved
of her cheerfulness and confidence, in defiance of all
difficulties, was now overcast by a depression which
she was clearly unable to dispel. I think she did make
one more attempt to buy her freedom, said Věra,
but after that she almost never left the building, she
shrank from opening the windows, she would sit
motionless for hours in the blue-velvet armchair in
the darkest corner of the drawing-room, or lie on
the sofa with her hands over her face. She was
simply waiting to see what happened next, and
above all she was waiting for post from England and
Paris. She had several addresses for Maximilian – a
hotel in the rue de l'Odéon, a small rented flat near
the Glacière Métro station, and a third place, said
Věra, in a district I no longer remember – and she
tormented herself by wondering whether at some

crucial moment she had mixed up these addresses, so
that it was her own fault if her correspondence had
gone astray, while at the same time she feared that
Maximilian's letters to her had been detained by the
security services on their arrival in Prague. And
indeed the letterbox was always empty up to the
winter of 1941, when Agáta was still living in the
Šporkova, so that as she said to me once, oddly, it
was as if those messages in which we placed our last
hopes were misdirected or swallowed up by the evil
spirits abroad in the air all around us. It was only
later, said Věra, that I realized how well this remark
of Agáta's conveyed the invisible terrors beneath
which the city of Prague lay cowering at the time,
only when I learned of the true extent of the per-
version of the law under the Germans, the acts of
violence they committed daily in the basement of
the Petschek palace, in the Pankrác prison, and at the
killing grounds out in Kobylisy. After ninety seconds
in which to defend yourself to a judge you could be
condemned to death for a trifle, some offence barely
worth mentioning, the merest contravention of
the regulations in force, and then you would be
hanged immediately in the execution room next to
the law-court, where there was an iron rail running

along the ceiling down which the lifeless bodies were pushed a little further as required. The bill for these cursory proceedings was sent to the relations of the hanged or guillotined victim, with the information that it could be settled in monthly instalments. Although little hint of it made its way out at the time, fear of the Germans spread through the whole city like a creeping miasma. Agáta said it even drifted in through the closed doors and windows, taking one's breath away. When I look back at the two years following the outbreak of the war, said Věra, it is as if at that time everything was caught in a vortex whirling downwards at ever-increasing speed. Bulletins came thick and fast over the wireless, read by the announcers in a curiously high-pitched tone of voice, as if forced out of the larynx: news of the never-ending exploits of the Wehrmacht, which had soon occupied the entire European continent, while its successive campaigns, with apparently conclusive logic, held out to the Germans the prospect of a vast world empire in which, thanks to the fact that they belonged to the chosen people, they would all be able to embark on the most glittering careers. I believe, Věra told me, said Austerlitz, that even the last remaining German sceptics were overcome by a kind of euphoria, such as one feels at high altitude, in these years when victory followed upon victory, while we, the oppressed, lived below sea level, as it were, and had to watch as the SS pervaded the economy of the entire country, and one business firm after another was handed over to German trustees. They had even aryanized the fez and slipper factory in Sternberg. The means Agáta still had at her disposal were barely enough for the necessities. Her bank accounts had been frozen ever since she was obliged to send in an eight-page statement of her assets, under dozens of headings. She was also strictly forbidden to dispose of any valuables such as pictures or antiques, and I remember, said Věra, how she once showed me a passage in one of those proclamations issued by the occupying power stating that in the case of any contravention of this regulation, both the Jew concerned in the transaction and the person acquiring the property must expect the most severe of measures to be taken by the State Police. The Jew concerned in the transaction! Agáta had cried, adding: Really, the way these people write! It's enough to make your head swim. I think it was in the late autumn of 1941, said Věra, that Agáta had to take her wireless, her gramophone and the records she loved so much, her binoculars and opera glasses, musical instruments, jewellery, furs and the clothes Maximilian had left behind to the so-called Compulsory Collection Centre. Because of some mistake she had made in complying with this order, she was sent to shovel snow on Ruzyně airfield on a freezing day – winter came very early that year, said Věra – and at three o'clock next morning, in the deepest part of the night, the two envoys of the Israelite religious community whom she had been expecting for some time arrived with the news that Agáta must prepare to be taken away within six days. These messengers, as Věra described them to me, said Austerlitz, who were strikingly alike and had faces that seemed somehow indistinct, with flickering outlines, wore jackets furnished with assorted pleats, pockets, button facings and a belt, garments which looked especially versatile although it was not clear what purpose they served. The pair spoke quietly to Agáta for some time, and gave her a sheaf of printed forms and instructions setting out everything down to the very smallest detail: where and when the person summoned must present herself, what items of clothing were to be brought – coat, raincoat, warm headgear, ear muffs, mittens, nightdress, underclothes, and so on – what articles of personal use it was advisable to bring, for instance sewing things, leather grease, a spirit stove and candles; the weight of the main item of luggage, which was not to exceed fifty kilos; what else could be brought in the way of hand baggage and provisions; how the luggage was to be labelled, with name, destination, and the number allotted to her; the proviso that all the attached forms were to be filled in and signed, that it was not permitted to bring cushions or other articles of furnishing, or to make rucksacks and travelling bags out of Persian rugs, winter coats, or other valuable remnants of fabric; and furthermore that matches, lighters and smoking were prohibited at the embarkation point and thereafter in general, and all orders issued by the official authorities were to be followed to the letter in every contingency. Agáta was unable, as I could see for myself, said Věra, to follow these nauseatingly phrased directives; instead, she simply flung a few wholly impractical items into a bag at random, like someone going away for the weekend, so that finally, difficult as it was for me and guilty as it made me feel, I did her packing while she simply stood at the window, turning away from me to look out at the empty street. Early in the morning of the appointed day we set off while it was still dark, with her luggage strapped to a toboggan, and without a word we made the long journey through the snow spinning down around us, along the left bank of the Vltava, past the Baumgarten, and further out still to the Trade Fair Palace at Holešovice. The closer we came to it, the more often did small groups of people carrying and dragging their heavy burdens emerge from the darkness, moving laboriously towards the same place through the snow, which was falling more thickly now, so that gradually a caravan strung out over a long distance formed, and it was with this caravan that we reached the Trade Fair entrance, faintly illuminated by a single electric light bulb, towards seven in the morning. We waited there in the crowd of those who had been summoned, a silent assembly stirred only, now and then, by an apprehensive murmur running through it. There were men and there were women, families with young children and solitary figures, there were the elderly and the infirm, ordinary folk and those who had been well to do, all of them, in accordance with the instructions they had received, with their transport numbers round their necks on pieces of string.

Agáta soon asked me to leave her. When we parted she embraced me and said: Stromovka Park is over there, would you walk there for me sometimes? I have loved that beautiful place so much. If you look into the dark water of the pools, perhaps one of these days you will see my face. Well, said Věra, so then I went home. It took me over two hours to walk back to the Šporkova. I tried to think where Agáta might be now, whether she was still waiting at the entrance or was already inside the Trade Fair precinct. I learned only years later, from one who had survived the ordeal, what it was like there. The people being taken away were herded into an unheated exhibition hall, a great barn-like building which was freezing in the middle of winter. It was a bleak place where, under faint, glaucous lamp-light, the utmost confusion reigned. Many of those who had just arrived had to have their baggage searched, and were obliged to hand over money, watches and other valuables to a Hauptscharführer called Fiedler who was feared for his brutality. A great mound of silver cutlery lay on a table, along with fox furs and Persian lamb capes. Personal details were taken down, questionnaires handed out, and identity papers stamped EVACUATED or

GHETTOIZED. The German officials and their Czech and Jewish assistants walked busily to and fro, and there was much shouting and cursing, and blows as well. Those who were to leave had to stay in the places allotted to them. Most of them were silent, some wept quietly, but outbursts of despair, loud shouting and fits of frenzied rage were not uncommon. They stayed in this cold Trade Fair building for several days, until finally, early one morning when scarcely anyone was out and about, they were marched under guard to nearby Holešovice railway station, where it took almost another three hours to load them on the trucks. Later, said Věra, I often walked out to Holešovice, to Stromovka Park and the Trade Fair precinct. On these occasions I usually visited the lapidarium installed there in the sixties and spent hours looking at the mineral samples in the glass cases – pyrite crystals, deep green Siberian malachites, specimens of Bohemian mica, granite, quartz, and limestone of an isabelline yellow hue – wondering at the nature of the foundations on which our world is built. On the very day when Agáta had been forced to leave her flat, Věra told me, said Austerlitz, a man from the Trusteeship Centre for Requisitioned Goods came to the Šporkova and put a paper seal on the doors. Then, between Christmas and the New Year, a troop of very shady characters arrived to clear away everything that had been left behind, the furniture, the lamps and candelabra, the carpets and curtains, the books and musical scores, the clothes from the wardrobes and drawers, the bedlinen, pillows, eiderdowns, blankets, china and kitchen utensils, the pot plants and umbrellas, even the bottled pears and cherries which had been standing forgotten in the cellar for years, and the remaining potatoes. They took everything, down to the very last spoon, off to one of the over fifty depots, where these abandoned objects were itemized separately with that thoroughness peculiar to the Germans, were valued, then washed, cleaned or mended as necessary, and finally stored, row upon row, on specially made shelves. Last of all, said Věra, a pest-control officer turned up in the Šporkova. He struck me as a particularly sinister figure, with an unpleasant look in his eye which went right through me. To this day he sometimes haunts my dreams, in which I see him surrounded by clouds of poisonous white smoke as he goes about fumigating the rooms. — When Věra had come to the end of her story, so Austerlitz continued that morning in Alderney

Street, she handed me, after a long pause in which the silence in the Šporkova flat seemed to grow deeper with every breath we drew, two small photographs measuring about three by four inches from the little occasional table beside her chair. She had found them by chance the previous evening inside one of the fifty-five carmine-red volumes of Balzac which she had happened to pick up, she did not know why. Věra said she could not remember unfastening the glass doors and taking the book off the shelf where it stood with its companions, she merely saw herself sitting here in this armchair and – for the first time since her late twenties, a point on which she laid special emphasis – turning the pages which tell the story of the great injustice suffered by Colonel Chabert. How the two pictures had slipped between the leaves was a mystery to her, said Věra. Perhaps Agáta had borrowed the small volume while she was still living here in the Šporkova, in the last weeks before the Germans marched in. In any case, one of the photographs showed the stage of a provincial theatre, perhaps in Reichenau or Olmütz or one of the other towns where Agáta sometimes performed before she was engaged to appear in Prague. At first glance, said Austerlitz, Věra said she had thought the two figures in the bottom left-hand corner were Agáta and Maximilian – they were so tiny that it was impossible to make them out well – but then of course she noticed that they were other people, perhaps the impresario, or a conjuror and his woman assistant. She had wondered, said Věra, what kind of play or opera had been staged in front of this alarming backdrop, and because of the high mountain range and the wild forest background she thought it might have been *Wilhelm Tell*, or *La Sonnambula*, or Ibsen's last play. The Swiss boy with the apple on his head appeared in my mind's eye, Věra continued; I sensed in me the moment of terror in which the narrow bridge gives way under the sleepwalker's foot, and imagined that, high in the rocks above, an avalanche was already breaking loose, about to sweep the poor folk who had lost their way (for what else would have brought them to these desolate surroundings?) down into the depths next moment. Minutes went by, said Austerlitz, in which I too thought I saw the cloud of snow crashing into the valley, before I heard Věra again, speaking of the mysterious quality peculiar to such photographs when they surface from oblivion. One has the impression, she said, of something stirring in them, as if one caught small sighs of despair, *gémissements de désespoir* was her expression, said Austerlitz, as if the pictures had a memory of their own and remembered us, remembered the roles that we, the survivors, and those no longer among us had played in our former lives. Yes, and the small boy in the other photograph, said Věra after a while, this is you, Jacquot, in February 1939, about six months before you left Prague. You were to accompany Agáta to a masked ball at the house of one of her influential admirers, and she had the snow-white costume made for you especially for the occasion. On the back it says *Jacquot Austerlitz, páže růžové královny*, in your grandfather's handwriting, for he happened to be visiting at the time. The picture lay before me, said Austerlitz, but I dared not touch it. The words *páže růžové královny, páže růžové královny* went round and round in my head, until their meaning came to me from far away, and once again I saw the live tableau with the Rose Queen and the little boy carrying her train at her side. Yet hard as I tried both that evening and later, I could not recollect myself in the part. I did recognize the unusual hairline running at a slant over the forehead, but otherwise all memory was extinguished in me by an overwhelming sense of the long years that had passed. I have studied the photograph many times since, the bare, level field where I am standing, although I cannot think where it was; the blurred, dark area above the horizon, the boy's curly hair, spectrally light around the outline of his head, the cape over his arm which appears to be held at an angle or, as I once thought, said Austerlitz, might have been broken or in a splint, the six large mother-of-pearl buttons, the extravagant hat with the heron's feather in it, even the folds of the stockings. I examined every detail under a magnifying glass without once finding the slightest clue. And in doing so I always felt the piercing, inquiring gaze of the page boy who had come to demand his dues, who was waiting in the grey light of dawn on the empty field for me to accept the challenge and avert the misfortune lying ahead of him. That evening in the Šporkova, when Věra put the picture of the child cavalier in front of me, I was not, as you might suppose, moved or distressed, said Austerlitz, only speechless and uncomprehending, incapable of any lucid thought. Even later nothing but blind panic filled me when I thought of the five-year-old page. Once I dreamed of returning to the flat in Prague after a long absence. All the furniture is in its proper place. I know that my parents will soon be back from their holiday, and there is something important which I must give them. I am not aware that they have been dead for years. I simply think they must be very old, around ninety or a hundred, as indeed they would be if they were still alive. But when at last they come through the door they are in their mid-thirties at the most. They enter the flat, walk round the rooms picking up this and that, sit in the drawing-room for a while and talk to each other in the mysterious language of deaf mutes. They take no notice of me. I suspect that they are about to set off again for the place somewhere in the mountains where they now live. It does not seem to me, Austerlitz added, that we understand the laws governing the return of the past, but I feel more and more as if time did not exist at all, only various spaces interlocking according to the rules of a higher form of stereometry, between which the living and the dead can move back and forth as they like, and the longer I think about it the more it seems to me that we who are still alive are unreal in the eyes of the dead, that only occasionally, in certain lights and atmospheric conditions, do we appear in their field of vision. As far back as I can remember, said Austerlitz, I have always felt as if I had no place in reality, as if I were not there at all, and I never had this impression more strongly than on that evening in the Šporkova when the eyes of the Rose Queen's page looked through me. Even next day, on my way to Terezín, I could not imagine who or what I was. I remember that I stood in a kind of trance on the platform of the bleak station at Holešovice, that the railway lines ran away into infinity on both sides, that I perceived everything indistinctly, and then that I leaned against a window in the corridor of the train, looking out at the northern suburbs as they passed by, at the water meadows of the Vltava and the villas and summer houses on the opposite bank. Once I saw a huge and now disused stone quarry on the other side of the river, then a number of cherry trees in blossom, a few villages far remote from one another, nothing else but the empty Bohemian countryside. When I got out of the train in Lovošice after about an hour, I felt as if I had been travelling for weeks, going further and further east and further and further back in time. The square in front of the station was empty except for a peasant woman wearing several layers of coats, and waiting behind a makeshift stall for someone to think about buying one of the cabbages she had piled up into a mighty bulwark in front of her. There was no taxi in sight, so I set off on foot from Lovosice in the direction of Terezín. As one leaves the town, the appearance of which I can no longer remember, said Austerlitz, a wide panorama opens up to the north: a field, poison-green in colour, in the foreground, behind it a petrochemicals plant half eaten away by rust, with clouds of smoke rising from its cooling towers and chimneys, as they must have done without cease for many long years. Further away I saw the conical Bohemian mountains surrounding the Bohuševice basin in a semicircle, their highest summits disappearing into the low sky this cold, grey morning. I walked on down the straight road, always looking ahead to see if the silhouette of the fortifications, which could not be more than an hour and a half's walk away, was in sight yet. The idea I had formed in my mind was of a mighty complex rising high above the level country, but in fact Terezín lies so far down in the damp lowlands around the confluence of the Eger and the Elbe that, as I read later, there is nothing to be seen of the town, even from the hills around Leitmeritz or indeed from its immediate vicinity, except the chimney of the brewery and the church tower. The brick walls built in the eighteenth century to a star-shaped ground plan, undoubtedly by serf labour, rise from a broad moat and stand not much higher than the outlying fields. In the course of time, moreover, all kinds of shrubs and bushes have covered the former glacis and the grass-grown ramparts, giving the impression that Terezín is not so much a fortified town as one half-hidden and sunk into the marshy ground of the flood plain. At any rate, as I made my way that morning to Terezín along the main road from Lovosice, I did not know until the last minute how close I already was to my journey's end. Several sycamores and chestnuts, their bark blackened by rain, still obstructed my view when I found myself standing among the façades of the old garrison buildings, and a few more steps brought me out on the central square, which was surrounded by a double avenue of trees. From the first, I felt that the most striking aspect of the place was its emptiness, said Austerlitz, something which to this day I still find incomprehensible. I knew from Věra that for many years now Terezín had been an ordinary town again. Despite this, it was almost a quarter of an hour before I saw the first human being on the other side of the square, a bent figure toiling very slowly forward and leaning on a stick, yet when I took my eye off it for a moment the figure had suddenly gone. Otherwise I met no one all morning in the straight, deserted streets of Terezín, except for a mentally disturbed man who crossed my path among the lime trees of the park with the fountain, telling I have no idea what tale in a kind of broken German while frantically waving his arms, before he too, still clutching the hundred-crown note I had given him, seemed to be swallowed up by the earth, as they say, even as he was running off. Although the sense of abandonment in this

fortified town, laid out like Campanella's ideal
sun state to a strictly geometrical grid, was extra-
ordinarily oppressive, yet more so was the for-
bidding aspect of the silent façades. Not a single
curtain moved behind their blank windows,
however often I glanced up at them. I could not

imagine, said Austerlitz, who might inhabit these
desolate buildings, or if anyone lived there at
all, although on the other hand I had noticed
that long rows of dustbins with large numbers
on them in red paint were ranged against the
walls of the back yards. What I found most un-
canny of all, however, were the gates and door-
ways of Terezín, all of them, as I thought I sensed,

obstructing access to a darkness never yet penetrated, a darkness in which I thought, said

Austerlitz, there was no more movement at all apart from the whitewash peeling off the walls and the spiders spinning their threads, scuttling on crooked legs across the floorboards, or hanging expectantly in their webs. Not long ago, on the verge of waking from sleep, I found myself looking into the interior of one of these Terezín barracks. It was filled from floor to ceiling with layer upon layer of the cobwebs woven by those ingenious creatures. I still remember how, in my half-conscious state, I tried to hold fast to my powdery grey dream image, which sometimes quivered in a slight breath of air, and to discover what it concealed, but it only dissolved all the more and was overlaid by the memory, surfacing in my mind at the same time, of the shining glass in the display windows of the ANTIKOS BAZAR on the west side of the town square, where I had stood for a long time around midday in what proved to be the vain hope that someone might arrive and open this curious emporium. As far as I could see, said Austerlitz, the ANTIKOS BAZAR is the only shop of any kind in Terezín apart from a tiny grocery store. It occupies the entire façade of one of the largest buildings, and I think its vaults reach back a long way as well. Of course I could see nothing but the items on display in the windows, which can have amounted to only a small part of the junk heaped up inside the shop. But even these four still lifes obviously composed entirely at random, which appeared to have grown quite naturally into the black branches of the lime trees standing around the square and reflected in the glass of the windows, exerted such a power of attraction on me that it was a long time before I could tear myself away from staring at the hundreds of different objects, my forehead pressed against the cold window, as if one of them or their relationship with each other must provide an unequivocal answer to the many questions I found it impossible to ask in my mind. What was the meaning of the festive white lace tablecloth hanging over the back of the ottoman, and the armchair with its worn brocade cover? What secret lay behind the three brass mortars of different sizes, which had about them the suggestion of an oracular utterance, or the cut-glass bowls, ceramic vases and earthenware jugs, the tin advertising sign bearing the words *Theresienstädter Wasser*, the little box of seashells, the miniature barrel organ, the globe-shaped paperweights with wonderful marine flowers swaying inside their glassy spheres, the model ship (some kind of corvette under full sail), the oak-leaf-embroidered jacket of light, pale, summery linen, the stag-horn buttons, the outsize Russian officer's cap and the olive-green uniform tunic with gilt epaulettes that went with it, the fishing rod, the hunter's bag, the Japanese fan, the endless landscape painted round a lampshade in fine brush-strokes, showing a river running quietly through perhaps Bohemia or perhaps Brazil? And then there was the stuffed squirrel, already moth-eaten here and there, perched on the stump of a branch in a showcase the size of a shoebox, which had its beady button eye implacably fixed on me, and whose Czech name — *veverka* — I now recalled like the name of a long-lost friend. What, I asked myself, said Austerlitz, might be the significance of the river never rising from any source, never flowing out into any sea but always back into itself, what was the meaning of *veverka*, the squirrel forever perched in the same position, or of the ivory-coloured porcelain group of a hero on horseback turning to look back, as his steed

rears up on its hindquarters, in order to raise up with his outstretched left arm an innocent girl already bereft of her last hope, and to save her from a cruel fate not revealed to the observer? They were all as timeless as that moment of rescue, perpetuated but for ever just occurring, these ornaments, utensils and mementoes stranded in the Terezín bazaar, objects that for reasons one could never know had outlived their former owners and survived the process of destruction, so that I could now see my own faint shadow image barely perceptible among them. As I waited outside the bazaar, Austerlitz resumed after a little while, a light rain had begun to fall, and since neither the proprietor of the shop, whose name was given as Augustýn Němeček, nor anyone else was in evidence, I finally walked on, going up and down a few streets until suddenly, on the north-east corner of the town square, I found myself outside the so-called Ghetto Museum, which I had overlooked before. I climbed the steps and entered the lobby, where a lady of uncertain age in a lilac blouse, her hair waved in an old-fashioned style, sat behind a kind of cash-desk. She put down the crochet work she was doing and leaned slightly forward to give me a ticket. When I asked if I was the only visitor today she said that the museum had only recently opened and not many people from outside the town came to see it, particularly at this time of year and in such weather. And the people of Terezín didn't come anyway, she added, picking up the white handkerchief she was edging with loops like flower petals. So I went round the exhibition by myself, said Austerlitz, through the rooms on the mezzanine floor and the floor above, stood in front of the display panels, sometimes skimming over the captions, sometimes reading them letter by letter, stared at the photographic reproductions, could not believe my eyes, and several times had to turn away and look out of a window into the garden behind the building, having for the first time acquired some idea of the history of the persecution which my avoidance system had kept from me for so long, and which now, in this place, surrounded me on all sides. I studied the maps of the Greater German Reich and its protectorates, which had never before been more than blank spaces in my otherwise well-developed sense of topography, I traced the railway lines running through them, felt blinded by the documentation recording the population policy of the National Socialists, by the evidence of their mania for order and purity, which was put into practice on a vast scale through measures partly improvised, partly devised with obsessive organizational zeal. I was confronted with incontrovertible proof of the setting up of a forced labour system throughout Central Europe, and learned of the deliberate wastage and discarding of the work-slaves themselves, of the origins and places of death of the victims, the routes by which they were taken to what destinations, what names they had borne in life and what they and their guards looked like. I understood it all now, yet I did not understand it, for every detail that was revealed to me as I went through the museum from room to room and back again, ignorant as I feared I had been through my own fault, far exceeded my comprehension. I saw pieces of luggage brought to Terezín by the internees from Prague and Pilsen, Würzburg and Vienna, Kufstein and Karlsbad and countless other places; the items such as handbags, belt buckles, clothes brushes and combs which they had made in the various workshops; meticulously worked out projects and production plans for the agricultural exploitation of the open areas behind the ramparts and on the glacis, where oats and hemp, hops and pumpkins and maize were to be grown on plots of land meticulously parcelled out. I saw balance sheets, registers of the dead, lists of every imaginable kind, and endless rows of numbers and figures, which must have served to reassure the administrators that nothing ever escaped their notice. And whenever I think of the museum in Terezín now, said Austerlitz, I see the framed ground-plan of the star-shaped fortifications, colour-washed in soft tones of grey-brown for Maria Theresia, her Imperial Highness in Vienna who had commissioned it, and fitting neatly into the folds of the surrounding terrain, the model of a world made by reason and regulated in all conceivable respects. This impregnable fortress has never been besieged, not even by the Prussians in 1866, but throughout the nineteenth century – if one disregards the fact that a considerable number of political prisoners of the Habsburg empire pined away in the casemates of one of its outworks – remained a quiet garrison for two or three regiments and some two thousand civilians throughout the nineteenth century, somewhat out of the way, a town with yellow-painted walls, galleried courtyards, well-clipped trees, bakeries, beerhouses, casinos, soldiers' quarters, armouries, bandstand concerts, occasional forays for the purpose of military manoeuvres, officers' wives who were bored to death, and service regulations which, it was believed, would never change for all eternity. When, towards the end of the day, the museum guardian came up to me and indicated that she would soon have to close, said Austerlitz, I had just been reading, several times over, a note on one of the display panels, to the effect that in the middle of December 1942, and thus at the very time when Agáta came to Terezín, some sixty thousand people were shut up together in the ghetto, a built-up area of one square kilometre at the most, and a little later, when I was out in the deserted town square again, it suddenly seemed to me, with the greatest clarity, that they had never been taken away after all, but were still living crammed into those buildings and basements and attics, as if they were incessantly going up and down the stairs, looking out of the windows, moving in vast numbers through the streets and alleys, and even, a silent assembly, filling the entire space occupied by the air, hatched with grey as it was by the fine rain. With this picture before my eyes I boarded the old-fashioned bus which had appeared out of nowhere, and stopped by the pavement directly in front of me a few paces from the entrance to the museum. It was one of those buses which travel from the country into the capital. The driver gave me change for a hundred-crown note without a word, and I remember that I held it clutched firmly in my hand all the way to Prague. Outside, the darkening Bohemian fields passed by, hop poles, deep-brown fields, flat, empty country all around. The bus was very overheated. I felt drops of perspiration break out on my forehead and a constriction in my chest. Once, when I looked over my shoulder, I saw that the other passengers, without exception, had fallen asleep, leaning and sprawling at awkward angles in their seats. Some had their heads dropped forward, others sideways or tipped back. Several were snoring quietly. Only the driver looked straight ahead at the ribbon of road gleaming in the rain. As so often when one is travelling south, I had the impression of going steadily downhill, particularly when we reached the suburbs of Prague and it seemed as if we were descending a kind of ramp into a labyrinth through which we moved very slowly, now this way and now that, until I had lost all sense of direction. When we reached the Prague bus station, an overcrowded traffic junction at this early hour of the evening, I therefore set out the wrong way through the great throng of people waiting there or getting in and out of buses. There were so many of them streaming towards me out in the street, said Austerlitz, most of them carrying large bags and with pale, sad faces, that I thought they could only be coming away from the city centre. Only later did I see from the map that I had reached the centre not in a more or less straight line, as I thought at first, but by way of a wide detour taking me almost to the Vyšehrad, and then through the New Town and along the banks of the Vltava back to my hotel on Kampa Island. It was already late by the time I lay down, exhausted from the day's walking, and tried to fall asleep by listening to the water rushing over the weir outside my window. But whether I kept my eyes wide open or closed, all through the night I saw pictures from Terezín and the Ghetto Museum, the bricks of the fortification walls, the display window of the Bazaar, the endless lists of names, a leather suitcase bearing a double sticker from the Hotels Bristol in Salzburg and Vienna, the closed gates I had photographed, the grass growing between the cobblestones, a pile of briquettes outside a cellar entrance, the squirrel's glass eye and the two forlorn figures of Agáta and Věra pulling the laden toboggan through the driving snow to the Trade Fair building at Holešovice. Only towards morning did I sleep briefly, but even then, in the deepest unconsciousness, the flow of pictures did not cease but instead condensed into a nightmare in which, from where I do not know, said Austerlitz, the north Bohemian town of Dux appeared to me situated in the middle of a devastated plain, a place of which all I had previously known was that Casanova spent the last years of his life there in Count Waldstein's castle writing his memoirs, a number of mathematical and esoteric tracts, and his five-volume futuristic novel *Icosameron*. In my dream I saw the old roué shrunk to the size of a boy, surrounded by the gold-stamped rows of books in Count Waldstein's library of more than forty thousand volumes, bending over his writing desk alone on a bleak November afternoon. He had taken off his powdered wig, and his own sparse hair was wafting above his head in a little white cloud, like a sign of the dissolution of his corporeal being. He wrote on and on, his left shoulder slightly raised. There was nothing to be heard but the scratching of his pen, which stopped only when the writer looked up for a couple of seconds and his watery eyes, already half blind for long-distance vision, sought what little brightness was still left in the sky above the park of

Dux. On the other side of the enclosed land, in deep darkness, lay the whole region extending from Teplice to Most and Chomutov. Over to the north, from end to end of the horizon, stood the black wall of the Grenzmark mountains, and in front of them, along their foothills, the torn and ravaged land, with slopes and terraces which dropped far below what had formerly been the surface of the earth. Where roads had once passed over firm ground, where human beings had lived, foxes had run across country and birds of many kinds had flown from bush to bush, now there was nothing but empty space, and at the bottom of it stones and gravel and stagnant water, untouched even by the natural movement of the air. The shadowy forms of power stations with their glowing furnaces drifted like ships in the sombre air: chalk-coloured buildings like blocks, cooling towers with jagged rims, tall chimneys above which motionless plumes of smoke stood white against the sickly colours streaking the western sky. A few stars showed only on the pallid, nocturnal side of the firmament, sooty, smoking lights extinguished one by one, leaving scab-like traces in the orbits through which they have always moved. To the south, in a broad semicircle, rose the cones of the

extinct Bohemian volcanoes, which I wished in my
nightmare would erupt and cover everything around
with black dust. — Not until around half-past two
next day, when I had to some degree pulled myself
together again, did I go from Kampa Island to the
Šporkova to pay what would be my last visit there for
the time being, Austerlitz continued. I had already
told Věra that I must retrace my journey from
Prague to London by train, all the way across Ger-
many, a country unknown to me, but that then I
would soon come back and perhaps take a flat some-
where near her for a few months. It was one of those
radiant spring days when the weather is clear as
glass. Věra was complaining of a dull pain behind her
eyes which had been troubling her since early that
morning, and she asked me to pull the curtains over
the windows on the sunny side of the room. Leaning
back in her red velvet armchair in the gloom, with
her tired eyelids closed, she listened as I told her
what I had seen in Terezín. I also asked Věra about
the Czech word for a squirrel, and after a while, with
a smile spreading slowly over her beautiful face, she
said it was *veverka*. And then, said Austerlitz, Věra
told me how in autumn we would often stand by the
upper enclosure wall of the Schönborn Garden to

watch the squirrels burying their treasures. When-
ever we came home afterwards, I had to read
aloud from your favourite book about the changing
seasons, said Věra, even though you knew it by heart
from the first line to the last, and she added that I
never tired of the winter pictures in particular,
scenes showing hares, deer and partridges transfixed
with astonishment as they stared at the ground
covered with newly fallen snow, and Věra said that
every time we reached the page which described the
snow falling through the branches of the trees, soon
to shroud the entire forest floor, I would look up at
her and ask: But if it's all white, how do the squirrels
know where they've buried their hoard? *Ale když
všechno zakryje sníh, jak veverky najdou to místo, kde si
schovaly zásoby?* Those were your very words, the
question which constantly troubled you. How
indeed do the squirrels know, what do we know
ourselves, how do we remember, and what is it we
find in the end? It was six years after their farewell
outside the gates of the Trade Fair in Holešovice, so
Věra continued, that she learned how Agáta was sent
east in September 1944 with one and a half thousand
others who had been interned in Terezín. For a long
time after that, said Věra, she herself had been almost

incapable of thinking of Agáta, of what must have become of her, and of her own life continuing into a pointless future. For weeks she was hardly in her right mind, she had felt a kind of dragging outside her body, she had tried to pick up broken threads and could not believe that everything had really happened as it did. None of her endless attempts later to find out my whereabouts in England or my father's in France had produced any results. Whatever she tried, it was as if all traces were lost in the sand, for at the time, with an army of censors causing havoc in the postal services, it often took months to get an answer from abroad. Perhaps, Věra surmised, said Austerlitz, it would have been different if she could have turned in person to the appropriate authorities, but she lacked both the opportunity and the means to do so. And in this way the years had raced by, seeming in retrospect like a single leaden day. She had indeed gone into the teaching profession and did what was necessary to maintain herself, but almost all her feelings had been extinguished, and she had not truly breathed since that time. Only in the books written in earlier times did she sometimes think she found some faint idea of what it might be like to be alive. Such remarks of Věra's were often followed by a long silence, said Austerlitz, as if neither of us knew what to say, and the hours passed by almost imperceptibly in the darkened flat in the Šporkova. Towards evening, when I said goodbye to Věra, holding her weightless hands in mine, she suddenly remembered how, on the day of my departure from the Wilsonova station, Agáta had turned to her when the train had disappeared from view, and said: We left from here for Marienbad only last summer. And now – where will we be going now? This reminiscence, which I did not fully take in at first, was soon occupying my mind so much that I made a call to Věra from the hotel on the island that evening, although in the normal way I never use the telephone. Yes, she said, in a voice very faint with weariness, yes, in the summer of 1938 we all went to Marienbad together, Agáta, Maximilian, Věra herself and me. We had spent three wonderful, almost blissful weeks there. The overweight or underweight spa guests, moving at a curiously slow pace through the grounds with their drinking glasses, radiated an extraordinary peacefulness, as Agáta once remarked in passing. We stayed at the Osborne-Balmoral boarding house behind the Palace Hotel. In the morning we generally went to the baths, and we took long walks in the country around Marienbad in the afternoons. I had retained no memory at all of that summer holiday when I was just four years old, said Austerlitz, and perhaps that was why when I was in that very place later, in Marienbad at the end of August 1972, I felt nothing but blind terror in the face of the better turn my life should have taken at that time. Marie de Verneuil, with whom I had been in correspondence since the time I spent in Paris, had invited me to accompany her on a visit to Bohemia, where she had to carry out some research for her studies on the architectural history of the spas of Europe, and I think I may now say, added Austerlitz, that she also hoped to try to liberate me from my self-inflicted isolation. She had arranged everything to perfection. Her cousin Frédéric Félix, attaché to the French embassy in Prague, had sent an enormous Tatra limousine to meet us at the airport and take us straight to Marienbad. We sat in the deeply upholstered back of the car for two or three hours as it drove west through the empty countryside, on a road which ran perfectly straight for long stretches of our journey, sometimes dipping down into valleys, then climbing again to extended plateaux over which one could see into the far distance, to the point, said Marie, where the wastes of Bohemia approach the Baltic. Sometimes we drove past low ranges of hills covered with blue forest, standing out sharp as a saw-blade against the uniformly grey sky. There were almost no other vehicles. Only occasionally did a small car of some kind come towards us, and now and then we overtook a truck crawling up the long gradients and trailing behind it great clouds of exhaust fumes. But ever since leaving Prague airport we had been followed by two uniformed motorcyclists who always preserved the same distance. They wore leather crash helmets and black goggles with their tunics and breeches, and their carbines were slung at an angle over their right shoulders. These two escorts made me very uneasy, said Austerlitz, particularly when we went over the top of one of the low hills and down again and they vanished from sight for a while, only to reappear outlined even more menacingly against the light. Marie, who was not so easily intimidated, merely laughed and said that the two shadowy riders were obviously the guard of honour specially provided by the ČSSR for visitors from France. As we approached Marienbad along a road running further and further downhill between wooded slopes, darkness had fallen, and I remember, said Austerlitz, that a slight sense of disquiet brushed me as we emerged from the firs growing all the way down to the outlying houses and slid into the town, which was sparsely illuminated by a few street lamps. The car stopped outside the Palace Hotel. Marie exchanged a few words with the chauffeur as he took out our luggage, and then we were in the foyer, which was made to look double its size, so to speak, by a row of tall mirrors along the walls. The place was so deathly still and deserted that you might have thought the time long after midnight. It was some while before the reception clerk at his desk in a cramped booth looked up from what he was reading and turned to his late-come guests with a barely audible murmur of *Dobrý večer*. This remarkably thin man – the first thing you noticed about him was that although he could not have been much over forty his forehead was wrinkled in fan-like folds above the root of his nose – went through the necessary formalities without another word, very slowly, almost as if he were moving in a denser atmosphere than ours, asked to see our visas, looked at our passports and his register, made an entry of some length on the squared paper of a school exercise book in laborious handwriting, gave us a questionnaire to fill in, looked in a drawer for our key and finally, ringing a bell, summoned as it seemed from nowhere a porter with a bent back, who was wearing a mouse-grey nylon coat that came down to his knees and, like the clerk at the reception desk, appeared to be afflicted by a chronic lethargy which incapacitated his limbs. When he preceded us up to the third floor with our two lightweight suitcases – the paternoster lift, Marie had pointed out to me as soon as we entered the foyer, had obviously been out of order for a very long time – he found it increasingly hard to climb the stairs and, like a mountaineer negotiating the last difficult ridge before attaining the summit, he had to stop several times for a rest, whereupon we too waited for a while a couple of steps below him. On the way up we met not a living soul except for another member of the hotel staff who, dressed in the same grey coat as his colleague and perhaps worn, I thought to myself, said Austerlitz, by all the employees of the state-owned spa hotels, was sitting asleep in a chair on the top landing with his head sunk forward, and a tin tray of broken glass on the floor beside him. The room unlocked for us was Number Thirty-Eight – a large room resembling a salon. The walls were covered with burgundy-red brocade wallpaper, very faded in places. The portières dated from a past time as well, and so did the bed standing in an alcove with its white pillows stacked at a curiously steep angle. Marie immediately began settling in, opened all the wardrobes, went into the bathroom, turned on the taps and the huge old-fashioned shower to make sure they were working, and inspected the whole place very closely. It was odd, she said at last, but she had the impression that although everything else was in perfect order the writing-desk had not been dusted for years. What can be the explanation, she asked me, said Austerlitz, of this remarkable phenomenon? Do ghosts haunt the desk, I wonder? I don't remember what I replied, said Austerlitz, but I do recall that as we sat together by the window for a couple of hours that evening Marie told me a great deal about the history of the spa, of the forests which still covered the valley floor at the beginning of the nineteenth century, the building of the first neo-classical houses and hotels set haphazard on the slopes, and the subsequent rapid rise in the fortunes of the resort. Architects, masons, decorators, tin- and locksmiths and stucco workers came from Prague and Vienna and from all the corners of the empire, many of them from as far afield as the Veneto. One of Prince Lobkowitz's court gardeners began turning what had once been woodland into a landscaped park in the English style, planted rare and native trees, laid out lawns surrounded by bushes and shrubs, avenues, arboured walks, and pavilions from which to admire the view. More and prouder hotels constantly rose from the ground, and so did assembly rooms, baths, reading-rooms, a concert hall and a theatre where all manner of eminent artistes were soon appearing. In 1873 the great cast-iron colonnade was built, and by now Marienbad was one of the most fashionable of European resorts. Marie claimed – and here, said Austerlitz, she launched, with her strong sense of the comical, into a positive verbal coloratura of medical and diagnostic terms – Marie claimed that the mineral waters and particularly the so-called Auschowitz Springs had gained a great reputation for curing the obesity then so common among the middle classes, as well as digestive disturbances, sluggishness of the intestinal canal and other stoppages of the lower abdomen, irregular menstruation, cirrhosis of the liver, disorders of bile secretion, gout, hypochondriacal spleen, diseases of the kidneys, the bladder and the urinary system, glandular swellings and scrofulous deformities, not to mention weakness of the nervous and muscular systems, fatigue, trembling of the limbs, paralysis, mucous and bloody fluxes, unsightly eruptions on the skin, and practically every other medical disorder known to the human race. I can just see them in my mind's eye, said Marie, a set of very corpulent men disregarding their doctors' advice and giving themselves up to the pleasures of the table, which even at a spa were lavish at the time, in order to suppress, by dint of their increasing girth, the anxiety for the security of their social position constantly stirring within them, and I see other patients, most of them ladies and rather pale and sallow already, deep in their own thoughts as they walk along the winding paths from one of the little temples which house fountains to the next, or else in elegiac mood, watching the play of the clouds moving over the narrow valley from the viewing points of the Amalienhöhe or Schloss Miramont. The rare sense of happiness that I felt as I listened to my companion talking, said Austerlitz, paradoxically enough gave me the idea that I myself, like the guests staying in Marienbad a hundred years ago, had contracted an insidious illness, and together

with that idea came the hope that I was now begin-
ning to be cured. Indeed, I had never in my life
passed over the threshold into sleep more securely
than on that first night I spent with Marie. I listened
to her regular breathing, and saw her beautiful face
next to me every so often for a split second in the
summer lightning that flashed across the sky. Then
the rain fell steadily outside, the white curtains blew
into the room, and as my mind became gradually
submerged I felt, like a slight easing behind my fore-
head, the belief rise within me that I had found
release at last. But nothing came of it. I woke before
dawn with such an abysmal sense of distress that
without even being able to look at Marie I sat up and,
like a man seasick, had to perch on the edge of the
bed. I had dreamed that one of the hotel servants
brought us a drink of a virulent green colour for
breakfast on a tin tray, with a French newspaper
bearing an article on the front page which held forth
on the necessity of reforming the spas, speaking
several times of the sad lot of the hotel employees
*qui portent*, so my dream newspaper put it, said
Austerlitz, *ces longues blouses grises comme en portent les*
*quincailliers*. The rest of the newspaper consisted
almost entirely of death announcements the size of

postage stamps, in tiny print which I could decipher only with great difficulty. The announcements were not just in French but also in German, Polish and Dutch. I still remember, said Austerlitz, Frederieke van Wincklmann, whose death notice said that she had *kalm en rustig van ons heengegaan*, I remember the strange word *rouwkamer* and the information that *De bloemen worden na de crematieplechtigheid neergelegd aan de voet van het Indisch Monument te Den Haag*. I had gone over to the window, where I looked down the main street, still wet with rain, and saw the grand hotels ranged in a semi-circle rising to the heights, the Pacifik, the Atlantic, the Metropole, the Polonia and Bohemia with their rows of balconies, their corner turrets and roof ridges emerging from the morning mist like ocean-going steamers from a dark sea. At some time in the past, I thought, I must have made a mistake, and now I am living the wrong life. Later, on a walk through the deserted town and up to the fountain colonnade, I kept feeling as if someone else were walking beside me, or as if something had brushed against me. Every new view that opened out before us as we turned a corner, every façade, every flight of steps looked to me both familiar and utterly alien. I felt that the decrepit state of these once magnificent buildings, with their broken gutters, walls blackened by rainwater, crumbling plaster revealing the coarse masonry beneath it, windows boarded up or clad with corrugated iron, precisely reflected my own state of mind, which I could not explain either to myself or to Marie, not on this first walk we took through the deserted park nor in the late afternoon, when we sat in the dimly lit *kavárna* of the Město Moskva under a picture of pink water-lilies measuring at least four square yards. I remember, said Austerlitz, that we ordered an ice cream, or rather, as it turned out, a confection resembling an ice cream, a plaster-like substance tasting of potato starch and notable chiefly for the fact that even after more than an hour it did not melt. Apart from us the only customers in the Město Moskva were two old gentlemen playing chess at one of the tables at the back. The waiter who was standing by the net curtains, which were discoloured with smoke, his hands behind his back and looking out, lost in thought, at the rubbish dump overgrown with giant hogweed on the other side of the road, was himself advanced in age. His white hair and moustache were carefully trimmed, and although he too wore one of those mouse-grey nylon coats it was easy to imagine him in deep-black, well-cut tails, with a velvet bow-tie above a starched shirt-front radiant with supernatural cleanliness, wearing shiny patent-leather shoes which reflected the lamplight of a grand hotel lobby. When he brought Marie a flat pack of forty Cuban cigarettes displaying a pretty palm-frond motif, and then gave her a light with an elegantly executed gesture, I could see that she greatly admired him. The Cuban tobacco smoke hung in blue drifts in the air between us, and some time went by before Marie asked what was in my mind, why I was so abstracted, so lost in thought; how could I have lapsed so suddenly from the happy mood which she had sensed in me yesterday? And all I could say was that I didn't know. I think, said Austerlitz, I tried to explain that something or other unknown wrenched at my heart here in Marienbad, something very obvious like an ordinary name or a term which one cannot remember for the sake of anyone or anything in the world. I do not now recall in detail how we spent those few days in Marienbad, said Austerlitz. I know that I often lay for hours in the bubbling mineral baths and the rest rooms, which did me good in one way but in another may have weakened the resistance I had put up for so many years against the emergence of memory. Once we went to a concert at the Gogol Theatre, where a Russian pianist called Bloch played the *Papillons* and *Kinderszenen* to an audience of half a dozen. On the way back to the hotel Marie spoke, almost as a warning, so it seemed to me, said Austerlitz, of the clouding of Schumann's mind as his madness came on and how at last, in the middle of carnival crowds in Düsseldorf, he took a leap over the parapet of the bridge into the icy waters of the Rhine, from which he was pulled out by two fishermen. He lived for a number of years after that, said Marie, in a private asylum for the mentally deranged near Bonn or Bad Godesberg, where he was visited by Clara and the young Brahms at intervals, and since it was impossible to converse with him any more, withdrawn from the world as he was and humming tunelessly to himself, they generally contented themselves with looking into his room for a while through a small trap in the door. As I listened to Marie and tried to imagine poor Schumann in his Bad Godesberg cell I had another picture constantly before my eyes, that of the pigeon loft we had passed on an excursion to Königswart. Like the country estate to which it belonged, this dovecote, which may have dated from the Metternich period, was in an advanced state of decay. The floor inside the brick walls was covered with pigeon droppings compressed under their own weight, yet already over two feet high, a hard, desiccated mass on which lay the bodies of some of the birds who had fallen from their niches, mortally sick, while their companions, surviving in a kind of senile dementia, cooed at one another in tones of quiet complaint in the darkness under the roof, and a few downy feathers, spinning round in a little whirlwind, slowly sank through the air. The torment inherent in both these images that came into my mind in Marienbad, the mad Schumann and the pigeons immured in that place of horror, made it impossible for me to attain even the lowest step on the way to self-knowledge. On the final day of our visit, Austerlitz continued at last, in the evening and as if to say goodbye, we walked through the park and down to the Auschowitz Springs. There is a prettily built and fully glazed pump-room there, all painted white inside. In this pump-room, illuminated by the rays of the setting sun, where, apart from the regular splashing of the water, silence reigned entirely, Marie moved closer to me and asked whether I had remembered that tomorrow was my birthday. When we wake up tomorrow, she said, I shall wish you every happiness, and it will be like telling a machine working by some unknown mechanism that I hope it will run well. Can't you tell me the reason, she asked, said Austerlitz, why you remain so unapproachable? Why, she said, have you been like a pool of frozen water ever since we came here? Why do I see your lips opening as if you were about to say something, maybe even cry out loud, and then I hear not the slightest sound? Why did you never unpack when we arrived, always preferring to live out of a rucksack, as it were? We stood there a couple of paces apart, like two actors on stage. The colour of

Marie's eyes changed as the light dimmed. And once again I tried to explain to her and to myself what incomprehensible feelings had been weighing on me over the last few days; how I kept thinking, like a madman, that there were mysterious signs and portents all around me here; how it even seemed to me as if the silent façades of the buildings knew something ominous about me, how I had always believed I must be alone, and in spite of my longing for her I now felt it more than ever before. But it isn't true, said Marie, it isn't true that we need absence and loneliness. It isn't true. It's only in your mind. You are afraid of I don't know what. You have always been rather remote, of course, I could tell that, but now it's as if you stood on a threshold and you dared not step over it. That evening in Marienbad, said Austerlitz, I could not admit to myself how right everything Marie said was, but today I know why I felt obliged to turn away when anyone came too close to me, I know that I thought this turning away made me safe, and that at the same time I saw myself transformed into a frightful and hideous creature, a man beyond the pale. Dusk was gathering as we walked back through the park. Dark trees and bushes lined both sides of the white sandy path curving ahead of us, and Marie, whom I lost entirely soon afterwards, by my own fault, was murmuring something quietly to herself. All I remember of it now is a phrase about the poor lovers *qui se promenaient dans les allées désertes du parc*. We were almost back in the town, said Austerlitz, when a little company of some ten or a dozen small people emerged from the dark as if out of nowhere, at a place where white mist was already rising from the ground, and crossed our path. They were the sort of visitors sent to the spa because of their failing health by some Czech enterprise or other, or perhaps they came from one of the neighbouring Socialist countries. They were strikingly short, almost dwarfish figures, slightly bent, moving along in single file, and each of them held one of those pitiful plastic mugs from which the water of the springs was drunk in Mariánske Lázne at the time. I also remember, added Austerlitz, that without exception they wore raincoats of thin blue-grey Perlon, the kind of thing that had been fashionable in the West in the late 1950s. To this day I can sometimes hear the dry rustling with which, as suddenly as they had appeared on one side of the path, they vanished again on the other. — I dwelt on my memories of Marienbad all night after my last visit to the Šporkova, continued Austerlitz. As soon as it began to grow light outside I packed, left the hotel on Kampa Island, and crossed the Charles Bridge, which was wrapped in early mist, walked through the streets of the Old Town and over the still deserted Wenceslaus Square, making my way to the main station on Wilsonova which, as it turned out, did not correspond in the least to the idea I had formed of it from Věra's narrative. Its Jugendstil architecture, once famous far beyond Prague, had been surrounded, obviously in the 1960s, by ugly glass façades and concrete blocks, and it took me some time to find a way into this forbidding complex over a taxi ramp leading down to the basement storey. The low-ceilinged hall I now entered was crowded with throngs of people who had spent the night there among piles of luggage, huddled together in groups of various sizes, most of them still asleep. A sickening red-hued light immersed the entire apparently boundless encampment in a positively infernal glare as it shone from a slightly raised platform measuring at least ten by twenty metres, on which about a hundred games machines were arranged in several batteries, idling to no purpose and chanting inanely to themselves. I stepped over some of the motionless bodies on the floor, went upstairs and downstairs but failed to find my way through this labyrinthine station, which seemed to consist of nothing but sales booths and stands of all kinds. Eventually I asked a uniformed man who came towards me: *Hlavní nádráží? Wilsonovo nádráží?* whereupon he took me carefully by the sleeve, like a lost child, guided me to a dark recess in a remote corner, and there showed me a memorial plaque saying that the station had been named in 1919 after the freedom-loving American President Wilson. When I had deciphered the memorial and nodded my thanks to the railway official, who had patiently stayed beside me, he led me round a few more corners and up several steps to a kind of mezzanine floor, from which I could look up at the mighty dome of the former Wilsonova station, or more accurately at half the dome, since the other half had been sliced away, so to speak, by the new construction towering up into it. Along the semi-circular lower rim of the dome ran a gallery with small café tables on it. When I had bought myself a ticket for the Hook of Holland I sat there for half an hour, until it was time for my train to leave, trying to think my way back through the decades, to remember what it had been like when, carried in Agáta's arms – as Věra had told me, said Austerlitz – I craned my neck, unable to take my eyes off the vault reaching such a vast height above us. But neither Agáta nor Věra nor I myself emerged from the past. Sometimes it seemed as if the veil would part; I thought, for one fleeting instant, that I could feel the touch of Agáta's shoulder or see the picture on the front of the Charlie Chaplin comic which Věra had bought me for the journey, but as soon as I tried to hold one of these fragments fast, or get it into better focus, as it were, it disappeared into the emptiness revolving over my head. It was all the more surprising and indeed alarming a little later, said Austerlitz, when I looked out of the corridor window of my carriage just before the train left at seven-thirteen, to find it dawning upon me with perfect certainty that I had seen the pattern of the glass and steel roof above the platforms before, made up as it was of triangles, round arches, horizontal and vertical lines and diagonals, and in the same half-light. As the train rolled very slowly out of the station, through a passage between the backs of blocks of flats and into the dark tunnel running under the New Town, and then crossed the Vltava with a regular beat, it really

seemed to me, said Austerlitz, as if time had stood still since the day when I first left Prague. It was a dark, oppressive morning. A small lamp with a pink pleated shade, the kind of thing one used to see in the windows of Belgian brothels, stood on the white cloth covering the little table in the Czech State Railways dining car, where I was sitting in order to get a better view. The chef, his toque at an angle on his head, leaned in the entrance to his galley smoking and talking to the waiter, a curly-haired, slight little man in a check waistcoat and yellow bow-tie. Outside, under the lowering sky, meadows and fields passed by, fishponds, woods, the curve of a bend in a river, a stand of alders, hills and valleys, and at Beroun, if I remember correctly, a lime-works extending over a square mile or more, with chimneys and towering silos disappearing into the low clouds above, huge square buildings of crumbling con-crete roofed with rusty corrugated iron, conveyor belts moving up and down, mills to grind the stone, conical mounds of gravel, huts and freight trucks, all of it uniformly covered with pale-grey sinter and dust. Then the wide countryside opened out again, and all the time I was looking out I never

saw a vehicle on the roads, or a single human bei.
except for the station masters who, whether from
boredom or habit or because of some regulation
which they had to observe, had come out on the
platform at even the smallest stations such as
Holoubkov, Chrást or Rokycany in their red uni-
form caps, most of them, it seemed to me, sport-
ing blond moustaches, and determined not to miss
the Prague express as it thundered by on this pallid
April morning. All I remember of Pilsen, where
we stopped for some time, said Austerlitz, is that I
went out on the platform to photograph the capital
of a cast-iron column which had touched some
chord of recognition in me. What made me uneasy
at the sight of it, however, was not the question of
whether the complex form of the capital, now
covered with a puce-tinged encrustation, had
really impressed itself on my mind when I passed
through Pilsen with the children's transport in the
summer of 1939, but the idea, ridiculous in itself,
that this cast iron column, which with its scaly
surface seemed almost to approach the nature of a
living being, might remember me and was, if I may
so put it, said Austerlitz, a witness to what I could
no longer recollect for myself. Beyond Pilsen the

line ran towards the mountains dividing Bohemia from Bavaria. Soon the gradient was delaying the tempo of the train, and dark forests were almost encroaching on the railway embankment. Swathes of mist or low, drifting cloud hung among the dripping pines, until after about an hour the line went downhill again, the valley gradually broadened, and we came out into pleasant countryside. I don't know what I had expected of Germany, said Austerlitz, but wherever I looked I saw trim towns and villages, neat yards around factories and industrial buildings, lovingly tended gardens, piles of firewood tidily stacked under cover, level asphalted cart tracks running through the meadows, roads with brightly coloured cars purring along them at great speed, well-managed woodland, regulated watercourses and new railway buildings where the station masters obviously felt under no obligation to come out. Parts of the sky had cleared, cheerful patches of sunlight lit up the country here and there, and the train, which had often seemed to be having difficulty in making any progress on the Czech side of the border, was now suddenly racing along with almost improbable ease. Around midday we reached Nuremberg, and when I saw the name on a signal box in its German spelling of Nürnberg, which was unfamiliar to me, I remembered what Věra had said about my father's account of the National Socialist Party rally of 1936 and the roars of acclamation rising from the people who had gathered here at the time. Although I had really meant to do no more than ask about my next connections, said Austerlitz, that recollection may have been why I walked out of Nuremberg station without pausing to think and on into that unknown city. I had never before set foot on German soil, I had always avoided learning anything at all about German topography, German history or modern German life, and so, said Austerlitz, Germany was probably more unfamiliar to me than any other country in the world, more foreign even than Afghanistan or Paraguay. As soon as I had emerged from the underpass in front of the station I was swept along by a huge crowd of people who were streaming down the entire breadth of the street, rather like water in a river bed, going in not just one but both directions, as if flowing simul-taneously up- and downstream. I think it was a Saturday, the day when people go to shop in town, inundating these pedestrian zones which apparently, as I was told later, said Austerlitz, exist in more or less the same form in all German cities. The first thing that caught my eye on this excursion was the great number of grey, brown and green loden coats and hats, and how well and sensibly everyone was dressed in general, how remarkably solid were the shoes of the pedestrians of Nuremberg. I avoided looking closely at the faces coming towards me, and thought it odd that few of these people raised their voices as they moved quietly through the city. Looking up at the façades on both sides of the street, even those of the older buildings which, judging by their style, must date from the sixteenth or fifteenth century, I was troubled to realize that I could not see a crooked line anywhere, not at the corners of the houses or on the gables, the window frames or the sills, nor was there any other trace of past history. I remember, said Austerlitz, that the paving under my feet sloped slightly downhill, that once, looking over the parapet of a bridge, I caught sight of two snow-white swans swimming on black water, and then, high above the rooftops, of the castle, somehow miniaturized and in postage-stamp format, so to speak. I could not bring myself to go into a café or buy anything from one of the many stalls and booths. When I turned to go back to the station after about an hour, I felt increasingly as if I had to struggle against a current growing ever stronger, perhaps because I was now going uphill, or maybe there were in fact more people moving one way than the other. In any case, said Austerlitz, I felt more panic-stricken with every passing minute, so that at last, although I was not at all far from the station, I had to stop under the red sandstone arch of a window displaying the pages of the local Nuremberg newspaper, where I waited until the crowds of shoppers had to some extent thinned out. I cannot now say for certain how long I stood there, my senses dazed, on the outer edge of this flood of Germans moving endlessly past me, said Austerlitz, but I think it was four or five o'clock by the time an elderly woman wearing a kind of Tyrolean hat with a cockerel's feather in it stopped beside me, probably taking me for one of the homeless because of my old rucksack, fetched a one-mark coin out of her purse with arthritic fingers, and carefully handed it to me as alms. I was still holding this coin, minted in 1956 with the head of Chancellor Adenauer on it, when I was finally in the train again late that afternoon, travelling towards Cologne, said Austerlitz. I stood in the corridor looking out of the window almost throughout this part of the journey. I think it was between Würzburg and Frankfurt that the line ran through a densely forested region with leafless stands of oak and beech trees, and mile upon mile of conifers. As I gazed out a distant memory came to me of a dream I often had both in the manse at Bala and later, a dream of a nameless land without borders and entirely overgrown by dark forests, which I had to cross without any idea where I was going, and it dawned upon me, said Austerlitz, that what I now saw going past outside the train was the original of the images that had haunted me for so many years. Then I recollected another idea which had obsessed me over a long period: the image of a twin brother who had been with me on that long journey, sitting motionless by the window of the compartment, staring out into the dark. I knew nothing about him, not even his name, and I had never exchanged so much as a word with him, but whenever I thought of him I was tormented by the notion that towards the end of the journey he had died of consumption and was stowed in the baggage net with the rest of our belongings. And then, Austerlitz continued, somewhere beyond Frankfurt, when I entered the Rhine valley for the second time in my life, the sight of the Mäuseturm in the part of the river known as the Binger Loch revealed, with absolute

certainty, why the tower in Lake Vyrnwy had always seemed to me so uncanny. I could not take my eyes off the great river Rhine flowing sluggishly along in the dusk, the apparently motionless barges lying low in the water, which almost lapped over their decks, the trees and bushes on the other bank, the fine cross-hatching of the vineyards, the stronger transverse lines of the walls supporting the terraces, the slate-grey rocks and ravines leading off sideways into what seemed to me a pre-historic and unexplored realm. While I was still under the spell of this landscape, to me a truly mythological one, said Austerlitz, the setting sun broke through the clouds, filled the entire valley with its radiance, and illuminated the heights on the other side where three gigantic chimneys towered into the sky at the place we were just passing, making the steep slopes on the eastern mountains look like hollow shells, mere camouflage for an underground industrial site covering many square miles. Passing through the valley of the Rhine, said Austerlitz, you can scarcely tell what century it is. As you look out of the train window it is difficult to say even of the castles standing high above the river, bearing such strange and somehow preposterous names as Reichenstein, Ehrenfels and Stahleck, whether they are medieval or were built by the industrial barons of the nineteenth century. Some of them, for instance Burg Katz and Burg Maus, seem to be rooted in legend, and even the ruins resemble a romantic stage set. At least, I no longer knew in what period of my life I was living as I journeyed down the Rhine valley. Through the

evening sunlight I saw the glow of a fiery dawn ris-
ing from my past above the other bank, pervading
the whole sky. Even today, Austerlitz continued,
when I think of my Rhine journeys, the second
of them hardly less terrifying than the first, every-
thing becomes confused in my head: my experi-
ences of that time, what I have read, memories
surfacing and then sinking out of sight again, con-
secutive images and distressing blank spots where
nothing at all is left. I see that German landscape,
said Austerlitz, as it was described by earlier
travellers, the great river not yet regulated in any
way, flooding its banks in places, salmon leaping
in the water, crayfish crawling over the fine sand;
I see Victor Hugo's sombre pen-and-ink drawings
of the Rhine castles, and Joseph Mallord Turner
sitting on a folding stool not far from the murder-
ous town of Bacharach, swiftly painting his water-
colours; I see the deep waters of Lake Vyrnwy
and the people of Llanwddyn submerged in them;
and I see, said Austerlitz, the great army of mice,
a grey horde said to have plagued the German
countryside, plunging into the river and swimming
desperately, their little throats raised only just
above the water, to reach the safety of the island.

—— Imperceptibly, the day had begun drawing to a close as Austerlitz talked, and the light was already fading when we left the house in Alderney Street together to walk a little way out of town, along the Mile End Road to the large Tower Hamlets cemetery, which is surrounded by a tall, dark brick wall and, like the adjoining complex of St Clement's Hospital, according to a remark made by Austerlitz in passing, was one of the scenes of this phase of his story. In the twilight slowly falling over London we walked along the paths of the cemetery, past monuments

erected by the Victorians to commemorate their dead, past mausoleums, marble crosses, stelae and obelisks, bulbous urns and statues of angels, many of them wingless or otherwise mutilated, turned to stone, so it seemed to me, at the very moment when they were about to take off

"UNTIL THE DAY BREAK, AND
THE SHADOWS FLEE AWAY."

from the earth. Most of these memorials had
long ago been tilted to one side or thrown over
entirely by the roots of the sycamores which were
shooting up everywhere. The sarcophagi covered
with pale-green, grey, ochre and orange lichens
were broken, some of the graves themselves had

risen above the ground or sunk into it, so that you might think an earthquake had shaken this abode of the departed, or else that, summoned to the Last Judgment, they had upset, as they rose from their resting places, the neat and tidy order we impose on them. In the first few weeks after his return from Bohemia, Austerlitz continued his tale as we walked on, he had learnt by heart the names and dates of birth and death of those buried here, he had taken home pebbles and ivy leaves and on one occasion a stone rose, and the stone hand broken off one of the angels, but however much my walks in Tower Hamlets might soothe me during the day, said Austerlitz, at night I was plagued by the most frightful anxiety attacks which sometimes lasted for hours on end. It was obviously of little use that I had discovered the sources of my distress and, looking back over all the past years, could now see myself with the utmost clarity as that child suddenly cast out of his familiar surroundings: reason was powerless against the sense of rejection and annihilation which I had always suppressed, and which was now breaking through the walls of its confinement. Soon I would be overcome by this terrible anxiety in the midst of the simplest actions: tying my shoelaces, washing up teacups, waiting for the kettle to boil. All of a sudden my tongue and palate would be as dry as if I had been lying in the desert for days, I had to fight harder and harder for breath, my heart began to flutter and palpitate in my throat, cold sweat broke out all over my body, even on the back of my trembling hand, and everything I looked at was veiled by a black mist. I felt like screaming but could not utter a sound, I wanted to walk out into the street but was unable to move from the spot; once, after a long and painful contraction, I actually visualized myself being broken up from within, so that parts of my body were scattered over a dark and distant terrain. I cannot say now, said Austerlitz, how many such attacks I suffered at the time, but one day, when I collapsed on my way to the kiosk at the end of Alderney Street, striking my head against the edge of the pavement, I was taken to St Clement's as the last in a series of various casualty departments and hospitals, and there found myself in one of the men's wards when at last I returned to my senses, after what I was told later had been nearly three weeks of mental absence which, though it did not impair the bodily functions, paralysed all thought processes and emotions.

I walked around in this place, said Austerlitz, his left
hand pointing to the tall brick façade of the hospital
building towering behind the wall, in the curiously
remote state of mind induced by the drugs I was
being given; both desolate and weirdly contented I
wandered, all through that winter, up and down the
long corridors, staring out for hours through one of
the dirty windows at the cemetery below, where

we are standing now, feeling nothing inside my
head but the four burnt-out walls of my brain.
Later, when there had been some improvement in
my condition, I looked through a telescope given to
me by one of the nurses and watched the foxes run-
ning wild in the cemetery in the grey dawn. I would
see squirrels dodging back and forth, or sitting quite
still, arrested, as it were, in mid-motion. I studied

the faces of those solitary people who visited the graveyard now and then, or I observed the slow wingbeats of an owl in its curving flight over the tombstones at nightfall. Occasionally I talked to one of the other hospital patients, a roofer, for instance, who said he could recollect with perfect clarity the moment when, just as he was about to fix a slate in place, something that had been stretched too taut inside him snapped at a particular spot behind his forehead, and for the first time he heard, coming over the crackling transistor wedged into the batten in front of him, the voices of those bearers of bad tidings which had haunted him ever since. While I was there I also thought quite often of Elias the minister lapsing into madness, and of the stone-built asylum in Denbigh where he died. But I found it impossible to think of myself, my own history, or my present state of mind. I was not discharged until the beginning of April, a year after returning from Prague. The last doctor whom I saw at the hospital advised me to look for some kind of light physical occupation, perhaps in horticulture, she suggested, and so for the next two years, at the time of day when office staff are pouring into the City, I went out the other way to Romford and my new place of work, a council-run nursery garden on the outskirts of a large park which employed, as well as the trained gardeners, a certain number of assistants who suffered from disabilities or required to have their minds set at rest by some quiet pursuit. I cannot say, said Austerlitz, why I began to recover in some degree out at Romford in the course of those months, whether it was because of the people in whose company I found myself, who though they all bore the scars of their mental sufferings often seemed carefree and very cheerful, or the constant warm, humid atmosphere in the greenhouses, the mossy, forest-ground fragrance filling the air, the rectilinear patterns presented to the eye, or simply the even tenor of the work itself, the careful pricking out and potting up of seedlings, transplanting them when they had grown larger, looking after the cold frames and watering the trays with a fine hose, which I liked perhaps best of all. At the time when I

was working as an assistant gardener in Romford, said Austerlitz, I began to spend my evenings and weekends poring over the heavy tome, running to almost eight hundred close-printed pages, which H. G. Adler, a name previously unknown to me, had written between 1945 and 1947 in the most difficult of circumstances, partly in Prague and partly in London, on the subject of the setting up, development and internal organization of the Theresienstadt ghetto, and which he had revised several times before it was brought out by a German publishing house in 1955. Reading this book, which

4. BEZIRK

← EGER

PRAG →

KLEINE FESTUNG

SCHLEUSENMÜHLE

E VII

E VI

E Vb

E V

DT. PARK

BAV. XX

HV

GVI

GV

ELBE ←

IV

BRUNNENPARK

E IIIb

E IIb

HR

LEITMERITZ ←

LOBOSIT
AUSSIG

E I

3. BEZIRK

WASSERWE

VERBINDUNG ZUR HAUPTSTRASSE

← EGER

ZUR EGER

L 6

D VI   C VI   B V

E Va   D V

C V

RAW XV

A V

D IV   C IV   B IV

E IIIa   D III   C III

KLEINER PARK

BAUSCHO-WITZER KESSEL

A IV

E IIa   C II   B II

A II

SÜDBERG

WESTBARACKEN

D I   B I

C I

ZUR KRETA

VERBINDUNG LEITMERITZ-BAUSCHOWITZ

SÜD-BARACKEN

KREMATORIUM

NORD   NACH BAUSCHOWITZ (BHF)

2. BEZIRK

line by line gave me an insight into matters I could never have imagined when I myself visited the fortified town, almost entirely ignorant as I was at that time, was a painstaking business because of my poor knowledge of German, and indeed, said Austerlitz, I might well say it was almost as difficult for me as deciphering an Egyptian or Babylonian text in hieroglyphic or cuneiform script. The long compounds, not listed in my dictionary, which were obviously being spawned the whole time by the pseudo-technical jargon governing everything in Theresienstadt had to be unravelled syllable by syllable. When I had finally discovered the meaning of such terms and concepts as *Barackenbestandteillager*, *Zusatzkostenberechnungsschein*, *Bagatellreparaturwerkstätte*, *Menagetransportkolonnen*, *Küchenbeschwerdeorgane*, *Reinlichkeitsreihenuntersuchung*, and *Entwesungsübersiedlung* – to my surprise, Austerlitz articulated these heterogeneous German compounds unhesitatingly and without the slightest trace of an accent – when I had worked out what they meant, he continued, I had to make just as much of an effort to fit the presumptive sense of my reconstructions into the sentences and the wider context, which kept threatening to elude me, first because it quite often took me until midnight to master a single page, and a good deal was lost in this lengthy process, and second because in its almost futuristic deformation of social life the ghetto system had something incomprehensible and unreal about it, even though Adler describes it down to the last detail in its objective actuality. It seems unpardonable to me today that I had blocked off the investigation of my most distant past for so many years, not on principle, to be sure, but still of my own accord, and that now it is too late for me to seek out Adler, who had lived in London until his death in the summer of 1988, and talk to him about that extra-territorial place where at the time, as I think I have mentioned before, said Austerlitz, some sixty thousand people were crammed together in an area little more than a square kilometre in size — industrialists and manufacturers, lawyers and doctors, rabbis and university professors, singers and composers, bank managers, businessmen, shorthand typists, housewives, farmers, labourers and millionaires, people from Prague and the rest of the Protectorate, from Slovakia, from Denmark and Holland, from Vienna and Munich, Cologne and Berlin, from the Palatinate, from Lower Franconia and Westphalia – each of

Verzeichnis der als Sonderweisungen bezeichneten Arbeiten.

1. Dienststelle
2. Kameradschaftsheim
3. SS-Garage
4. Kleine Festung
5. Deutsche Dienstpost
6. Reserve-Lazarett
7. Berliner Dienststelle
8. Gendarmerie
9. Reichssippenforschung
10. Landwirtschaft
11. Torfabladen
12. Schleusenmühle
13. Eisenbahnbau Ing. Figlovský
14. Eisenbahnbau eig. Rechnung
15. Feuerlöschteiche E I, H IV
16. Straßenbau Leitmeritz
17. Straßenbau f. Rechnung Ing. Figlovský (T 321)
18. Uhrenreparaturenwerkstätte
19. Zentralamt f. d. Regelung der Judenfrage in Prag
20. Bau des Wasserwerks (T 423)
    a) Ing. Figlovský            b) Artesia, Prag
    c) Ing. C. Pštross, Prag     d) sonstige Posten
21. Silagenbau Ing. Figlovský
    (Hilfsdienst          )
22. Kanalisationsarbeiten (T 45)
23. Kanalisationsarbeiten für Rechnung Ing. Figlovský
24. Bau der Silagegrube Ing. Figlovský
25. Steinbruch Kamaik
26. Krematoriumbau
27. Hilfsarbeiten und Schießstätte Kamaik-Leitmeritz
28. Kreta-Bauten und deren Erhaltungskosten
29. Chemische Kontrollarbeiten
30. Gruppe Dr. Weidmann [s. 19. Kap.]
31. Bucherfassungsgruppe [s. 19. Kap.]
32. Schutzbrillenerzeugung
33. Uniformkonfektion
34. Rindsledergaloschen
35. Zentralbad (arische Abt.)
36. Glimmerspalten
37. Kaninchenhaarscheren
38. Tintenpulversäckchenfüllen
39. Elektrizitätswerk
40. Kartonagenwerkstätte
41. Lehrspiele
42. Marketenderwarenerzeugung (früher Galanterie)
43. Instandhaltung von Uniformen
44. Jutesäcke-Reparatur
45. Bijouterie
46. Straßenerhaltung und Straßenreinigung
47. Arbeitsgruppe Jungfern-Breschan
48. Projektierte Hydrozentrale
49. NSFK-Flugplatz
50. Schlachthof
51. Schieß-Stand
52. Holzkohleerzeugung

whom had to make do with about two square metres
of space in which to exist and all of them, in so far as
they were in any condition to do so or until they
were loaded into trucks and sent on east, obliged to

work entirely without remuneration in one of the primitive factories set up, with a view to generating actual profit, by the External Trade Section, assigned to the bandage-weaving workshop, to the handbag and satchel assembly line, the production of horn buttons and other haberdashery items, the manufacturing of wooden soles for footwear and of cowhide galoshes, to the charcoal yard, the making of such board games as Nine Men's Morris and Catch the Hat, the splitting of mica, the shearing of rabbit fur, the bottling of ink dust, the silkworm-breeding station run under the aegis of the SS or, alternatively, employed in one of the operations serving the ghetto's internal economy, in the clothing store, for instance, in one of the precinct mending and darning rooms, the shredding section, the rag depot, the book reception and sorting unit, the kitchen brigade, the potato-peeling platoon, the bone-crushing mill, the glue-boiling plant or the mattress department, as medical and nursing auxiliaries, in the disinfestation and rodent-control service, the floor-space-allocation office, the central registration bureau, the self-administration housed in barrack block BV, known as 'The Castle', or in the transport of goods maintained within the walls of the fortress by means of a medley of carts of every conceivable kind and four dozen ancient hearses brought from the now defunct Jewish communities in the Bohemian countryside to Terezín, where they moved along the crowded streets with two men harnessed between the shafts and four to eight pushing or putting their weight against the spokes of the wheels of these oddly swaying conveyances, which were covered by ulcerations of peeling black varnish and from which, before long, the rickety superstructures, high-built coach-boxes and silver-bronzed canopies resting on turned columns had been roughly sawn away, so that the lower parts, on the sides of which rows of letters and numbers were coarsely painted in lime-wash, scarcely betrayed their former function, a function, said Austerlitz, for which they were still frequently employed even now, since much of the load carted round Theresienstadt every day was made up of the dead, of whom there were always a great many because the high population density and poor diet rendered it impossible for the course of such infectious diseases as scarlet fever, enteritis, diphtheria, jaundice and tuberculosis to be stemmed, and because the average age of those brought from all regions of the German Reich to the ghetto was over

seventy, and these people, who before they were
sent away had been led to believe some tale about
a pleasant resort in Bohemia called Theresienbad,
with beautiful gardens, promenades, boarding
houses and villas, and many of whom had been
persuaded or forced to sign contracts, so-called
*Heimeinkaufsverträge*, said Austerlitz, offering them,
against deposits of up to eighty thousand Reichs-
marks, the right of residence in what was described

to them as a most salubrious place, these people,
Austerlitz continued, had come to Theresienstadt,
completely misled by the illusions implanted in
their minds, carrying in their luggage all manner of
personal items and mementoes which could be of
no conceivable use in the life that awaited them in
the ghetto, often arriving already ravaged in body
and spirit, no longer in their right minds, delirious,
frequently unable to remember their own names,

surviving the procedure of being sluiced in, as it was
termed, either not at all or only by a few days, in
which latter case, on account of the extreme psycho-
pathic personality changes which they had under-
gone and which generally resulted in a kind of
infantilism divorcing them from reality and entailing
an almost total loss of the ability to speak and act,
they were immediately sectioned in the casemate of
the Cavalier Barracks, which served as a psychiatric
ward and where they usually perished within a week
under the dreadful conditions prevailing there, so
that although there was no shortage of doctors and
surgeons in Theresienstadt who cared for their
fellow prisoners as best they could, and in spite of
the steam-disinfection boiler installed in the malting
kiln of the former brewery, the hydrogen-cyanide
chamber and other hygienic measures introduced by
the Kommandantur in an all-out campaign against
infestation with lice, the number of the dead –
entirely in line, said Austerlitz, with the intentions
of the masters of the ghetto – rose to well above
twenty thousand in the ten months between August
1942 and May 1943 alone, as a result of which the
joiner's workshop in the former riding school could
no longer make enough deal coffins, there were

sometimes more than five hundred dead bodies stacked in layers on top of each other in the central morgue in the casemate by the gateway to the Bohuševice road, and the four naphtha-fired incinerators of the crematorium, kept going day and night in cycles of forty minutes at a time, were stretched to the utmost limits of their capacity, said Austerlitz, and this comprehensive system of internment and forced labour which, in Theresienstadt as elsewhere, was ultimately directed, so he continued, solely at the extinction of life and was built on an organizational plan regulating all functions and responsibilities, as Adler's reconstruction shows, with a crazed administrative zeal – from the use of whole troops of workers in building the branch railway line from Bohuševice to the fort, to the one man whose job it was to keep the clock mechanism in the closed Catholic church in order – this system had to be constantly supervised and statistically accounted for, particularly with respect to the total number of inmates of the ghetto, an uncommonly time-consuming business going far beyond civilian requirements when you remember that new transports were arriving all the time, and people were regularly weeded out to be sent elsewhere with their files marked *R.N.E.* for *Rückkehr Nicht Erwünscht*, Return Not Desired, a purpose for which the SS men responsible, who regarded numerical accuracy as one of their highest principles, had a census taken several times, on one occasion, if I remember correctly, said Austerlitz, on 10 November 1943 outside the gates in the open fields of the Bohuševice basin, when the entire population of the ghetto – children, old people and any of the sick at all able to walk not excepted – was marched out after assembling in the barracks yards at dawn to be drawn up in block formation behind numbered wooden boards, and there, throughout the whole of this cold and damp day, as the fog drifted over the fields, they were forced to wait, guarded by armed police and not permitted to step out of line even for a minute, for the SS men to arrive, as they eventually did on their motorbikes at three o'clock, to carry out the count of heads and then repeat it twice before they could feel convinced that the final result, including those few still within the walls, did in fact tally with the expected number of forty thousand one hundred and forty-five, whereupon they rode away again in some haste, entirely forgetting to give any orders for the inmates' return, so that this great crowd of many thousands stood out in the Bohuševice basin on that grey tenth of November drenched to the skin and increasingly distressed until well after dark, bowed and swaying like reeds in the showers that now swept over the countryside, before finally, driven to it by a wave of panic, they poured back into the town from which most of them had never emerged except for this one time since their transfer to Theresienstadt, where soon after the beginning of the new year, said Austerlitz, what was described as a *Verschönerungsaktion* or general improvement campaign was undertaken, with an eye to the imminent visit in the early summer of 1944 of a Red Cross commission, an event regarded by those authorities of the Reich responsible as a good opportunity to dissimulate the true nature of their deportation policy, and consequently it was decided to organize the ghetto inmates under the command of the SS for the purpose of a vast cleaning-up programme: pathways and a grove with a columbarium were laid out, park benches and signposts were set up, the latter adorned in the German fashion with jolly carvings and floral decoration, over a thousand rose-bushes were planted, a children's nursery and crèche or *Kriechlingskrippe*, as it was termed, said Austerlitz, in

one of those perverse formulations, were adorned
with pretty fairy-tale friezes and equipped with sand-
pits, paddling pools and merry-go-rounds, whilst
the former OREL cinema, which until now had
served as a dumping ground for the oldest inmates of
the ghetto and where a huge chandelier still hung
from the ceiling in the dark space inside, was con-
verted within a few weeks into a concert hall and
theatre, and elsewhere shops stocked with goods
from the SS storehouses were opened for the sale of
food and household utensils, ladies' and gentlemen's
clothing, shoes, underwear, travel requisites and
suitcases; there were also a convalescent home, a
chapel, a lending library, a gymnasium, a post office,
a bank where the manager's office was furnished
with a sort of field marshal's desk and a suite of easy
chairs, not to mention a coffee-house with sun
umbrellas and folding chairs outside it to suggest the
agreeable atmosphere of a resort inviting all passers-
by to linger for a while, and indeed there was no end
to the improvements and embellishments, with
much sawing, hammering and painting until the time
of the visit itself approached and Theresienstadt,
after another seven and a half thousand of the less
presentable inmates had been sent east amidst all this

busy activity, to thin out the population, so to speak, became a Potemkin village or sham Eldorado which may have dazzled even some of the inhabitants themselves and where, when the appointed day came, the commission of two Danes and one Swiss official, having been guided, in conformity with a precise plan and a timetable drawn up by the Kommandant's office, through the streets and over the spotless pavements, scrubbed with soap early that morning, could see for themselves the friendly, happy folk who had been spared the horrors of war and were looking out of the windows, could see how smartly they were all dressed, how well the few sick people were cared for, how they were given proper meals served on plates, how the bread ration was handed out by people in white drill gloves, how posters advertising sporting events, cabarets, theatrical performances and concerts were being put up on every corner and how, when the day's work was over, the residents of the town flocked out in their thousands on the ramparts and bastions to take the air, almost as if they were passengers enjoying an evening stroll on the deck of an ocean-going steamer, a most reassuring spectacle, all things considered, which the Germans, whether for propaganda purposes or in order to justify their actions and conduct to themselves, thought fit after the end of the Red Cross visit to record in a film, which Adler tells us, said Austerlitz, was given a soundtrack of Jewish folk music in March 1945, when a considerable number of the people who had appeared in it were no longer alive, and a copy of which, again according to Adler, had apparently turned up in the British-occupied zone after the war, although he, Adler himself, said Austerlitz, never saw it, and thought it was now lost without trace. For months, said Austerlitz, I tried in vain, through the good offices of the Imperial War Museum and other agencies, to find any clue to the present location of that film, since although I had been to Theresienstadt before leaving Prague, and despite Adler's meticulous account, which I had read down to the last footnote with the greatest attention, I found myself unable to cast my mind back to the ghetto and picture my mother Agáta there at the time. I kept thinking that if only the film could be found I might perhaps be able to see or gain some inkling of what it was really like, and then I imagined recognizing Agáta, beyond any possibility of doubt, a young woman as she would be by comparison with me today, perhaps among the guests outside the fake coffee-house, or a saleswoman in the haberdashery shop, just taking a fine pair of gloves carefully out of one of the drawers, or singing the part of Olympia in the *Tales of Hoffmann* which, so Adler says, was staged in Theresienstadt in the course of the improvements campaign. I imagined seeing her walking down the street in a summer dress and lightweight gabardine coat, said Austerlitz: among a group of ghetto residents out for a stroll, she alone seemed to make straight for me, coming closer with every step, until at last I thought I could sense her stepping out of the frame and passing over into me. It was wishful fantasies such as these which cast me into a state of great excitement when the Imperial War Museum finally succeeded, through the Federal Archives in Berlin, in obtaining a cassette copy of the film of Theresienstadt for which I had been searching. I remember very clearly, said Austerlitz, how I sat in one of the museum's video viewing rooms, placed the cassette in the black opening of the recorder with trembling hands, and then, although unable to take in any of it, watched various tasks being carried out at the anvil and forge of a smithy, in the pottery and wood-carving workshop, in the handbag-making and shoe-manufacturing sections —

a constant, pointless to-do of hammering, metal-beating and welding, cutting, gluing and stitching; I saw an unbroken succession of strangers' faces emerge before me for a few seconds, I saw workers leaving the huts when the siren had sounded and crossing an empty field beneath a sky filled with motionless white clouds, a game of football in the inner court of one of the barrack buildings, with hundreds of cheerful spectators crowding the arcades and the galleries on the first and second floors, I saw men under the showers in the central bathhouse, books being borrowed from the library by gentlemen of soigné appearance, I saw a full-scale orchestral concert and, in the moat surrounding the fortified town, kitchen gardens neatly laid out where several dozen people were raking the vegetable beds, watering beans and tomatoes, searching brassica leaves for Cabbage White caterpillars, whilst at the end of the day others were sitting on benches outside the houses, apparently in perfect contentment, letting the children play a little longer, one man reading a book, a woman talking to her neighbour, many of them just taking their ease at their windows, arms folded, in a way once common at the onset of dusk. At first I could get none of these images into my head; they merely flickered before my eyes as the source of continual irritation or vexation, which was further reinforced when, to my horror, it turned out that the Berlin cassette inscribed with the original title of *Der Führer schenkt den Juden eine Stadt* had on it only a patchwork of scenes cobbled together and lasting some fourteen minutes, scarcely more than an opening sequence in which, despite the hopes I had entertained, I could not see Agáta anywhere, however often I ran the tape and however hard I strained to make her out among those fleeting faces. In the end the impossibility of seeing anything more closely in those pictures, which seemed to dissolve even as they appeared, said Austerlitz, gave me the idea of having a slow-motion copy of this fragment from Theresienstadt made, one which would last a whole hour, and indeed once the scant document was extended to four times its original length, it did reveal previously hidden objects and people, creating, by default as it were, a different sort of film altogether, which I have since watched over and over again. The men and women employed in the workshops now looked as if they were toiling in their sleep, so long did it take them to draw needle and thread through the air as they

stitched, so heavily did their eyelids sink, so slowly did their lips move as they looked wearily up at the camera. They seemed to be hovering rather than walking, as if their feet no longer quite touched the ground. The contours of their bodies were blurred and, particularly in the scenes shot out of doors in broad daylight, had dissolved at the edges, resembling, as it occurred to me, said Austerlitz, the frayed outlines of the human hand shown in the fluidal pictures and electrographs taken by Louis Draget in Paris around the turn of the century. The many damaged sections of the tape, which I had hardly noticed before, now melted the image from its centre or from the edges, blotting it out and instead making patterns of bright white sprinkled with black which reminded me of aerial photographs taken in the far north, or a drop of water seen under the microscope. Strangest of all, however, said Austerlitz, was the transformation of sounds in this slow-motion version. In a brief sequence at the very beginning, showing red-hot iron being worked in a smithy to shoe a draught ox, the merry polka by some Austrian operetta composer on the soundtrack of the Berlin copy had become a funeral march dragging along at a grotesquely sluggish pace, and the rest of the musical pieces accompanying the film, among which I could identify only the can-can from *La Vie Parisienne* and the scherzo from Mendelssohn's *Midsummer Night's Dream*, also moved in a kind of subterranean world, through the most nightmarish depths, said Austerlitz, to which no human voice has ever descended. None of the words of the commentary could be distinguished any more. At the point where, on the original Berlin copy, a male voice, in high-pitched, strenuous tones forced through the larynx, had spoken of task forces and cohorts of workers deployed, as circumstances required, in various different ways, or if necessary retrained, so that everyone willing to work – *jeder Arbeitswillige!*, so Austerlitz interrupted himself – had an opportunity of fitting seamlessly into the production process, at this point of the tape all that could now be made out, Austerlitz continued, was a menacing growl such as I had heard only once before in my life, on an unseasonably hot May Day many years ago in the Jardin des Plantes in Paris when, after one of the peculiar turns that often came over me in those days, I rested for a while on a park bench beside an aviary not far from the big cats' house, where the lions and tigers, invisible from my vantage point and, as it struck me at the time, said Austerlitz, driven out of their minds in captivity, raised their hollow roars of lament hour after hour without ceasing. And then, Austerlitz continued, towards the end of the film there was the comparatively long sequence showing the first performance of a piece of music composed in Theresienstadt, Pavel Haas's study for string orchestra, if I am not mistaken. The series of frames begins with a view into the hall from the back. The windows are wide open, and a large audience is sitting not in rows as usual at a concert, but as if they were in some sort of tavern or hotel dining-room, in groups of four around tables. The chairs, probably made specially for the occasion in the carpentry workshop of the ghetto, are of pseudo-Tyrolean design with heart shapes sawn out of their backs. In the course of the performance the camera lingers in close-up over several members of the audience, including an old gentleman whose cropped grey head fills the right-hand side of the picture, while at the left-hand side, set a little way back and close to the upper edge of the frame, the face of a young woman appears, barely emerging from the black shadows around it, which is why I did not notice it at all at first. Around her neck, said Austerlitz, she is

wearing a three-stringed and delicately draped neck
lace which scarcely stands out from her dark, high-
necked dress, and there is, I think, a white flower in
her hair. She looks, so I tell myself as I watch, just as
I imagined the singer Agáta from my faint memories
and the few other clues to her appearance that
I now have, and I gaze and gaze again at that face,
which seems to me both strange and familiar, said
Austerlitz, I run the tape back repeatedly, looking at
the time indicator in the top left-hand corner of the
screen, where the figures covering part of her fore-
head show the minutes and seconds, from 10:53 to
10:57, while the hundredths of a second flash by so
fast that you cannot read and capture them. — At

the beginning of this year, Austerlitz finally contin-
ued his narrative, after lapsing, as so often, into
deep abstraction in the middle of it, at the begin-
ning of this year, he said, not long after our last
meeting, I went to Prague for a second time,
resumed my conversations with Věra, set up a kind
of pension fund at a bank for her and did what else
I could to ease her life in the Šporkova. When it
was not too cold out of doors we called a taxi
driver, whom I had engaged to be at Věra's dis-
posal should she need him, to take us to some of
the places she had mentioned and which she herself
had not seen, as she put it, for an eternity. We
looked down at the city again from the observation
tower on Petřín Hill, watching the cars and trains
crawling slowly along the banks of the Vltava and
over the bridges. We walked for a little while
through the Baumgarten by the river in the pale
winter sunlight, we sat for an hour or so in the
planetarium on the Holešovice exhibition grounds,
repeating the names of those heavenly constella-
tions we could recognize, first in French and then
in Czech or vice versa, and once we went out to the
game park at Liboc where, surrounded on all sides
by lovely meadows, there is a star-shaped house

built as his summer residence by Archduke Ferdinand of the Tyrol, which Věra had told me was a favourite destination of Agáta and Maximilian on their excursions out of the city. I also spent several days searching the records for the years 1938 and 1939 in the Prague theatrical archives in the Celetná, and there, among letters, files on employees, programmes and faded newspaper cuttings, I came upon the photograph of an anonymous actress who seemed to resemble my dim memory of my mother, and in whom Věra, who had already spent some time studying the face of the woman in the concert audience which I had copied from the Theresienstadt film, before shaking her head and putting it aside, immediately and without a shadow of doubt, as she said, recognized

Agáta as she had then been. —— During this part of his tale, Austerlitz and I had walked from the cemetery behind St Clement's Hospital all the way back to Liverpool Street. When we took leave of each other outside the railway station, Auster-litz gave me an envelope which he had with him and which contained the photograph from the theatrical archives in Prague, as a memento, he said, for he told me that he was now about to go to Paris to search for traces of his father's last move-ments, and to transport himself back to the time when he too had lived there, in one way feeling liberated from the false pretences of his English life, but in another oppressed by the vague sense that he did not belong in this city either, or indeed anywhere else in the world.

*

It was in September of the same year that I received a postcard from Austerlitz giving me his new address (6 rue des cinq Diamants, in the thirteenth arrondissement), which I knew was in the nature of an invitation to visit him as soon as it could be arranged. When I arrived at the Gare du Nord, high summer temperatures still prevailed, at the end of a drought which had been parching large parts of the country for over two months, and they did not begin to drop until October. The thermometer rose to over twenty-five degrees quite early in the morning, and towards midday the city was groaning beneath the heavy haze of lead and petrol fumes weighing down like a bell jar on the entire Ile de France. The blue-grey air was motionless and took one's breath away. The traffic inched along the boulevards, the tall stone façades quivered like mirages in the shimmering light, the leaves of the trees in the Tuileries and the Jardin du Luxembourg were scorched, the passengers in the Métro trains and the endless underpasses through which a hot desert wind blew were exhausted. I met Austerlitz, as agreed, on the day after my arrival, in the Le Havane bistro bar on the boulevard Auguste Blanqui, not far from the Glacière Métro station. As I entered the bar, which was rather dark even in the middle of the day, a television screen measuring at least two square metres and fixed high on the wall was just transmitting pictures of the great palls of smoke which had been stifling the towns and villages of Indonesia for weeks on end, and dusting grey ash over the heads of all who for any reason ventured out of doors, wearing masks to protect their faces. We both watched these calamitous images from the other end of the earth for some time before Austerlitz, as usual without any preamble, continued his story. When I was first in Paris at the end of the 1950s, he said, turning to me, I had a room in the apartment of an elderly lady of almost transparent appearance called Amélie Cerf, who lived at No. 6, rue Emile Zola, not far from the Pont Mirabeau, a shapeless concrete block which I still sometimes see in my nightmares today. On my return now I had really meant to find somewhere to stay in the same street, but then after all I decided to rent a place here in the thirteenth arrondissement, since my father, Maximilian Aychenwald, whose last known address was in the rue Barrault, must have frequented this area at least for a while before, as it seems, he disappeared irrevocably and without trace. At any rate, my inquiries at the house in the rue Barrault, most of which is now empty, were fruitless, and so were my inquiries at various agencies in the prefecture, partly because of the proverbially unhelpful attitude of Parisian officials, which was even more marked than usual on account of

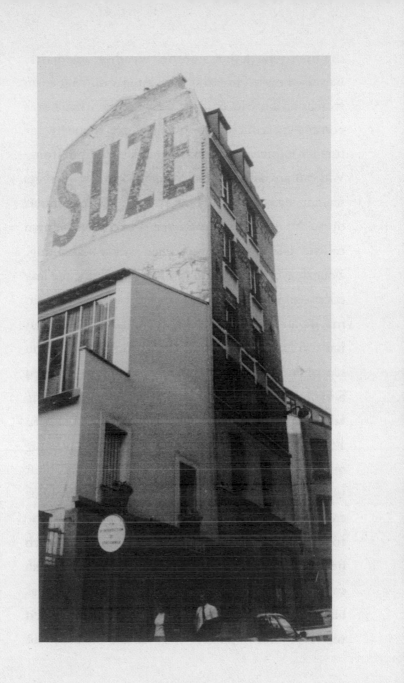

the interminable hot summer weather, and partly because I myself found it increasingly difficult to go from one bureau to another making what I was coming to conclude were useless requests for further information. Soon I was merely wandering without any aim or plan in mind down the streets leading away from the boulevard Auguste Blanqui, up to the Place d'Italie on one side and back down to the Glacière on the other, always thinking, against all reason, that I might suddenly see my father appear out of nowhere, coming towards me or stepping out of an entrance. I sat in this bar too for hours on end, trying to imagine him in his plum-coloured double-breasted suit, perhaps a little threadbare now, bent over one of the café tables and writing those letters to his loved ones in Prague which never arrived. I kept wondering whether he had been interned in the half-built housing estate out at Drancy after the first police raid in Paris in August 1941, or not until July of the following year, when a whole army of French gendarmes took thirteen thousand of their Jewish fellow citizens from their homes, in what was called the *grande rafle*, during which over a hundred of their victims jumped out of the windows in desperation or found some other way of committing suicide. I sometimes thought I saw the window-less police cars racing through a city frozen with terror, the crowd of detainees camping out in the open in the Vélodrome d'Hiver, and the trains on which they were soon deported from Drancy and Bobigny; I pictured their journey through the Greater German Reich, I saw my father still in his good suit and his black velour hat, calm and upright among all those frightened people. Then again, I thought that Maximilian would surely have left Paris in time, had gone south on foot across the Pyrenees, and perished somewhere along his way. Or I felt, as I was saying, said Austerlitz, as if my father were still in Paris and just waiting, so to speak, for a good opportunity to reveal himself. Such ideas infallibly come to me in places which have more of the past about them than the present. For instance, if I am walking through the city and look into one of those quiet courtyards where nothing has changed for decades, I feel, almost physically, the current of time slowing down in the gravitational field of oblivion. It seems to me then as if all the moments of our life occupy the same space, as if future events already existed and were only waiting for us to find our way to them at last, just as when we have accepted an invitation we duly arrive in a certain house at a given time. And might it not be, continued Austerlitz, that we also have appointments to keep in the past, in what has gone before and is for the most part extinguished, and must go there in search of places and people who have some connection with us on the far side of time, so to speak? For instance, one curiously gloomy morning recently I was in the Cimetière de Montparnasse, laid out by the Hospitallers in the seventeenth century on land belonging to the Hôtel de Dieu and now surrounded by towering office blocks, walking among the gravestones erected in a vaguely segregated part in memory of members of the Woelfflin, Wormser, Mayerbeer, Ginsberg, Franck and many other Jewish families, and I felt as if, despite knowing nothing of my origins for so long, I had lingered among them before, or as if they were still accompanying me. I read all their euphonious German names and retained them in my mind – thinking of my land-lady in the rue Emile Zola and of a certain Hippolyte Cerf who was born in Neuf Brisach in

1807, probably as Hippolyt Hirsch, and according
to the inscription had died in Paris on the eighth of
March 1890, the sixteenth of Adar 5650, many
years after his marriage to one Antoinette Fulda of
Frankfurt. Among the children of these forebears
who had moved from Germany to the French capital
were Adolphe and Alfonse, together with Jeanne
and Pauline, who had brought Messrs Lanzberg and
Ochs into the family as sons-in-law, and a genera-
tion later came Hugo and Lucie Sussfeld, née
Ochs, who had a memorial plaque half hidden
by a dried-up asparagus fern inside the cramped
mausoleum, informing visitors to the grave that the
couple had died on being deported in 1944. Since
that time which, as I told myself while attempting
to decipher, through the sparse stems of the aspara-
gus fern, the letters forming the words *morts en
déportation*, was now half a century ago, since that
time, said Austerlitz, not much more than a dozen
years had passed before I moved into Amélie
Cerf's apartment in the rue Emile Zola with my
few belongings. What, I wondered, are twelve or
thirteen such years, if not a single moment of un-
alterable pain? Was Amélie Cerf, whom I remem-
ber as physically almost non-existent, perhaps the

last surviving member of her tribe? Was there no one left to put up a memorial to her in the family mausoleum? Did she ever come to lie in that tomb at all, or did she dissolve into the empty air like Hugo and Lucie? As for myself, Austerlitz continued his story after a long pause, during my first stay in Paris, and indeed later in my life as well, I tried not to let anything distract me from my studies. In the week I went daily to the Bibliothèque Nationale in the rue Richelieu, and usually remained in my place there until evening, in silent solidarity with the many others immersed in their intellectual labours, losing myself in the small print of the footnotes to the works I was reading, in the books I found mentioned in those notes, then in the footnotes to those books in their own turn, and so escaping from factual, scholarly accounts to the strangest of details, in a kind of continual regression expressed in the form of my own marginal remarks and glosses, which increasingly diverged into the most varied and impenetrable of ramifications. My neighbour was usually an elderly gentleman with carefully trimmed hair and sleeve protectors, who had been working for decades on an encyclopaedia of church history, a project which had now reached the letter K, so that it was obvious he would never be able to complete it. Without the slightest hesitation, and never making any corrections, he filled in one after another of his index cards in tiny copperplate handwriting, subsequently setting them out in front of him in meticulous order. Some years later, said Austerlitz, when I was watching a short black and white film about the Bibliothèque Nationale and saw messages racing by pneumatic post from the reading-rooms to the stacks, along what might be described as the library's nervous system, it struck me that the scholars, together with the whole apparatus of the library, formed an immensely complex and constantly evolving creature which had to be fed with myriads of words, in order to bring forth myriads of words in its own turn. I think that this film, which I saw only once but which assumed ever more monstrous and fantastic dimensions in my imagination, was entitled *Toute la mémoire du monde* and was made by Alain Resnais. Even before then my mind often dwelt on the question of whether there in the reading-room of the library, which was full of a quiet humming, rustling and clearing of throats, I was on the Islands of the

Blest or, on the contrary, in a penal colony, and that conundrum, said Austerlitz, was going round in my head again on a day which has lodged itself with particular tenacity in my memory, a day when I spent perhaps as much as an hour in the manuscripts and records department on the first floor, where I was temporarily working, looking out at the tall rows of windows on the opposite side of the building, which reflected the dark slates of the roof, at the narrow brick-red chimneys, the bright and icy-blue sky, and the snow-white metal weather vane with the shape of a swallow cut out of it, soaring upwards and as blue as the azure of the sky itself. The reflections in the old glass panes were slightly irregular or undulating, and I remember, said Austerlitz, that at the sight of them, for some reason I could not understand, tears came to my eyes. It was on the same day, added Austerlitz, that Marie de Verneuil, who was working in the records department too and must have noticed my strange fit of melancholy, pushed a note over to me asking me to join her for a cup of coffee. In the state I was in at the time I did not stop to reflect on the unconventionality of her conduct, but nodded in silent acceptance of her invitation and went out with her, almost obediently, one might say, said Austerlitz, downstairs, across the inner courtyard and through the library gates, down several of the streets so full of pleasant air that fresh and somehow festive morning, and over to the Palais Royal, where we sat for a long time under the arcades beside a shop window in which, as I recollect, said Austerlitz, hundreds and hundreds of tin soldiers in the brightly coloured uniforms of the Napoleonic army were drawn up in marching order and battle formation. On that first encounter, and indeed later, Marie told me very little about herself and her background, perhaps because she came from a very distinguished family, while as she probably guessed I was from nowhere, so to speak. Once we had discovered our common interests, our conversation in the café under the arcade, during which Marie alternately ordered peppermint tea and vanilla ice cream, turned mainly on subjects of architectural history, including, as I still remember very clearly, said Austerlitz, a paper-mill in the Charente which Marie had visited with a cousin of hers not long before and which by her account of it was one of the strangest places she had ever seen. This enormous building, made of oak beams and sometimes groaning under its own weight, said Marie, stands half hidden among trees and bushes on the bend of a river with waters of a deep, almost unnatural green. Inside the mill two brothers, each proficient in his own skills, one of whom had a squint and the other a crooked shoulder, turn great masses of soaked paper and rags of fabric into clean sheets of blank paper, which are then dried on the racks of a large airing loft at the top of the mill. You are surrounded by a quiet twilight there, said Marie, you see the light of day outside through cracks in the slatted blinds, you hear water running gently over the weir, and the heavy turning of the mill wheel, and you wish for nothing more but eternal peace. Everything Marie meant to me from then on, said Austerlitz, was summed up in this tale of the paper-mill in which, without speaking of herself, she revealed her inner being to me. In the weeks and months that followed, Austerlitz continued, we often strolled together in the Jardin du Luxembourg, the Tuileries and the Jardin des Plantes, walking up and down the esplanade between the well-pruned plane trees with the west front of the Natural History Museum now on our right and now on our left, going into the palm house and coming out of it again, tracing the convoluted paths of the Alpine garden, or traversing the dreary terrain of the old zoo where large animals from the African colonies had once been put on display, said Austerlitz, elephants, giraffes, rhinoceroses, dromedaries and crocodiles, although most of the enclosures, decked out with pitiful remnants of natural objects – tree stumps, artificial rocks and pools of water – were now empty and deserted. On these walks it was not unusual for us to hear one of the children whose adult companions still took them to the zoo calling out, in some exasperation: *Mais il est où? Pourquoi il se cache? Pourquoi il ne bouge pas? Est-ce qu'il est mort?* I recollect that I myself saw a family of fallow deer gathered together by a manger of hay near the perimeter fence of a dusty enclosure where no grass grew, a living picture of mutual trust and harmony which also had about it an air of constant vigilance and alarm. Marie particularly asked me to take a photograph of this beautiful group, and as she did so, said Austerlitz, she said something which I have never forgotten, she said that captive animals and we ourselves, their human counterparts, view one another *à travers une*

*brèche d'incompréhension.* Marie spent every second
or third weekend, continued Austerlitz, his narra-
tive taking another direction, with her parents or
wider family, who owned several estates in the
wooded country around Compiègne or further
north in Picardy. At those times when she was
not in Paris, which always cast me into an anxious
mood, I regularly set off to explore the out-
lying districts of the city, taking the Métro out
to Montreuil, Malakoff, Charenton, Bobigny,
Bagnolet, Le Pré St Germain, St Denis, St Mandé

or elsewhere, to walk through the empty Sunday streets taking hundreds of *banlieu*-photographs, as I called them, pictures which in their very emptiness, as I realized only later, reflected my orphaned frame of mind. It was on such a suburban expedition, one unusually oppressive Sunday in September when grey storm-clouds were rolling over the sky from the south-west, that I went out to Maisons-Alfort and there discovered the museum of veterinary medicine, of which I had never heard before, in the extensive grounds of the Ecole Vétérinaire, itself founded two hundred years ago. An old Moroccan sat at the entrance, wearing a kind of burnous, with a fez on his head. I still have the twenty-franc ticket he sold me in my wallet, said Austerlitz, and taking it out he handed it to me over the table of the bistro where we were

sitting as if there were something very special about it. Inside the museum, Austerlitz continued, I did not meet another living soul, either in the well-proportioned stairway or in the three exhibition rooms on the first floor. All the more uncanny in the ambient silence, which was merely emphasized by the creaking of the floorboards beneath my feet, seemed the exhibits assembled in the glass-fronted cases reaching almost to the ceiling, and dating without exception from the end of the eighteenth or the beginning of the nineteenth century. There were plaster casts of the jaws of many different kinds of ruminants and rodents; kidney stones which had been found in circus camels, as large and spherically perfect as skittle-balls; the cross-section of a piglet only a few hours old, its organs rendered transparent by a process of chemical diaphanization and now floating in the liquid around it like a deep-sea fish which would never see the light of day; the pale-blue foetus of a foal, where the quicksilver injected as a contrast medium into the network of veins beneath its thin skin had formed patterns like frost flowers as it leeched out; the skulls and skeletons of many different creatures; whole digestive systems in formaldehyde; pathologically malformed organs, shrunken hearts and bloated livers; trees of bronchial tubes, some of them three feet high, their petrified and rust-coloured branches looking

like coral growths; and in the teratological depart-
ment there were monstrosities of every imaginable
and unimaginable kind, Janus-faced and two-
headed calves, Cyclopean beasts with outsized
foreheads, a human infant born in Maisons-Alfort
on the day when the Emperor was exiled to the
island of St Helena, its legs fused together so that
it resembled a mermaid, a ten-legged sheep, and
truly horrific creatures consisting of little more
than a scrap of skin, a crooked wing and half a claw.
Far the most awesome of all, however, so said
Austerlitz, was the exhibit in a glass case at the back
of the last cabinet of the museum, the life-sized
figure of a horseman, very skilfully flayed in the
post-Revolutionary period by the anatomist and
dissector Honoré Fragonard, who was then at the
height of his fame, so that every strand in the
tensed muscles of the rider and his mount, which
was racing forward with a panic-stricken expres-
sion, was clearly visible in the colours of congealed
blood, together with the blue of the veins and
the ochre yellow of the sinews and ligaments.
Fragonard, who was descended from the famous
family of Provençal perfumiers, said Austerlitz,
had apparently dissected over three thousand

bodies and parts of bodies in the course of his career, and consequently he, an agnostic who did not believe in the immortality of the soul, must have spent all the hours of his days and nights intent upon death, surrounded by the sweet smell of decay, and, as I imagine, moved by a desire to secure for the frail body at least some semblance of eternal life through a process of vitrification, by translating its so readily corruptible substance into a miracle of pure glass. In the weeks following my visit to the museum of veterinary science, Austerlitz continued his story, gazing now at the boulevard outside, I was unable to recall any of what I have just told you, for it was in the Métro on my way back from Maisons-Alfort that I had the first of the several fainting fits I was to suffer, causing temporary but complete loss of memory, a condition described in psychiatric textbooks, as far as I am aware, Austerlitz added, as hysterical epilepsy. Only when I developed the photographs I had taken that Sunday in September at Maisons-Alfort was I able, with their aid and guided by Marie's patient questioning, to reconstruct my buried experiences. Then I remembered the courtyards of the veterinary school lying white in the afternoon heat as I left the museum, I recollected that as I walked along beside the wall I felt that I had reached steep and impassable terrain, and that I had wanted to sit down but none the less walked on, into the bright rays of the sun, until I came to the Métro station where I had to wait endlessly, as it seemed to me, in the brooding darkness of the tunnel for the next train to come in. The carriage in which I travelled towards the Bastille, said Austerlitz, was not very full. Later I remembered a gypsy playing the accordion, and a very dark Indo-Chinese woman with an alarmingly thin face and eyes sunk deep in their sockets. Of the few other passengers, I could recollect only that they were all looking out of the side windows of the train into the darkness, where there was nothing to be seen but a pallid reflection of the carriage where they sat. Gradually I also came to remember suddenly feeling unwell during the journey, with a phantom pain spreading through my chest, and thinking I was about to die of the weak heart I have inherited, from whom I do not know. I did not return to my senses until I was in the Salpêtrière, to which I had been taken and where I was now lying in one of the men's wards, containing perhaps forty patients or more, somewhere in that gigantic complex of buildings where the borders between hospital and penitentiary have always been blurred, and which seems to have grown and spread of its own volition over the centuries until it now forms a universe of its own between the Jardin des Plantes and the Gare d'Austerlitz. I lay there in my semi-conscious condition for several days, and in that state I saw myself wandering around a maze of long passages, vaults, galleries and grottoes where the names of various Métro stations – Campo Formio, Crimée, Elysée, Iéna, Invalides, Oberkampf, Simplon, Solferino, Stalingrad – and certain discolorations and shadings in the air seemed to indicate that this was a place of exile for those who had fallen on the field of honour, or lost their lives in some other violent way. I saw armies of these unredeemed souls thronging over bridges to the opposite bank, or coming towards me down the tunnels, their eyes fixed, cold and dead. Sometimes they manifested themselves in one of the dark catacombs where, covered in frayed and dusty plumage, they were crouching on the stony floor and, turning silently towards one another, made digging motions with their earth-stained hands. And when at last I began to improve, said Austerlitz, I also recollected how once, while my mind was still quite submerged, I had seen myself standing, filled with a painful sense that something within me was trying to surface from oblivion, in front of a poster painted in bold brushstrokes which was pasted to the tunnel wall and showed a happy family on a winter holiday in Chamonix. The peaks of the mountains towered snow white in the background, with a wonderful blue sky above them, the straight upper edge of which did not entirely hide a yellowed notice issued by the Paris city council in July 1943. Who knows, said Austerlitz, what would have become of me there in the Salpêtrière – when I could remember nothing about myself, or my own previous history, or anything else whatsoever, and as I was told later I kept babbling disconnectedly in various languages – who knows what would have become of me had it not been for one of the nursing staff, a man with fiery red hair and flickering eyes called Quentin Quignard, who looked in my notebook and under the barely legible initials M. de V. found the address 7, place des Vosges, written by Marie in a blank space among my notes after our first conversation at the café in the arcades of the Palais Royal? When they had fetched her, said Austerlitz, she sat beside my bed for hours and days on end, talking calmly to me, whilst at first I remained quite unaware of who she was, even though I felt a deep longing for her, particularly when I sank into the weariness that weighed so heavily on me and tried, in a last stirring of consciousness, to bring my hand out from under the blankets, as a sign of both farewell and the hope that she would soon return. On one of her regular visits to my sickbed in the Salpêtrière, Marie brought me a book from her grandfather's library, published in Dijon in 1755, a little medical work *pour toutes sortes de maladies, internes et externes, invétérées et difficiles à guérir*, as the title page said, a beautiful specimen of the art of printing, in the preface to which the printer himself, one Jean Ressayre, reminds the pious and charitable ladies of the upper classes that they had been chosen as instruments of divine mercy by the highest authority governing our fate, and that if they turned their hearts to the abandoned and afflicted in their misery, it would draw upon themselves and their families the heavenly rewards of grace, prosperity and happiness. I read every line of this delightful foreword several times, said Austerlitz, and studied the prescriptions for making aromatic oils, powders, essences and infusions to soothe over-wrought nerves, cleanse the blood of secretions of black bile and dispel melancholy by means of such ingredients as pale and dark rose-leaves, March violets, peach blossom, saffron, melissa and eye-bright, and indeed by immersing myself in the better world of this little book, whole passages of which I still know by heart, said Austerlitz, I regained my lost sense of myself and my memory, gradually mastering the crippling physical weak-ness which had overcome me after my visit to the veterinary museum, so that I could soon walk on Marie's arm down the long corridors of the Salpêtrière, through the diffuse, dusty grey light which pervades everything in that institution. After I had been discharged from the fortress-like hospital, which covers a site of thirty hectares and, with its four thousand patients, represents at any given time almost the entire range of disorders from which humanity can suffer, so Austerlitz con-tinued, we resumed our walks in the city. Among the images I have retained in my memory from these excursions is one of a little girl with a rebellious mop of hair and green eyes the colour of iced water who stumbled over the hem of her raincoat, which was much too long for her, as she was playing with her skipping rope in one of the lime-white squares in the Luxembourg gardens and grazed her right knee, a scene regarded by Marie as a *déjà vu* because, she said, over twenty years ago just the same accident had happened to her at exactly the same place, an incident which at the time seemed to her shameful and aroused in her the first premonitions of death. Not long afterwards, one Saturday afternoon when a cold mist hung low in the air, we wandered through the half-deserted area between the tracks of the Gare d'Austerlitz and the Quai d'Austerlitz on the left bank of the Seine, slowly finding our way among abandoned dockyards, boarded-up warehouses, goods depots, customs halls and a few garages and car-repair shops. In one of the empty spaces not far from the station itself, the Bastiani Travelling Circus had erected its small tent, much mended and wreathed in strings of orange electric lights. By tacit agreement, we entered just as the performance was coming to a close. A few dozen women and children were seated on low stools round the ring – not that it was really a ring, said Austerlitz, rather it was a vague sort of rondelle on which a few shovelfuls of sawdust had been thrown, so hemmed in by the front row of spectators that even a pony could hardly have trotted round it in a circle. We were just in time for the last number, featuring a conjuror in a dark-blue cloak who produced from his top hat a bantam cockerel with wonderfully coloured plumage, not much bigger than a magpie or a raven. This brightly hued bird, obviously completely tame, went over a kind of miniature show-jumping course consisting of all manner of little steps, ladders and other obstacles which he had to negotiate, gave the right answer to sums such as two times three or four minus one by clattering his beak when the conjurer showed him cards with the figures written on them, at a whispered command lay down on the ground to fall asleep, resting in a curious position on his side with his wings outspread, and finally disappeared into the top hat again. After the conjuror's exit the lights slowly dimmed, and when our eyes were used to the darkness we saw a quantity of stars traced in luminous paint inside the top of the tent, giving the impression that we were really out of doors.

We were still looking up with a certain sense of awe at this artificial firmament which, as I recollect, said Austerlitz, was almost close enough for us to touch its lower rim, when the whole circus troupe came in one by one, the conjuror and his wife, who was very beautiful, with their equally beautiful, black-haired children, the last of them carrying a lantern and accompanied by a snow-white goose. Each of these artistes had a musical instrument. If I remember correctly, said Auster-litz, they played a transverse flute, a rather battered tuba, a drum, a bandoneon and a fiddle, and they all wore Oriental clothing with long, fur-edged cloaks, while the men had pale-green turbans on their heads. At a signal between themselves they began playing in a restrained yet penetrating manner which, although or perhaps because I have been left almost untouched by any kind of music all my life, affected me profoundly from the very first bar. I cannot say what it was that the five circus performers played that Saturday afternoon in the circus tent beyond the Gare d'Austerlitz for their tiny audience, drawn from heaven knows where, said Austerlitz, but it seemed to me, he added, as if the music came from somewhere very distant, from the East, I thought, from the Caucasus or Turkey. Nor can I say what was suggested to my mind by the sounds produced by the players, none of whom, I am sure, could read musical notation. Sometimes I seemed to hear a long-forgotten Welsh hymn in their melodies, or then again, very softly yet making the senses swirl, the revolutions of a waltz, a ländler theme, or the slow sound of a funeral march, which put me in mind of the curiously halting progress of a uniformed guard of honour escorting a body to its last resting place, and of how, in their ceremonious manner, they pause every time before taking the next step, with one foot suspended an inch above the ground for the briefest of moments. I still do not understand, said Austerlitz, what was happening within me as I listened to this extraordinarily foreign nocturnal music conjured out of thin air, so to speak, by the circus performers with their slightly out-of-tune instruments, nor could I have said at the time whether my heart was contracting in pain or expanding with happiness for the first time in my life. Why certain tonal colours, subtleties of key and syncopations can take such a hold on the mind is something that an entirely

unmusical person like myself can never under-
stand, said Austerlitz, but today, looking back, it
seems to me as if the mystery which touched me at
the time was summed up in the image of the snow-
white goose standing motionless and steadfast
among the musicians as long as they played. Neck
craning forward slightly, pale eyelids slightly
lowered, it listened there in the tent beneath
that shimmering firmament of painted stars
until the last notes had died away, as if it knew its
own future and the fate of its present companions.
— As I might perhaps be aware, said Austerlitz,
taking up his tale again at our next meeting at

the Brasserie Le Havane, the new Bibliothèque Nationale bearing the name of the French President now stands on what over the years had become the increasingly dilapidated area on the left bank of the Seine, where he and Marie de Verneuil had once attended that unforgettable circus performance. The old library in the rue Richelieu has been closed, as I saw for myself not long ago, said Austerlitz, the domed hall with its green porcelain lampshades which cast such a soothing, pleasant light is deserted, the books have been taken off the shelves, and the readers, who once sat at the desks numbered with little enamel plates, in close contact with their neighbours and silent harmony with those who had gone before them, might have vanished from the face of the earth. I do not think, said Austerlitz, that many of the old readers go out to the new library on the Quai François Mauriac. In order to reach the Grande Bibliothèque you have to travel through a desolate no-man's-land in one of those robot-driven Métro trains steered by a ghostly voice, or alternatively you have to catch a bus in the Place Valhubert and then walk along the windswept river bank towards the hideous, outsize building, the monumental dimensions of which were evidently inspired by the late President's wish to perpetuate his memory whilst, perhaps because it had to serve this purpose, it was so conceived that it is, as I realized on my first visit, said Austerlitz, both in its outer appearance and inner constitution unwelcoming if not inimical to human beings, and runs counter, on principle, one might say, to the requirements of any true reader. If you approach the new Bibliothèque Nationale from the Place Valhubert you find yourself at the foot of a flight of steps which, made out of countless grooved hardwood boards and measuring three hundred by a hundred and fifty metres, surrounds the entire complex on the two sides facing the street like the lower storey of a ziggurat. Once you have climbed the steps, at least four dozen in number and as closely set as they are steep, a venture not entirely without its dangers even for younger visitors, said Austerlitz, you are standing on an esplanade which positively overwhelms the eye, built of the same grooved wood as the steps, and extending over an area about the size of nine football pitches between the four corner towers of the library which thrust their way twenty-two floors up into the air. You might think, especially on days when the wind drives rain over this totally exposed platform, as it quite often does, said Austerlitz, that by some mistake you had found your way to the deck of the *Berengaria* or one of the other ocean-going giants, and you would be not in the least surprised if, to the sound of a wailing foghorn, the horizon of the city of Paris suddenly began rising and falling against the gauge of the towers as the great steamer pounded onwards through mountainous waves, or if one of the tiny figures, having unwisely ventured on deck, were swept over the rail by a gust of wind and carried far out into the

wastes of the Atlantic waters. The four glazed towers themselves, named in a manner reminiscent of a futuristic novel *La tour des lois*, *La tour des temps*, *La tour des nombres* and *La tour des lettres*, make a positively Babylonian impression on anyone who looks up at their façades and wonders about the still largely empty space behind their closed blinds. When I first stood on the promenade deck of the new Bibliothèque Nationale, said Austerlitz, it took me a little while to find the place where the visitor is carried down on a conveyor belt to what appears to be a basement storey but, in reality, is the ground floor. This downwards journey, when you have just laboriously ascended to the plateau, struck me as an utter absurdity, something that must have been devised – I can think of no other explanation, said Austerlitz – on purpose to instil a sense of insecurity and humiliation in the poor readers, especially as it ends in front of a sliding door of makeshift appearance which had a chain across it on the day of my first visit, and where you have to let yourself be searched by semi-uniformed security men. The floor of the large hall which you then enter is laid with rust-red carpet, on which a few low seats are placed far apart, backless

upholstered benches and small chairs like folding
stools where visitors to the library can perch only
in such a way that their knees are almost level with
their heads, so that my first thought at the sight of
them, said Austerlitz, was that the people whom
I saw crouching so close to the ground, some by
themselves and some in small groups, were mem-
bers of a wandering tribe encamped here on their
way through the Sahara or the Sinai desert in the
last glow of the setting sun, in order to await the
coming of darkness. And of course, Austerlitz
continued, you cannot leave the red Sinai hall for
the inner citadel of the library without more ado;
first you have to put your request at an information
point staffed by half a dozen ladies, whereupon, if
this request to any degree exceeds the very
simplest contingency, you take a number, like a
visitor to a tax office; you then have to wait, often
for half an hour or more, until another member of
staff calls you into a separate cubicle, as if you were
on business of an extremely dubious nature, or at
least had to be dealt with away from the public
gaze, and here you must say again what it is you
have come for and receive the relevant instruc-
tions. Despite such measures of control I finally

succeeded, said Austerlitz, in gaining admission to the newly opened *Haut-de-jardin* public reading-room, where I subsequently sat for many hours and days on end, looking out abstractedly, as my habit now is, at the inner courtyard and the curious nature reserve cut, so to speak, from the surface of the promenade deck and sunk two or three storeys deep, which has been planted with about a hundred full-grown stone pines from the Forêt de Bord transported, how I do not know, to this place of banishment. If one looks down from the deck at the spreading grey-green crowns of the trees, some of which perhaps are still thinking of their home in Normandy, it is like looking across an uneven expanse of moorland, while from the reading-room you can see only the blotched red trunks which, although fixed in place with steel hawsers rising at an oblique angle, sway slightly back and forth on stormy days like water-weed in an aquarium. In the daydreams into which I fell in the reading-room, said Austerlitz, I sometimes felt as if I saw circus acrobats climbing the cables slanting up from the ground to the evergreen canopy, placing one foot in front of the other as they made their way upwards with the ends of their balancing poles quivering, or as if, always on the edge of invisibility, I saw dodging now here, now there, those two mythical squirrels said to have been brought to the library in the hope that they will increase and multiply, founding a large colony of their species in this artificial pine grove to entertain any readers who look up from their books now and then. And several times, said Austerlitz, birds which had lost their way in the library forest flew into the mirror images of the trees in the reading-room windows, struck the glass with a dull thud, and fell lifeless to the ground. Sitting at my place in the reading-room, said Austerlitz, I thought at length about the way in which such unforeseen accidents, the fall of a single creature to its death when diverted from its natural path, or the recurrent symptoms of paralysis affecting the electronic data retrieval system, relate to the Cartesian overall plan of the Bibliothèque Nationale, and I came to the conclusion that in any project we design and develop, the size and degree of complexity of the information and control systems inscribed in it are the crucial factors, so that the all-embracing and absolute perfection of the concept can in practice coincide, indeed ultimately must coincide, with its chronic dysfunction and constitutional instability. At any rate, as far as I myself was concerned, a man who, after all, had devoted almost the whole of his life to the study of books and who had been equally at home in the Bodleian, the British Museum and the rue Richelieu, I for my part, said Austerlitz, found that this gigantic new library, which according to one of the loathsome phrases now current is supposed to serve as the treasure-house of our entire literary heritage, proved useless in my search for any traces of my father who had disappeared from Paris more than fifty years ago. Confronted day after day by a system which appeared to consist entirely of obstructions and was placing an increasing strain on my nerves, I set aside my researches for a while and one morning, when for some reason or other the fifty-five carmine-red volumes in Věra's bookcase came into my mind, I instead began reading the novels of Balzac, hitherto unknown to me, starting with the story of Colonel Chabert, a man whose glorious career in the service of the Emperor ends abruptly on the battlefield of Eylau, when he receives a sabre blow and sinks unconscious to the ground. Years later, after long wanderings across Germany, the colonel, risen from the dead, so to speak, returns to Paris to claim his rights to his estates, to his wife the Comtesse Ferraud who has now remarried, and to his own name. He is presented as a ghostly figure, said Austerlitz, standing in the lawyer Derville's office, a gaunt and desiccated old soldier, as we are told at this point. His eyes appear half-blind, veiled as they are by a mother-of-pearl gleam, flickering unsteadily like candle flames. His face is pale, its lines sharp as a knife edge. Around his neck he wears a shabby cravat of black silk. *Je suis le Colonel Chabert, celui qui est mort à Eylau* are the words with which he introduces himself, and then he tells the tale of the mass grave (a *fosse des morts*, as Balzac describes it, said Austerlitz), into which he was thrown the day after the battle along with the rest of the fallen, and where he finally came to himself, as he says, in excruciating pain. *J'entendis, ou crus entendre*, Austerlitz quoted from memory, looking out of the brasserie window at the boulevard August Blanqui, *des gémissements poussés par le monde des cadavres au milieu duquel je gisais. Et quoique la mémoire de ces moments soit bien ténébreuse, quoique mes souvenirs soient bien confus, malgré les impressions de souffrances encore plus profondes que je devais éprouver et qui ont brouillé mes idées, il y a des nuits où je crois encore entendre ces soupirs étouffés.* Only a few days after reading this book, the more melodramatic aspects of which, Austerlitz continued, reinforced the suspicion I had always entertained that the border between life and death is less impermeable than we commonly think, I was in the reading-room again and, on opening an American architectural journal – this was at exactly six in the evening – I came upon a large-format photograph showing the room filled with open shelves up to the ceiling where the files on the prisoners in the little fortress of Terezín, as it is called, are kept today. I remembered, said Austerlitz, that at the time of my first visit to the Bohemian ghetto I could not bring myself to enter the outworks on the glacis to the south of the star-shaped town, and perhaps that was why, at the sight of the records room, a kind of *idée fixe* forced itself upon me that, all along, my true place of work should have been there in the little fortress of Terezín, where so many had perished in the cold, damp casemates, and it was my own fault that I had not taken it up.

As I was tormenting myself with such thoughts, distinctly aware, so Austerlitz continued, that my face was being marked by the signs of that anguish which so often assails me, I was approached by one of the library staff called Henri Lemoine, who had recognized me from those early years of mine in Paris when I went daily to the rue Richelieu. Jacques Austerlitz, inquired Lemoine, stopping by my desk and leaning slightly down to me, and so, said Austerlitz, we began a long, whispered conversation in the *Haut-de-jardin* reading-room, which was gradually emptying now, about the dissolution, in line with the inexorable spread of processed data, of our capacity to remember, and about the collapse, *l'effondrement*, as Lemoine put it, of the Bibliothèque Nationale which is already underway. The new library building, which in both its entire layout and its near-ludicrous internal regulation seeks to exclude the reader as a potential enemy, might be described, so Lemoine thought, said Austerlitz, as the official manifestation of the increasingly importunate urge to break with everything which still has some living connection to the past. At a certain point in our conversation, said Austerlitz, and in response to a casual request of mine, Lemoine took me up to the eighteenth floor of the south-east tower, where one can look down from the so-called belvedere at the entire urban agglomeration which has risen over the millennia from the land beneath its foundations, which is now entirely hollowed out: a pale limestone range, a kind of excrescence extending the concentric spread of its incrustations far beyond the boulevards Davout, Soult, Poniatowski, Masséna and Kellermann, and on into the outermost periphery beyond the suburbs, which now lay in the haze of twilight. A few miles to the south-east there was a faint green mark in the even grey, with a kind of blunt cone rising from it which Lemoine identified as the monkeys' hill in the Bois de Vincennes. Closer to hand, we saw the convoluted traffic routes on which trains and cars crawled back and forth like black beetles and caterpillars. It was strange, said Lemoine, but up here he always had the impression that life moved silently and slowly down below, that the body of the city had been infected by an obscure disease spreading underground, and I remembered, said Austerlitz, when Lemoine made this remark, the winter months of the year 1959 during which I was studying the six-volume work pointing me the way in my own research, on *Paris, ses organes, ses fonctions et sa vie dans la seconde moitié du XIXème siècle*, which Maxime du Camp, who had previously travelled the deserts of the Orient that are formed, as he said, from the dust of the dead, began to write around 1890, after he was inspired by an overwhelming vision on the Pont Neuf, and which he finished only seven years later. From the other side of the belvedere storey, said Austerlitz, you looked north over the transverse ribbon of the Seine, the Marais quarter and the Bastille. An inky wall of storm-clouds was building up above the city as it sank into shadow, and soon no more could be distinguished of its towers, palaces and monuments than the spectral white dome of the Sacré-Coeur. We were standing only a foot behind the glass panels which reach all the way to the ground. As soon as you looked down at the light-coloured promenade deck and the darker crowns of the trees emerging from it, the pull exerted by the abyss below took hold of you, forcing you to step back. Sometimes, so Lemoine told me, said Austerlitz, he felt the current of time streaming round his temples and brow when he was up here, but per-

haps, he added, that is only a reflex of the aware-
ness formed in my mind over the years of the vari-
ous layers which have been superimposed on each
other to form the carapace of the city. Thus, on the
waste land between the marshalling yard of the
Gare d'Austerlitz and the Pont Tolbiac where this
Babylonian library now rises, there stood until the
end of the war an extensive warehousing complex
to which the Germans brought all the loot they had
taken from the homes of the Jews of Paris. I believe
they cleared some forty thousand apartments at
that time, said Lemoine, in an operation lasting
months, for which purpose they requisitioned the
entire pantechnicon fleet of the Paris Union of
Furniture Removers, and an army of no fewer than
fifteen hundred removal men was brought into
action. All who had taken part in any way in this
highly organized programme of expropriation and
reutilization, said Lemoine, the people in charge of
it, the sometimes rival staffs of the occupying
power and the financial and fiscal authorities, the
residents' and property registries, the banks and
insurance agencies, the police, the transport firms,
the landlords and caretakers of the apartment
buildings, must undoubtedly have known that

scarcely any of those interned in Drancy would ever come back. For the most part the valuables, bank deposits, the shares and the houses and business premises ruthlessly seized at the time, said Lemoine, remain in the hands of the city and the state to this day. In the years from 1942 onwards everything our civilization has produced, whether for the embellishment of life or merely for everyday use, from Louis XVI chests of drawers, Meissen porcelain, Persian rugs and whole libraries, down to the last salt-cellar and pepper-mill, was stacked there in the Austerlitz-Tolbiac storage depot. A man who had worked in it told me not long ago, said Lemoine, that there were even special cardboard cartons set aside to hold the rosin removed, for the sake of greater cleanliness, from confiscated violin cases. Over five hundred art historians, antique dealers, restorers, joiners, clockmakers, furriers and couturiers brought in from Drancy and guarded by a contingent of Indo-Chinese soldiers were employed day after day, in fourteen-hours shifts, to put the goods coming into the depot in proper order and sort them by value and kind – silver cutlery with silver cutlery, cooking pans with cooking pans, toys with toys, and so forth. More than seven hundred train-loads left from here for the ruined cities of the Reich. Not infrequently, said Lemoine, Party grandees on visits from Germany and high-ranking SS and Wehrmacht officers stationed in Paris would walk around the halls of the depot, known to the prisoners as Les Galéries d'Austerlitz, with their wives or other ladies, choosing drawing-room furniture for a Grunewald villa, or a Sèvres dinner service, a fur coat or a Pleyel piano. The most valuable items, of course, were not sent off wholesale to the bombed cities, and no one will now admit to knowing where they went, for the fact is that the whole affair is buried in the most literal sense beneath the foundations of our pharaonic President's Grande Bibliothèque, said Lemoine. The last of the light faded away down on the empty promenades. The tree-tops of the pine grove, which from this high vantage point had resembled moss-covered ground, now formed a regular black rectangle. For a while, said Austerlitz, we stood together in silence on the library belvedere, looking out over the city where it lay now sparkling in the light of its lamps.

*

When I met Austerlitz again for morning coffee on the boulevard Auguste Blanqui, shortly before I left Paris, he told me that the previous day he had heard, from one of the staff at the records centre in the rue Geoffroy-l'Asnier, that Maximilian Aychenwald had been interned during the latter part of 1942 in the camp at Gurs, a place in the Pyrenean foothills which he, Austerlitz, must now seek out. Curiously enough, said Austerlitz, a few hours after our last meeting, when he had come back from the Bibliothèque Nationale and changed

trains at the Gare d'Austerlitz, he had felt a
premonition that he was coming closer to his
father. As I might know, he said, part of the rail-
way network had been paralysed by a strike last
Wednesday, and in the unusual silence which,
as a consequence, had descended on the Gare
d'Austerlitz, an idea came to him of his father's
leaving Paris from this station, close as it was to
his flat in the rue Barrault, soon after the Germans
entered the city. I imagined, said Austerlitz, that
I saw him leaning out of the window of his

compartment as the train left, and I saw the white clouds of smoke rising from the locomotive as it began to move ponderously away. After that I wandered round the deserted station half dazed, through the labyrinthine underpasses, over foot-bridges, up flights of steps on one side and down on the other. That station, said Austerlitz, has always seemed to me the most mysterious of all the railway terminals of Paris. I spent many hours in it during my student days, and even wrote a kind of memorandum on its layout and history. At the time I was particularly fascinated by the way the Métro trains coming from the Bastille, having crossed the Seine, roll over the iron viaduct into the station's upper storey, quite as if the façade were swallowing them up. And I also remember that I felt an uneasiness induced by the hall behind this façade, filled with a feeble light and almost entirely empty, where, on a platform roughly assembled out of beams and boards, there stood a scaffolding reminiscent of a gallows with all kinds of rusty iron hooks, which I was told later was used as a bicycle store. When I first set foot on this platform years ago, on a Sunday afternoon in the middle of the vacation period, however, there was

not a bicycle to be seen, and perhaps for that rea-
son, or perhaps because of the plucked pigeon
feathers lying all over the floorboards, an impres-
sion forced itself upon me of being on the scene
of some unexpiated crime. What is more, said
Austerlitz, that sinister wooden structure still
exists. Even the grey pigeon feathers have not yet
blown away. And there are dark patches, of leaked
axle grease, perhaps, or carbolineum, or some-
thing altogether different, one can't tell. More-
over, I was disturbed by the fact that, as I stood on
the scaffolding that Sunday afternoon looking up
through the dim light at the ornate ironwork of
the north façade, two tiny figures which I had
noticed only after some time were moving about

on ropes, carrying out repair work, like black spiders in their web. — I don't know, said Austerlitz, what all this means, and so I am going to continue looking for my father, and for Marie de Verneuil as well. It was nearly twelve o'clock when we took leave of each other outside the Glacière Métro station. Years ago, Austerlitz said as we parted, there were great swamps here where people skated in winter, just as they did outside Bishopsgate in London, and then he gave me the key to his house in Alderney Street. I could stay there whenever I liked, he said, and study the black and white photographs which, one day, would be all that was left of his life. And I should not omit, he added, to ring the bell at the gateway in the brick wall adjoining his house, for behind that wall, although he had never been able to see it from any of his windows, there was a plot where lime trees and lilacs grew and in which members of the Ashkenazi community had been buried ever since the eighteenth century, including Rabbi David Tevele Schiff and Rabbi Samuel Falk, the Baal Shem of London. He had discovered the cemetery, from which, as he now suspected, the moths used to fly into his house, said Austerlitz,

only a few days before he left London, when the
gate in the wall stood open for the first time in all
the years he had lived in Alderney Street. Inside, a
very small, almost dwarf-like woman of perhaps
seventy years old – the cemetery caretaker, as it
turned out – was walking along the paths between
the graves in her slippers. Beside her, almost as

tall as she was, walked a Belgian sheepdog now
grey with age who answered to the name of Billie
and was very timid. In the bright spring light shin-
ing through the newly opened leaves of the lime
trees you might have thought, Austerlitz told me,
that you had entered a fairy tale which, like life
itself, had grown older with the passing of time. I
for my part could not get the story of the ceme-
tery in Alderney Street with which Austerlitz had

taken his leave of me out of my head, and that may
have been why I stopped in Antwerp on my way
back from Paris, to see the Nocturama again
and go out to Breendonk once more. I spent
a disturbed night in a hotel on the Astridsplein, in
an ugly room with brown wallpaper looking out
on fire-walls, ventilation chimneys and flat roofs
separated from each other by barbed wire at the

back of the building. I think there was some kind
of popular festival going on in the city at the time;
in any case, the wailing of ambulance and police
sirens went on until early in the morning. When
at last I woke from a bad dream I saw the tiny
silver arrows of aeroplanes passing at intervals of
ten or twelve minutes through the bright-blue
space above the neighbouring houses, which still
lay in twilight. On leaving the Flamingo Hotel –

such was its name, if I remember correctly – at about eight o'clock, I saw a pale-faced woman of about forty with her eyes turned away lying on a high trolley down by the reception desk, where there was no one in evidence. Two ambulance men were talking out on the pavement. I crossed the Astridsplein to the station, bought myself a coffee, and took the next suburban train to Mechelen, then walking the ten remaining kilometres to Willebroek through the suburbs and the now built-up outskirts of the town. I retained hardly anything of what I saw on my way. All I remember is a peculiarly narrow house, in fact no more than one room wide, built of puce-coloured brick and standing in an equally narrow strip of garden surrounded by a tall thuya hedge. A canal ran beside this house, and a long barge laden with cabbages as big and round as cannonballs was gliding along it just as I passed, apparently without any boatman to steer it and leaving not a trace on the black surface of the water. It had turned unusually hot, just as it was thirty years ago, by the time I reached Willebroek. The fortifications lay unchanged on the blue-green island, but the number of visitors had increased. There were several coaches in the car park, while inside the porter's lodge a troop of schoolchildren in brightly coloured clothes was crowding around the cash desk and the small kiosk. Some of them had already gone ahead of the rest over the bridge to the dark gate through which, yet again, I could not bring myself to pass even after long hesitation. I spent some time in one of the hut-like wooden buildings where the SS had set up a printing shop for the manufacture of various official forms and greetings cards. The roof and the walls creaked in the heat, and the thought passed through my mind that the hair on my head might catch fire, as St Julian's did on his way through the desert. Later I sat beside the moat surrounding the fortress. In the distance, beyond the penal colony, the fence and the watch towers, I saw the high-rise blocks of Mechelen encroaching further and further on the fields and the countryside. A grey goose was swimming on the dark water, going a little way in one direction and then a little way back in the other. After a while it scrambled up on the bank and settled on the grass not far from me. I took the book Austerlitz had given me on our first meeting in Paris out of my rucksack. It was by Dan Jacobson (a colleague of his, although unknown to him all these years, Austerlitz had said), and it described the author's search for his grandfather Rabbi Yisrael Yehoshua Melamed, known as Heshel. All that had come down from Heshel to his grandson was a pocket calendar, his Russian identity papers, a worn spectacle case containing not only his glasses but a faded and already disintegrating piece of silk, and a studio photograph of Heshel in a black coat with a black velour top hat on his head. His one eye, or so at least it looks on the cover of the book, is shaded; in the other it is just possible to make out a white fleck, the light of life extinguished when Heshel died of a heart attack at the age of fifty-three soon after the First World War. It was this premature death which made Menuchah, the rabbi's wife, decide in 1920 to emigrate with her nine children from Lithuania to South Africa, and that was also the reason why Jacobson himself spent most of his childhood in the town of Kimberley, near the diamond mines of the same name. Most of the mines, so I read as I sat there opposite the fortifications of Breendonk, were already disused at the time, including the two largest, the Kimberley and De Beers mines, and since they were not fenced off anyone who liked could venture to the edge of those vast pits and look down to a depth of several thousand feet. Jacobson writes that it was truly terrifying to see such emptiness open up a foot away from firm ground, to realize that there was no transition, only this dividing line, with ordinary life on one side and its unimaginable opposite on the other. The chasm into which no ray of light could penetrate was Jacobson's image of the vanished past of his family and his people which, as he knows, can never be brought up from those depths again. On his travels in Lithuania Jacobson finds scarcely any trace of his forebears, only signs everywhere of the annihilation from which Heshel's weak heart had preserved his immediate family when it stopped beating. Of the town of Kaunas, where Heshel had his photograph taken all those years ago, Jacobson tells us that the Russians built a ring of twelve fortresses around it in the late nineteenth century, which then in 1914, despite the elevated positions on which they had been constructed, and for all the great number of their cannon, the thickness of their walls and their labyrinthine corridors, proved entirely useless.

Some of the forts, writes Jacobson, fell into disrepair later, others served the Lithuanians and then the Russians once more as prisons. In 1941 they fell into German hands, including the notorious Fort IX where Wehrmacht command posts were set up and where more than thirty thousand people were killed over the next three years. Their remains, says Jacobson, lie under a field of oats a hundred metres outside the walls. Transports from the west kept coming to Kaunas until May 1944, when the war had long since been lost, as the last messages from those locked in the dungeons of the fortress bear witness. One of them, writes Jacobson, scratched the words *Nous sommes neuf cents Français* on the cold limestone wall of the bunker. Others left only a date and place of origin with their names: Lob, Marcel, de St. Nazaire; Wechsler, Abram, de Limoges; Max Stern, Paris, 18.5.44. Sitting by the moat of the fortress of Breendonk, I read to the end of the fifteenth chapter of *Heshel's Kingdom*, and then set out on my way back to Mechelen, reaching the town as evening began to fall.

# W. G. SEBALD

## ACROSS THE LAND AND THE WATER: SELECTED POEMS 1964-2001

When W. G. Sebald died in 2001, he was internationally acknowledged as one of the most important German writers of our era. Now, thanks to Iain Galbraith's vibrant translations, the full breadth of his poetry is available in English for the first time.

This volume brings together poems published during Sebald's lifetime with an additional selection of those which were found in his literary archives in Marbach and never published while he was alive. Arranged chronologically, from work published during his student days in the 1960s to the longer narratives he produced during the 1980s, the poems touch on the themes which were closest to Sebald – nature and history; forgetting and remembering; borders, journeys and landscapes – and express in short, lyrical form the same distinctive insight and sensitivity that shaped his great works of prose fiction.

*Across the Land and the Water* is available as a Hamish Hamilton hardback from 3rd November 2011.

# W.G. SEBALD

## CAMPO SANTO

Sebald's final collection of essays provides a powerful insight into the themes that came to dominate his life. Four of them pay homage to Corsica, weaving elegiacally between past and present. In others, Sebald examines the works of writers such as Günter Grass, Bruce Chatwin and Kafka, showing both how literature can provide restitution for the injustices of the world and how such literature came to have so great an influence on him.

'Sebald's writing has a turbulent power to disturb the sediments of thought and history . . . *Campo Santo* will come to be seen as indispensable to an understanding of his work' *Sunday Times*

'Full of a sense of liberation and lightness . . . these [pieces] abound in energy and work the authentic Sebaldian magic' *Literary Review*

'A precious addition to the canon' *Independent*

# W.G. SEBALD

## ON THE NATURAL HISTORY OF DESTRUCTION

In the last years of World War II, the Allies dropped a million tons of bombs on Germany. Yet the German people have been silent about the resulting devastation and loss of life, failing to recognize that the terrible shadow that destruction from the air cast over their land. Here W.G. Sebald, one of the most brilliant writers of the twentieth century, asks why it is we turn our backs on the horrors of war, and, in addressing our responses to the past, bravely offers insights into how we live now.

'Brilliant and disturbing. Sebald was probably the greatest intellect and voice of the late twentieth century' *The Times*

'Demands to be read for its grand emotional power, born of clean, clear thought; it absorbs and horrifies and illuminates' *Scotsman*

'The work of a brilliant mind' *Sunday Telegraph*